CODEX

CODEX

A NOVEL

Megan Fatheree

ISBN: 978-1-7359411-0-3

For Abbie

Because every girl should have at least one epic love story
dedicated to them.

These are the chronicles of an impossible man. I would like to deny it. I would like to assure that this intrigue is merely a terrible jest, befit to me for the regrets of my life. I cannot, for there is no jest here.

I thought myself inane to believe these things I saw, however, there is naught but to believe them now. This morn, under a cloud-less and azure sky, I buried the son of my closest acquaintance. He lived, by God's grace, sixty-three years here on this earth. There were many more laughter lines on his aged face than wrinkles brought about by sorrow.

Where he has begotten a son, loved a woman, and died after a long and full life, I have not aged a day.

It is not for lack of want or trying. Would things truly change if I painted lines on my face and stooped to walk? I think not. For what I had feared is now come to pass. It seems I cannot age, and thus I cannot see when my end will come about. How many must I live to bury?

[EPISODE 1]
EVERYDAY LIFE, INTERRUPTED

There was no reason to go to work, but there was no reason to stay home, either. Amorette chose the lesser of two evils.

The others still slept when she crawled from her bed. She would have to hurry if she wanted to arrive on time. Melodia wouldn't mind it, but Amorette hated to be late. It showed a lack of work ethic on her part and she refused to slack off.

One day, something would go right. It didn't have to be today, but she would look forward to it while she waited.

The sky was overcast again, Amorette noted as she stepped onto the sidewalk. Why did it always have to rain when she had places to be? It wasn't fair. Fate must somehow think she deserved punishment.

"What did I ever do to upset you this much?" Amorette asked the sky.

Only a chilled, whispering wind answered her. Of course, Fate wouldn't answer. Amorette had always known Fate to be a cruel mistress, especially to her. With a sigh, she tugged her hood over her head, prepared for the impending drizzle.

"Miss. Miss!" A woman on the side of the road waved a hand to garner Amorette's attention.

Amorette stopped to turn to the older woman. A woman with laugh lines around her eyes and mouth, her teeth still perfect despite her age. She was strikingly beautiful, in an envy-inducing sort of way.

In a semi-polite gesture, Amorette tugged one earphone out of her ear.

The woman held out some sort of wrapped sandwich. "Here. Take this. Everyone needs a good meal."

Amorette wrinkled her brow. Questions flitted through her mind like bees around their hive. "I don't have any money."

"Did I say you had to pay?" The woman clucked her tongue and shoved the sandwich closer to Amorette's hands. "It's free. It's for you."

Free wasn't usually a word in Amorette's vocabulary, but she couldn't deny that the sandwich sounded delicious. If she believed in fairy-tales, this might be one of those poisoned apple situations. Thankfully, Amorette stopped believing in those lie-filled stories a long time ago.

"Thank you." Amorette accepted the sandwich with a tiny smile. All she could manage today. Especially after the events of the last few days. "I'll pay you back somehow."

"Child..." The woman chuckled. "There is no need. I have other ways to take care of myself."

Amorette held the sandwich to her chest like a precious treasure. Today, she would eat more than one meal. Small happinesses were the best, especially when they involved food.

The rain started as Amorette stepped over the threshold into Melodia's shop. Another small happiness for today.

"I'm here!" Amorette ditched her backpack behind the counter and set the sandwich on a shelf. Part of her didn't want to eat it. Gifts like that were so few and far between. The more logical side of her brain insisted she not let it go to waste.

Melodia floated from the back room, her arms stuffed to the brim with books. Her face lit at the sight of her only employee. "Just in time! A new shipment came in. Help me shelve them."

Amorette nodded as she tugged her hair into a ponytail, high atop her head. "Old or new?"

"Both." Melodia waltzed to a nearby shelf and hummed a soft tune as she organized the books thereupon.

Amorette shook her head at the fairy-like woman. It was amazing Melodia afforded any new shipments with the clientele she attracted. Which, in fact, was none.

Oh, occasionally a passerby or curious neighborhood resident would darken their door, but for the most part the quaint and cluttered bookstore remained tragically empty. Still, somehow, the paychecks kept coming and the little store managed to stay afloat. Amorette didn't have enough guts to ask how Melodia managed it.

Melodia had burrowed her nose deep in a romance novel by the time Amorette returned with a crate of ancient, weathered texts. It wasn't odd for Melodia to get distracted so easily, and it was a little amusing. Amorette didn't mind letting Melodia chase her own thoughts. At least then Amorette could take her time stocking each book with a kind and loving hand.

Today, the books all seemed to be old enough to take precautions with them. Amorette pulled on a pair of white gloves and took special care with each cracked leather tome. Some names she couldn't read, due to age or language of origin. Others came with lengthy, descriptive titles. One, in particular, caught her attention. There was no title on the cover, nor on the spine. Only a black leather casing and a strap to bind it closed.

Amorette blew a loose strand of hair from her eye. Her fingers grazed gently over the cover. Some sense of foreboding seemed to reverberate in the room around her, even though she knew that was stupid. It was just a book. She worked for its owner. There was nothing to get anxious over. Nothing at all.

With a firm but gentle tug, Amorette unwrapped the bindings and spread the book open. The first date shocked her, drew her in. The first sentence confused her entirely.

"The chronicles of an impossible man..." Amorette muttered the words to herself. She was half afraid to read on.

Surely this was a cleverly designed work of fiction. Meant to look like a diary but in actuality penned to give young women something to fantasize about. It was the only logical explanation.

Amorette snapped it closed a little too hard. Still, even if she didn't read all of it, she wanted this novel. Something to look at on her poorer days. "Melodia, how much do you want for this?"

Melodia waved a hand in the air. "Take it."

"It wouldn't be right. I'll pay you for it." Amorette rose to her feet, the other books forgotten in light of the most intriguing one.

"You do enough for me. Just take it. It's a gift."

"Are you sure?" Odd, that she would receive two free gifts in one day. Something felt fishy about it.

Melodia nodded and waved her hand again. "I'm sure. Lunchtime. Go on break and take your book with you."

"I've only been here two hours." Amorette couldn't say she had any clue what went through Melodia's mind at any given moment.

"Okay, so early lunch." Melodia sighed and glanced up from her book. "It's getting good. Come on, Amy, cut me some slack and take a break! Read that... that weirdly epic looking book of yours."

Amorette followed Melodia's gaze to the black leather tucked in her arms. Amorette would rather be somewhere quiet and alone to dig her way through this particular story. "I'll eat my lunch then."

"That's what I thought." Melodia went right back to her book, choosing to lean her back against the counter as she did.

Amorette rolled her eyes. Melodia was more mystery than anyone else Amorette knew. With the gentlest of fingers, Amorette settled the book in her backpack and sealed it away. The time would come, one day, to delve into its secrets. Right now, she had a sandwich to savor.

Thunder rolled loudly overhead, allowing the rain to come in sheets.

⊱━━

Eadric watched a single droplet trail down the thick window before him. Life was a lot like that droplet sometimes, its path redirected by obstacles around it. It's course intersecting with others and carrying them along with it. Direct yet evasive. Complicated.

A light knock brought him out of his reverie, back to the present inside this office.

Eadric turned from the window, his hands folded behind his back. "Yes?"

The dark metal door opened with a click. "Sir?" Otto bowed as he entered the room, his weathered face serious but pleasant. Exactly how Eadric came to think of him over the past few decades.

Eadric couldn't help but smile at his aging friend. "Otto. Please come in. Have a seat."

"Thank you, sir." Otto hobbled a bit, his left knee giving him problems due to the weather. "I won't stay long, but there are certain instructions that need to be gone over. Is Doon here yet?"

"I haven't been alerted to his presence, no." Eadric crossed his office to assist Otto down into a chair. "Is he so old already?"

Otto laughed. "He is just turned twenty-seven, my lord. I trust he will serve you very well."

"We speak of the same precocious young man I met... oh... twenty years ago?" Eadric couldn't help but smile back. Being in Otto's presence was soothing to his soul. Only a great friend, one who knew everything, could have such an effect.

"Yes, sir. And he is still as precocious as ever." Otto shook his head. "I fear he may not be the best choice to care for you. If I may say so, he is quite selfish and incompassionate toward others."

"Everyone has such moments in their lifetime." Eadric nodded in understanding. He never expected the young man to be as excellent as Otto. Their family had served him well through the years, but there were always the few who had no respect for the position.

With a sigh, Eadric scooped up his tablet from the glass table and opened it. A quick message to the front desk should suffice, he supposed. He requested Doon's whereabouts and set the gadget back down. "I'm sure security will find him soon enough."

A mischievous smile spread over Eadric's face. It had been a long time since he dealt with disobedience in those serving him.

It might be quite humorous to toy with the young man.

Otto sighed and folded his hands in his lap. "I have done my best to keep him in line, but..." he shook his head again.

Eadric leaned forward to pat the old man's knee. "Have you ever known me to meet a challenge I cannot overcome?"

"Not in my lifetime."

"Then don't worry yourself. I know how to handle him." Eadric grinned wider when he heard a commotion in the hall. "That will be him."

On cue, the door opened with a bang. Two security guards shoved their captive into the office.

"He was in the server room," one offered by way of explanation.

"You may go now." Eadric nodded in gratitude to each of them, then folded his arms over his chest. Doon turned to leave with them. Eadric uttered two words to stop him. "Not you."

Doon stopped mid-step, his eyes falling shut as if he knew the trouble that awaited him. With the widest, most insincere smile Eadric had ever seen, Doon spun to face him. "Mister Hawkmore! Wow. I didn't know you owned this entire company. That's awesome."

"Mm. I run it, too." Eadric jerked his chin toward a chair. "Sit."

Doon collapsed into the chair with an audible gulp. "Mister Hawkmore, I-"

"Silence yourself and listen to what your grandfather tells you." Eadric arched a brow menacingly. If there was one thing he was good at, it was intimidating those who needed intimidation.

Doon rolled his lips together and lowered his gaze.

Otto cleared his throat and turned slightly. "It's time for me to step down from my lord's service, but I cannot leave him without a valet."

"Grandpa, do you really think he needs a valet?"

"Doon." Eadric lowered his voice dangerously.

Doon wasn't about to be dissuaded from his spiel just yet. "I mean, he owns this whole company. If you ask me, our family is far too generous to him. And why do you call him 'my lord' anyway? It's weird. I was born to be more than a manservant!"

"These things will be explained given time." Otto reached to pat Doon's shoulder, an affectionate gesture. "Until then, please serve your lord well. He is not a man that refuses reward to those who obey his orders."

Doon froze, the connotations of that sinking in one slow second at a time. That ridiculous smile returned as he spun in his chair. "My lord! Is there anything you need? Laundry? Housecleaning? Coffee? I'll get you some coffee." He was out of the chair as quickly as he sank into it.

"Sit down, I don't drink coffee." Eadric couldn't believe he was about to have this conversation with the hyper, overactive man now sitting across from him. But there was no choice. "I need you to find something for me. It's a very precious article that has been lost for far too long. Do well and we'll see about that credit card you keep asking your grandfather to collect for you."

Doon gave a sheepish nod. "Okay, okay. What is this little thing you need me to find?"

Eadric stood and retrieved a photograph from his desk. He held it out to the new steward with a heavy, regretful sigh. "This."

Doon stared at the photo for a long time before he looked up. Only one outraged word left his lips, in disbelief or utter fear, Eadric wasn't sure. "This?!"

⚷

Amorette tiptoed through the front door. Just once, she would like a peaceful return instead of the welcome she usually got. For the first time in a long time, she made a wish. A wish that she would be able to make it silently to her room.

The living area appeared empty, which usually meant they were out or in their own rooms. Amorette blew out a quiet sigh and stepped into the room.

A rolled newspaper whacked her arm, then her head, then her other arm as she lifted it to shield herself.

"Wicked girl!" Her stepmother screeched as the newspaper came down against Amorette's side. "We've been waiting for dinner for hours! Where were you? Who were you with? Were you trying to desert us?"

"Why would I desert you? Ow!" Amorette shied far enough away that her stepmother stopped hitting her.

Her stepmother hissed at her like a feral cat. Not a bad description of the woman. Amorette never liked her much. "Stop being selfish. We're all hungry. Go cook something."

"Is it so hard for you to cook something for yourself?" Amorette rubbed at her arm where the first, strongest blow had landed. "I worked all day and you can't even reheat something left in the fridge?"

"Why, you..." Amorette's stepmother raised her hand to strike again, then took a breath and managed to lower her arm. "It doesn't matter. There was nothing left in the refrigerator. Go make soup or something. We're starving."

Amorette rolled her eyes, but pushed past her stepmother to bolt for the kitchen. She learned a long time ago that it didn't matter what she did or didn't do. It would never be enough. Her stepmother never loved Amorette. Not for a single second since they first met.

"Ugh, what was your father thinking? Leaving his first daughter with me..." She clicked her tongue.

Amorette would have liked to know the same thing. Her father must not have known how horribly his second wife hated Amorette. A true Cinderella story, but without the happy ending. Amorette had no other place to lay her head, so she needed to keep her stepmother happy.

There were few ingredients in the refrigerator, perhaps because certain residents were more concerned with beauty products and expensive fashion than their own stomachs. In the end, Amorette began work on a simple chicken soup with vegetables. It would have to be enough, despite the fact that they would all complain.

One thing made it a little easier to push through her exhaustion and finish cooking. An old, black leather book still nestled in her backpack. Maybe tonight she would get around to starting it.

"Is it almost done?" Leah whined from the doorway. Amorette's stepmother's precious youngest, always begging to have her way.

"Just a few minutes." Amorette stirred the boiling soup and willed it to cook faster. Anything to get away from these people for a few minutes.

By the time the carrots were soft and the celery no longer crunchy, Leah's unruly brother Lucas had joined her at the table. Amorette chose to ignore the whispering they did about her. Things she would never do or even think of. Their tongues never stopped wagging when it came to degrading their stepsister.

Amorette pulled three bowls from the cabinet and filled each with a generous portion of soup. The instant she set them on the table, the vultures swooped in to devour them. Amorette merely rolled her eyes again and headed for her room. It wasn't worth sticking around to hear the abuse. They'd used it all on her before, anyway.

"Be sure to come back and clean it!" Her stepmother called as she joined the vulture twins.

Amorette waved a hand over her head at them, a dismissive motion meant to replace her harsh words. "Whatever."

"Hey, don't be so flippant!" Her stepmother shrieked.

Too late. Amorette had already shut her door and dumped her backpack on the ground. It wasn't that her room was silent by any means, but it was at least quieter. And she could be alone. That was the important thing.

Amorette snatched her bag and tossed it onto the bed beside her. There was only one way to drown out the screeching argument from the other room. She would lose herself in a book. As soon as she was comfortable.

Amorette pulled out the book and set it on the bed. She grabbed an over-sized sweatshirt and a pair of shorts, then headed into her tiny bathroom. At least it was hers. That was all she could ask for at this point.

Fifteen minutes later she crawled into bed, clean and comfy. The book waited patiently beside her pillow. A pillow which she squished into something to cuddle against her chest.

"Alright, impossible man. What's your secret?" Amorette flipped open the ancient journal and began to read. Anything to keep the impending tears at bay.

Eadric wrinkled his nose at the graphics on his screen. He'd never seen worse characters from the planning department. With an exasperated sigh, he sent a quick email to request a meeting with these particular designers. How did they get hired if they couldn't do their jobs?

He scrubbed his hands back through his hair, unsure why he was so angry this morning. Perhaps the knowledge that one of his personal journals was floating out there, lost and in the wrong hands. He couldn't let Codex find it.

His cell phone vibrated on the desk beside him. Eadric snatched it up without looking at the caller identification.

"Hello?"

"Mister Hawkmore!" Doon's voice sounded distant, muffled.

Eadric knit his brow and glanced at the phone. "Where are you?"

"That's not important right now." The distinct sound of chewing came over the line. "What is important is that I think I found that item you're looking for."

It seemed Doon was actually a useful person when he put his mind to it. Hopefully, he would continue to serve Eadric as well in the future.

"Well, I'm waiting. Where is it? Do you have it?"

"No. You didn't tell me what to do once I found it and that legendary temper of yours isn't something I want to run into." Doon huffed, followed by the distinct sound of a food wrapper.

Eadric rubbed the bridge of his nose with two fingers. "Where is it, Doon?"

"I told you, I don't have it." This time he most definitely spoke with his mouth full.

Eadric was done with these games. He needed the beginning of his story back. The last of his calm demeanor dissolved. "Doon! Tell me its whereabouts."

"Okay, okay..." Doon fell silent, presumably to look at the address. "It's some little bookstore hidden in some crevice of an old strip mall..."

"Text me the address. I'll go myself." Eadric stood and gathered his things. This could finally be the real thing.

"Of course. Mister Hawkmore, about that credit card-"

Eadric hung up and slung his jackets onto his shoulders. Finally, after all this time, he could once more see his journal back where it belonged.

One of the security personnel fell in step behind him as Eadric stormed for the doors. He immediately turned and held out a hand. "I'll be fine. Thank you for doing your job, but I'm more than capable of caring for this matter alone."

The man folded his hands in front of himself with a nod. "Yes, sir."

Eadric didn't bother to say anything else. Their discussion ended with his command. He sailed out the doors and toward his car. His phone chimed in his pocket as he turned the engine. He would never tire of the soft purr his SUV emitted. Nor was he anything but convinced that the text message was the address Doon found for him.

It was time to fish for information on his own. Time to meet whoever held the beginning of his story in their clutches.

Eadric tapped the address into the GPS and pressed the gas pedal to the floor.

He arrived at the address in record time. There wasn't much

to show for it, just a glass door with a single title on its top pane. The Nook. Aptly named, he supposed, especially for the tiny shop nestled in the corner of the run-down strip mall.

How was it possible for something so small to find its way across oceans and into this pathetic little shop? Eadric sighed and climbed out of his car.

It could be wrong information. Otto searched for years. Eadric had gotten used to getting his hopes up and then finding it wasn't what he searched for.

Today felt different. Somehow, Eadric was certain Doon found the real artifact. All he had to do was retrieve it.

A passel of bells jingled over the door as he pushed it open. The sound was quaint and somehow soothing. The scent of paper and glue, new and ancient, drew him further into the dim atmosphere.

"Hello there. Welcome to The Nook."

Eadric glanced to the source of the voice, a thin woman with blonde hair and her nose buried in the latest romance novel. What kind of hired help did a place like this put up with nowadays?

"I'm looking for the proprietor."

"You found her." The woman jerked a thumb toward her own chest.

Oh, good heavens, no. This woman was the epitome of the stigma surrounding fair-haired young women. "Surely you jest."

"Nope." She snapped the book shut and slammed it down on the counter. "Melodia Morris, at your service. What can I help you find?"

"I'm looking for an old... volume. Bound in black and handwritten. Held together with cords of the same leather." Eadric folded his hands behind his back, perusing the books nearby. "Have you seen it?" He turned his head, staring at Melodia as if he could see her very soul.

Melodia tilted her head, studying him right back. "I don't have that book anymore."

"Anymore?" Eadric took a step closer, sizing up how much intimidation it might take to break her.

"I run a store. I sold it." Melodia shrugged a shoulder. "You should have come sooner."

"I came as soon as I could." Eadric ventured closer, taking in each corner of the little store. "It seems unlikely that you'd have sold it already. Who but me would have interest in such a volume?"

"There are plenty of people who collect old and rare books." Melodia reached for her novel again. "Sometimes even journals. And, no, I can't give out my customers' personal information."

"I never said it was a journal." Eadric shot a narrowed gaze her direction.

Melodia shrugged again. "You described it as a journal. Handwritten, black leather with binding. A journal."

Eadric relaxed a fraction of an inch, but something still felt fishy to him. His fingers traced the spines of the nearby books, seeking a spot on the shelf to place the small electronic device in his hand.

"If that's all you're here for, and I no longer have it, I suggest you leave." Melodia opened her book and turned her attention from Eadric.

"Of course." Eadric pasted on a fake smile. He turned for the door, reached up to caress the bells before he exited. They would offer a safer, clearer view of the shop anyway. "I suppose it would be too much to ask you to contact me if it's returned."

"It won't be."

She seemed so certain, but Eadric wasn't quite at the point to believe her. He blew out an exasperated breath and stormed out. Maybe it wasn't really gone. Maybe it was still sitting somewhere in her storeroom. He'd have to look.

With a furtive glance in each direction, Eadric jogged to his car and headed for the alley behind the strip mall.

[EPISODE 2]
FIRST ENCOUNTERS

"Mi Amor!"

Amorette spun to catch sight of the owner of the voice. She couldn't help a grin when she saw Hunter jogging her direction. She waved. Her bag hung heavy on her shoulders, but for Hunter she would make time.

"How have you been?" Hunter pulled her into a quick hug. "We haven't seen each other in too long. Are you doing okay? How's your family treating you?"

"You're still calling me by that ridiculous nickname?" Amorette ducked her head. Her thumb brushed against the leather of the book in her arms. Even if she had fallen asleep before she got to read it, she couldn't seem to put it down.

"I don't think it's so ridiculous. It makes you smile." Hunter rocked on his heels, his grin wider when she blushed. "You're still excellent at changing the subject, I see."

Amorette giggled and shook her head. "There's not a good answer for any of the questions you asked me."

"And now I'm depressed." Hunter sighed. His hands, he

shoved in his pockets. "It isn't fair for them to treat you like this because you don't belong to their clan."

"If we're being honest, she treats her own kids like that too. I'm not special." Amorette dragged her thumb against the corner of the book in her arms. Somehow, it was comforting to hold it close. To imagine that her impossible man cared what happened to her and watched over her. Stupid, that she thought like that. Life wasn't a fairy-tale. Especially not for Amorette.

"I'm sorry, Mi Amor." Hunter rested a hand against her shoulder. "I'm only a phone call away though. What's your number?"

Amorette stared at him quizzically, but recited the numbers by heart. It was one of her most precious possessions, paid for by her own money.

Hunter grinned again as Amorette's phone chimed in her pocket. "And now you have my number, too. Don't be a stranger. We should hang out more."

Amorette was so shocked that she almost dropped the book.

Hunter reached out and caught it as it slipped. "Be careful. That looks old."

"It is." Amorette clutched it tightly again. Today, she didn't need a story to make her feel better.

She smiled one last time at Hunter before she turned and headed for the storeroom door. She had sorting to do.

The door already stood ajar as Amorette approached it. She frowned. Maybe she hadn't pulled it all the way shut when she left the day before. Hopefully, Melodia hadn't noticed.

Amorette stepped into the dim interior and glanced around. Everything seemed in order, but... what was that noise? Like someone shuffling through a crate. She tiptoed through the aisles, searching for the source of the mysterious sound. What she found instead was a row of open crates and scattered books.

"What in the world?"

Amorette glanced across the mess. Someone had little care for the newer books, but judging by the stack of old tomes, they knew better than to throw history to and fro.

Footsteps clicked across the concrete behind her.

Amorette spun, wielding the black book like a weapon against whoever approached. "I know you're there! Come out and no one will get hurt."

A man stepped out of the shadows and into the warehouse lights. He was beautiful, in a strange way. With dark, shaggy hair and eyes both sad and wise. His lips settled into a firm line as he surveyed her. Amorette wasn't good with math or proportions, but this man had to be at least a foot taller than her, with broad shoulders and an elegant posture.

He motioned to the book in her hands. "How much should I pay you for you to give me that volume?"

Amorette blinked. She caught him rummaging through Melodia's warehouse and all he wanted to know was how much for a book that wasn't for sale?

"I asked, how much for the tome you carry?" The man took a step closer.

Amorette stepped back, away from his authoritative presence. "Stop there! Don't come closer." She waved the book slightly. "I don't have any problem using this."

"Child..." He sighed. "It will go better for everyone if you tell me your price now."

"I'm not a child!" Amorette made a face at him. "And it's not for sale."

"To own that title is to borrow trouble on your own head. It's quite dangerous, you see. I'm attempting to spare both of us the headache of cleaning up this complicated mess later." He lifted his chin and held out his hand as if he expected her to hand it over.

Amorette swallowed. "What if I asked for a million dollars?"

"Alright. I'll have the money transferred." He didn't even blink.

"That's not the price, I was just asking." Amorette tucked the book back against her chest. How much could she get out of this deal? Did she really want to sell the book before she had a chance to read it? "What are you doing in our storeroom?"

"What is your price?"

"I haven't decided yet." Amorette took another step back. The further away from him she could get, the better. Something about him unnerved her.

"Decide quickly." He folded his hands behind his back. "I don't have all day."

"Amorette? Are you back here?" Melodia called from the door to the front room.

Amorette sidestepped into another aisle. "Coming!"

"What about my book?"

"It's still mine since you haven't bought it from me." Amorette walked backward toward the front room. "You should get out of our storeroom, mister. It's trespassing and I'm sure I could have you thrown in jail. And you'd better not take any books out with you unless you plan to buy them."

"I only want the one."

"It's not for sale." Amorette turned and sprinted for the front before he could try anything less than proper.

It was strange enough that he broke in just to buy her book. She couldn't imagine what else he had planned. Crazy people were always the worst. This guy was definitely not an exception.

⚷⟶

Eadric slammed a hand against his door, willing himself to be calm even if he wasn't.

It was there. He saw it. Inches from him, and he didn't have the guts to reach out and take it. Of course, at the time he was trying to be civil. If that girl paid for it, he wanted to at least reimburse her. Except that plan backfired immediately.

Eadric growled and stomped through the house to his bedroom. That girl had no idea what kind of danger she put herself in by keeping the blasted journal.

A flick of his wrist brought his computer to life. A few keystrokes brought up the camera he planted in the bells. Small, but functional. Able to transmit audio and video to his remote server.

The proprietress still stood with her nose in a book, this time chewing a piece of gum. The other girl scrambled around shelving and straightening books, an infuriating smile plastered on her face. It took everything in him to take another breath.

He tried to warn her. Tried to keep her out of his long and complicated life. Did she listen? No. Why must she be so stubborn? At this point, he didn't think she'd even allow him to buy the volume from her. Which left only one option for keeping her safe, deaf and dumb to the danger around them.

Eadric sank into his desk chair and picked up his phone. What had her name been? Ah, yes. Amorette. Well, it shouldn't be too hard to find information on her. He already knew where she worked. His sources were discreet, if a bit legally questionable. No matter how much he disliked the child, he wasn't cold-hearted.

Not always.

Eadric sent the orders with the request. Observe. Report. Keep an eye and an ear out for Codex and their cronies. It seemed they were everywhere nowadays, slowly closing in on those who dared defy logic.

Eadric sneered at the screen, at the delightful little woman flitting around the bookstore. Even more irritating than her boss. He clicked out of the screen and picked up his tablet instead. He had things to approve for work. He couldn't spend his time obsessing over something he already took care of. Good riddance.

Eadric had opened the files he needed to review when a soft alarm sounded.

Someone had entered his humble abode. Too bad he wasn't in a mood to indulge any burglars.

Eadric rose to his feet and pocketed his phone. Finally, some kind of stress relief when he needed it. He smiled at the broadsword mounted against his wall. It had been years since he used it properly. Eadric pulled it from its mount.

The house seemed too quiet even for him. Eadric made his way down the stairs, toward the front door. A smart burglar wouldn't have come in that way, but burglars weren't known for their intelligence.

A shadow moved near the entryway.

Eadric spun into action. Two quick steps brought him into the walkway. A single flick of his wrist brought the very tip of the sword up under the intruder's chin.

"Holy—" Doon skittered back a step and threw his arms over his head. "I'm sorry! I'm sorry! Whatever I did, I'll fix it, just... put the sword down. Please?"

"Pity." Eadric sighed and brought the sword back to his side. "I was looking forward to a good duel."

"D-duel?" Doon's eyes didn't leave the massive sword, even when he phrased his question to Eadric. "Grandpa told me to come check on you. You're not actually going to stab me with that right?"

Eadric rolled his eyes and turned to walk away. "I suppose he told you the wrong alarm code, too, then."

"No, I forgot. He's always telling me to write things down. I just don't." Doon, still hesitant, followed Eadric into the spacious living and dining room. "May I have the alarm code, Mister Hawkmore? I'll be silent next time I come to check on you. Promise."

Eadric laid the sword longways on the dining table. "I suppose you do work for me now. It's still difficult to realize you'll be taking Otto's place."

"Trust me, it's unbelievable for me, too." Doon glanced around the rich interior of Eadric's home. "Anyway, the code?"

"1401."

Doon nodded, distracted by the abstract chandelier hanging from the center of a floating candle display.

Eadric pulled his phone from his pocket and rolled his eyes. "You should write it down now, before you forget again."

"Oh! Yeah." Doon fished through his own pockets until he found his phone. "Let's see... notes... hm, what color?"

"Make it red," Eadric didn't even glance up at him. "To remind you that if you don't remember the code, I'll kill you.

Accidental incident, of course."

Doon froze, his only motion the bobbing of his Adam's apple when he swallowed.

Eadric looked up and made eye contact with him. His lips turned in the barest hint of a sadistic smile. "I do not jest in this."

Doon gulped, looked away, and typed his note as quickly as he could.

Eadric smiled in satisfaction. "You can tell your grandfather I have the situation well in hand. There is no need to worry."

"Situation?" Doon scrambled to follow Eadric into the kitchen next. "We have a situation? What kind of situation? Didn't you find the stupid... I mean, the journal?"

"Found, yes. Acquired... it's complicated." Eadric dug a drink from the refrigerator. The lid popped open with a satisfying hiss. "I have it well in hand, so don't fret yourself. This is no longer any concern of yours."

"Seeing as how it's now my job to make sure you're taken care of, it's most definitely my concern." Doon folded his arms petulantly.

"Do you want to meet the end of my blade again?" Eadric rose a brow, knowing it would be more than enough.

Surprisingly, Doon only lifted his own eyebrows. "You think I'm scared? I'm more frightened of what my grandfather will do to me if I don't do my job. He's a scary old man."

Despite all his attempts to hold it in, a single laugh escaped Eadric's lips. He couldn't have described Otto better himself. Perhaps Doon was useful for more than one thing around here. Even if he did get on Eadric's nerves.

"So, what's going on?" Doon grinned as if he won the lottery.

Eadric shook his head. "If you need to know at any point, I'll be the one to tell you. Go study the books your grandfather gave you. It will be helpful for you to know those things." He didn't bother to wait around for Doon's reaction. He grabbed his sword in one hand and marched back to his room. If it was anything like his usual stress, Eadric knew he wouldn't be sleeping at all tonight.

⚷—

Amorette set down her pencil and rubbed her tired eyes. It had been a good idea to start with, but it was also painstaking and took too much focus. She should go to sleep. She had an early morning the next day.

With a sigh, Amorette put away the things she'd been using and carried her work with her to bed. She curled under the covers, her fingers tracing over the black leather of that book, but sweet dreams wouldn't come. Amorette tossed and turned, increasingly agitated that she couldn't fall asleep.

A loud crash sounded from the living room.

It wasn't unusual to hear a fight break out between her stepmother and step-siblings, but that particular sound never happened before.

Amorette leaped out of bed and tugged her door open, just a crack. Enough to see the front room and a half-dozen intruders that definitely didn't belong there. She pressed the door shut again.

"What do I do? What do I do?" Amorette paced toward her window, then back toward the door. There weren't many options, but she didn't want to let them get away with much, if anything at all. This house may be full of bittersweet memories for her, but it was still Amorette's home.

The intruders never expected a small woman to use a leather-bound journal as a weapon, but that's exactly what happened.

The very second someone opened her door and stepped into her room, Amorette jumped out from behind the door. The journal slammed across the taller man's chin with an audible clap.

The burglar stumbled backward. Two more came flying through the door, presumably to his rescue.

"The book," the first man mumbled to one of the two.

Amorette lashed out again, this time at one of the other intruders. She landed a wallop against his shoulder.

The third man got a hold of her next, one arm wrapped around her shoulders and the other trapping her arms at her sides.

The first man recovered some from the shock of the attack. He appeared before her, his sneer wide and his eyes homicidal. His hand came up to wrap around Amorette's throat in a vise-like grip.

"Pity you were awake. If you were asleep, this wouldn't be necessary." He clucked his tongue. "Such a pretty thing too."

His grip tightened.

Amorette coughed. Her mouth opened wide, searching for air that didn't come. Her eyes watered, the moisture running down her cheeks like tears. This must be the end. How everything caught up to her and took her life. There was no way out.

A sharp buzz, accompanied by a flash of light near the attacker's neck, sent him sprawling on the floor.

Amorette sputtered and gasped, still held by one of the intruders but very much still alive.

"Release her unless you want similar treatment. We have

specific instructions to take any measures necessary to ensure her safety."

Amorette looked up to see a man in a dark suit. One of those large, retired military types. Still, he didn't look familiar. If anything, he seemed stranger because she didn't know him. Another quick glance around her room revealed two more similar strangers.

When the burglar holding Amorette didn't move, the first man sprang into action. Faster than Amorette could blink, the taser he used on the first man made contact with the man holding Amorette. He cried out and loosened his hold enough that she could struggle free.

Amorette sprinted for the door. No way she was staying there with any of those people. She didn't know them. She didn't trust them. She wasn't stupid. Something weird was going on.

"Grab her."

The command was barely out of his mouth when two more ex-military types stepped into Amorette's path. Even though one could have easily detained her, they each took one of her arms and lifted her just far enough her feet couldn't touch the floor.

"Oh, come on! This is so unfair!" Amorette struggled against them, careful not to lose her grip on the leather journal. "Put me down, you idiots!"

The man in the suit stepped out of Amorette's bedroom and sighed. "I'm afraid you'll be going on a little excursion with them. It shouldn't take long. We'll have this cleaned up by the time you return. Sorry for the inconvenience."

Amorette didn't even have time to curse him before the brutes dragged her out the door and toward a waiting van.

The doorbell rang.

Eadric frowned and stood immediately from his desk. Doon and Otto wouldn't ring the doorbell, which meant only one thing. Something happened. He wasted no time sailing down his stairs and pressing the button to unlock the front door.

The doors didn't open right away but rather left Eadric in a state of suspense. Finally, two of his company's security personnel shoved their way through the double doors and down the entryway steps.

Between them, a small woman struggled with all her might, her lungs as powerful as the impact of her bare feet.

The large men dropped her to the steps.

Amorette landed with a thud and a pout. Eadric half expected her to get up and start slapping people, but instead she fell silent and clutched the book to her chest. His book.

She looked tiny and pathetic sitting on his floor like that. Most of her hair fell in wisps around her face, even though it had clearly been piled into a ponytail before. The oversized sweatshirt hid only a pair of shorts beneath it. He could only see those because of the way she rested her chin on her clutched knees.

Despite any compassion that tugged at Eadric's heart, it couldn't be helped. Better to cut ties and let her run.

With a heavy sigh, Eadric knelt before her and draped his arms across his knees. "I did try to warn you. Possessing this journal is dangerous. Do you see that now?"

Amorette didn't answer. A soft huff parted her lips, but that was it. Her eyes remained downcast. Her thumb absently moved against the corner of the pages.

"Give it to me, then." Eadric held out a hand, palm up.

Part of him wondered if she would listen to him this time. Another part didn't want to wait to find out. He waited for her to make a move and, when she didn't, he reached out and snatched the book from her grasp.

Amorette didn't say a word. That's what tipped him off.

"Something the matter?" Eadric raised a brow sardonically.

She was too quiet and demure. This wasn't the woman he met in the back room of the bookstore. Nor the one who'd been skipping across his computer monitor all day.

Amorette whipped her head to look up at him, fury sizzling in her eyes and the heavy rise and fall of her chest. "No. Why would something be the matter? I mean, obviously you sent those thugs to scare me into giving you what you want, so no. Nothing's the matter. Fine. You win. Don't send any more."

"I didn't send them." Eadric gently unwound the bindings on the journal. They felt newer than he had expected after so many years of being passed around from historian to antique dealer and back again.

"Liar." Amorette stood to her feet and tugged her hooded sweatshirt down. "I'm leaving now."

"Fine. Do what you will." Eadric shrugged a shoulder and waved her toward the door. He was far too focused on his own piece of history to care about what she was thinking or feeling.

The leather fell open against his palm. His own words stared back at him, but... it wasn't right. Eadric quickly flipped through the book. Only to find... nothing.

In three strides, Eadric caught up with the runaway. He snatched her arm, but managed only to snag the sleeve of her hoodie. It slid from her shoulder and stuck.

Amorette halted and looked back over her now-bare shoulder at him.

"What is this?" Eadric held up the book in a single, furious motion. How dare she try to pull one over on him?

Still, Amorette looked at him with an expression beyond reproof, the epitome of innocence. "I don't know what you're talking about." She tugged at her arm in an attempt to get away from his hold.

Eadric released her with a soft shove. He tossed the book her direction, surprised when she caught it. "This isn't the journal. There's only one entry."

Amorette's face went white as a sheet. Her eyes darted around the room. "That can't be right." But she didn't bother to open the journal and look.

"What happened to the journal?" Eadric took a step closer, into her personal space.

"I..."

"*What. Happened?*"

Amorette winced and took a step back from his looming presence. "I... I... it's... g-gone."

"Gone?" Eadric couldn't deny that his heart stopped beating. That could mean so many things. Stolen. Given away. Destroyed.

"Y-yes..." Amorette clutched this new journal to her chest. "B-but I... read the whole thing! I read it and I remember it so I was trying to put it down exactly how I read it. I know everything and I can put it down for you so you can't kill me or you'll never get it back."

"If you've lost it, find it," Eadric growled. He didn't spend so many years hunting down his journal for it to slip through his grasp now.

"I didn't lose it!" Amorette glared up at him now.

"Then whatever happened, I suggest you get it back. Because I assure you, until that journal is back in my hands, you won't be safe from any of those hooligans." Eadric took one step closer to her. "Is that understood?"

"Crystal clear." Amorette pulled her hair over one shoulder, leaving that exposed patch of skin open to the air.

Eadric blinked and stepped closer still, until he could grab her arms and study the mark against her pale skin.

No. No, this couldn't be possible. It was a mistake. A fluke. She was never meant to meet him and he was never meant to find her. He had to get her out of there.

Amorette caught him by surprise when she shoved him away. Eadric stumbled back a step.

"I don't care if you believe me." Amorette tucked a stray hair behind her ear. "I don't have the journal. You think I would have brought this if I did?" She held up the almost-empty diary.

"Go home, Amorette." Eadric turned to walk away. "It's best if we never see each other again. I'll have my men keep an eye on you in case you happen to find the journal you misplaced."

"Fine," Amorette called after him. Too loudly, as though she expected him to come back. "What should I do with this one?"

"Keep it." Eadric slammed the office door as he passed through it. It wasn't worth fighting with her. The company personnel would escort her home and that would be the end of it. He would never see her again.

Except, something told him it wasn't entirely true. Someone had targeted her, or his security personnel wouldn't have intervened this evening. Which meant, perhaps, she was in danger despite his distance from her. Eadric sighed and sank into a chair. All he could do was keep his people on alert.

No matter what happened, he wouldn't let anyone else get hurt on his behalf.

[EPISODE 3]
A SERIES OF CATALYSTIC EVENTS

True to their word, the ones who stayed behind did have the house cleaned up by the time Amorette got home that night. She wasn't quite sure how they didn't wake up her step-family, but she wasn't about to complain. There was no need to pull those monsters into this mess.

Amorette sank onto the end of her bed and set the new journal down beside her.

She didn't know why she lied to him. It seemed like the right thing to do at the time. Less complicated if he thought she didn't have it any more, right? Besides, at the time, she was afraid that What's-His-Face would kill her where she stood. If she made a story wherein he needed her alive, she would save herself.

Apparently, it worked. But it was still weird. Everything that happened was weird. From the first thug that broke her front door to the way the tall, elegant man's dark eyes glittered in the lamplight.

He was so serious, but somehow she wanted to see him again. It felt like she could solve a puzzle if she saw him enough times.

"Never gonna happen, Amorette. Pull yourself together." She rolled her eyes at her own naivete. He wasn't even that attractive. A sad smile and mysterious eyes did not a handsome man make.

Still, try as she might, she couldn't erase his face from her memory. Great. Now she was thinking about him again. Not the most brilliant thing she'd ever done. Not the stupidest either.

Amorette crawled up to her pillows and pulled out the old journal. She had to start it tonight. She had to know what she was dealing with. The man wanted this too badly for it to be just a story. Even she could recognize coincidence when it wasn't a coincidence at all.

"What big secret do you have inside, hm?" Amorette stroked the leather lovingly, imagining that it might purr if it had a real life.

She couldn't explain why she loved this journal so much without having read it. But it called to her, somehow. She wasn't about to give that up without figuring out why. Amorette was always a curious soul.

The next thing she knew, Amorette opened her eyes to bright sunshine streaming through her window. She blinked against the light.

Nothing else happened last night. Nothing that harmed her or woke her. Perhaps the entire ordeal was a dream.

Amorette rolled out of bed and snatched the journal up into her arms. In case last night hadn't been a dream, she should keep it close. She didn't know why she feared for its safety above her own, but she did. It wasn't right or fair, it didn't make sense, but she needed the journal close.

With the new day came new worries, like what mood her step-mother would be in this morning. If she hurried, perhaps the woman would sleep through the ruckus in the kitchen.

Hopeful, Amorette dashed through her morning routine and scrambled to the kitchen. There wasn't an awful lot of food in the fridge or cabinets, but she could come up with something. Leftovers were out of the question, they would only get her yelled at later. They had some flour and sugar. She could make pancakes.

Amorette went digging in the cabinets, in search of something suitable for the picky eaters she catered to.

About the time she found the ingredients, her phone buzzed in her pocket. At first, she frowned, but one look at the name over the text had her smiling again. Hunter.

Morning, Mi Amor. Hope your morning is going well. Let me drive you to work?

Amorette nibbled at her lip. She shouldn't grin like an idiot about that, but Hunter had never asked something like that before.

She had always had a bit of a crush on him, ever since the nickname he gave her, but Hunter never seemed to reciprocate. Until now. Maybe he changed his mind.

She hustled to set the flour and sugar on the counter. Her fingers flew over the keyboard, the one word sure but her emotions less so. *Yes.*

"What are you doing? Where's my breakfast?" Her stepmother stormed into the kitchen.

Amorette winced and sent the message. "I'm getting it. I'm sorry."

"Sorry? Is that what you say when you've done nothing the past few days? I've been generous, letting you stay here for free when I could be charging rent for that room of yours. Don't think there's no end to my generosity."

"I'm sorry." It was all Amorette could say. Nothing else would suffice, nor would anything calm her stepmother. She tucked her phone against her chest.

"Who are you talking to? Are you running up your phone bill? Let me see." Her stepmother snatched at the device.

Amorette stepped back and shied away from her reach. "It's mine. I don't think it's legal for you to demand it. Isn't that stealing?"

"Insolent child! Who pays for that plan on the phone?" She reached for it again.

"Who paid for the phone?" Amorette stood her ground. She was so tired of being treated like an outcast in her own home.

Her stepmother snarled and smacked at the device, hitting it hard enough that Amorette lost her grip.

The phone went clattering to the floor. It hit the corner of a metal cabinet on the way down. The battery skittered one direction, the shattered pieces of the phone in the other.

Amorette blinked against the sudden tears. She saved for months to buy that. What would she do now? She'd only had the phone a few weeks. It was supposed to be the sturdiest model on the market. Why did it break so easily?

With an outraged, hurt cry, Amorette scooped up the pieces of her broken phone and pushed past her stepmother. She didn't want to deal with that woman any more this morning. Last night was bad enough. Why should she have to put up with verbal abuse as well?

She made it all the way to the sidewalk before the tears started in earnest. They ran down her cheeks in rivers, dripped off her chin to the pavement below.

Amorette was so intent on putting one foot in front of the other, she hardly noticed the sleek red car that slowed to drive alongside her.

"Mi Amor?" Hunter's voice floated through the morning air. "What happened? What's wrong?"

Amorette shook her head. "Stupid corporations, thinking they can sell low-end products for high-end prices."

"Mi Amor?" Hunter asked again, this time more out of confusion than anything else. "Let me drive you to work."

"I'm not going to work." Amorette made up her mind in a split second of emotion and rage. "Drive me somewhere else? I can't get there by walking. It's too far."

Hunter hesitated but a moment before he nodded his head. He reached across the passenger seat and popped the door open. "Get in."

⚷

"This makes no sense!" Doon flew through the office door without knocking. "There is no record of the sale. Trust me, I checked everywhere. She definitely didn't sell the journal even if she said she did."

"Something is wrong." Unable to sit calmly any longer, Eadric shot to his feet. "The proprietor insisted she sold it. I saw the younger woman with it in her hands, but she appears to work in the place. I don't understand why either of them are so intent on protecting it. It isn't their life on the line."

"For now." Doon blew out a breath and flopped into a chair. "I mean, really. What are they? Are you sure they're not Codex?"

Eadric stopped to look over at Doon. The boy had a point. How could they be sure that neither of the women were Codex?

A pair of wide eyes and a wispy birthmark materialized in his memory.

Eadric huffed and shook his head. "The smaller one isn't. That's a certain fact."

"But how do you know?"

"I just do!" Eadric clenched his fists to calm himself. He couldn't get riled up this early in the morning. He had an entire day to get through. Things to accomplish. Things to fix. "There are some things I know beyond a shadow of a doubt. That girl is not Codex, though I can't say as much for the proprietor of that store."

Doon nodded, taking in the information and processing it before he opened his mouth again. "But how do you know?"

"Because she has the mark." Eadric shot him a glare.

He refused to say more about it. For someone to bear the mark meant many things. It wouldn't bode well for him to get himself involved with her. Trouble always followed.

"What mark?"

"Doon!" If Doon asked one more question, Eadric feared he may permanently damage the poor child's head. He never expected him to be so quizzical. Otto made it out to sound like Doon didn't care, but from Eadric's perspective, he cared a bit too much. "I swear if you ask one more question I'll run you through this time."

"Okay, got it. Curiosity squashed." Doon ran a finger over his lips in a zipping motion.

At least he learned quickly. Many self-centered young men such as Doon didn't know when to stop, even for their own good. Perhaps there was still humanity behind his apathetic exterior.

Eadric motioned for him to follow. "I'm hungry. Let's go."

"Food?" Doon was on his feet in seconds. He fell into step beside Eadric as they headed down the hall. "Are you buying? Because that's a first."

Before Eadric could answer, a security guard stepped into their path, his arms spread. "I'm sorry, sir. We're dealing with a problem at the front desk in the lobby. I'm afraid we can't let you leave yet. Just in case."

"What kind of problem?" Eadric tuned out Doon to listen to whatever his subordinate had to say.

The man retrieved his company phone and held it out.

Eadric took the device and squinted at the screen. The live feed showed all he needed to know. A young woman, hair falling from a ponytail, waving her hands around like a madwoman. She seemed upset, like she needed something desperately.

"She's been complaining for an hour. She won't leave."

Eadric handed the device back and folded his arms across his chest. "Bring her to me."

The guard blinked. "Excuse me?"

"What?" Doon tugged at his arm in a silent demand to leave it alone.

Eadric shrugged him off. He knew the woman at a glance, something he would ponder over later. Right now, he was more curious than cautious. "I said, bring her to me. I'll settle the matter."

"I don't think that's the wisest idea, sir..." The guard cleared his throat, clearly flustered at the demand.

"I didn't ask for your opinion. I gave an order. Bring the girl to my office." Eadric spun on his heel, intent on seeing this through.

Why would Amorette be at his company, of all places? It must be some kind of cruel joke on someone's part, to have him deal with her so many times in the span of a week. He should get a reward for it.

Doon trailed him back into the office, his eyes wide and his lips in constant motion. "What do you mean? Who is she? You never deal with things yourself, that's what grandpa said. Why this one? What are you planning? She's innocent, don't hurt her or anything just because you're angry with me."

"Doon." Eadric faced him and took a step closer. He held out his own company credit card. "Go have lunch on me. Bring something back for me to eat. Don't lose this card."

As expected, that shut Doon's mouth faster than any explanation. He grabbed the card from Eadric's hands and bowed slightly. "Yes, sir. Of course, sir. I wouldn't dream of it, sir." Doon left the office muttering something about "the most beautiful thing he'd ever seen."

Eadric had to chuckle at his young naivete. Doon still had much to learn about life.

Eadric heard the woman before he saw anything. He didn't know she could be so deafening. Somehow, through her entire rant, she managed to avoid any expletives. An impressive achievement.

The security personnel hauled a struggling Amorette through the office door and dumped her on the couch.

Eadric waved them out. He could definitely take care of the little woman on his own. She never had presented much of a problem, aside from her stubborn attitude and that mark on her shoulder. She shouldn't be much of a problem now.

Amorette sprang to her feet and charged after the security personnel until she met the closed door. Her fist slammed against the metal. "Cowards! Come back here and fight your own battles! Don't pawn me off on some politician!"

"Did you bring the journal?" Eadric rested against the side of his desk.

Amorette froze, her fist midair. He couldn't tell what she was thinking since she faced away from him, but her shoulders slumped before they stiffened.

"I don't know what you're talking about." She spun to face him. "In fact, I didn't even know you worked here. I'm sorry, I was looking for the CEO or someone in charge."

"Mm, yes. That would be me."

It was amusing, at least, the way her eyes went wide. Right before she squared her shoulders again. "I'm sorry, I didn't know you ran this company." Amorette turned for the door again.

"You're going to run off because I frighten you? After you've been complaining and screaming for an hour?" Eadric clucked his tongue. She was a strange girl, after all.

Amorette froze, which at this point was just about the reaction he expected from her. "Fine." She spun back to him so fast it almost gave Eadric whiplash. "If you really want to hear it, I'll tell you." Angry and fierce, she lifted her palms to reveal a shattered cellular phone. "Replace my phone."

"You came all the way here for that?" Eadric scoffed. "Phones break all the time. What business is it of mine?"

"Your company created this phone!" Amorette stepped closer to drop the pieces onto the coffee table in the middle of the room. "They promised it was the sturdiest, longest-lasting model on the market. I've only had this for two weeks! This is false advertising and I'll scream it to the world if you don't replace my phone this instant!"

"If you've only had it two weeks, it should be under warranty, yes?"

Amorette's shoulders stiffened again, a bad habit of hers when she was at a disadvantage. She looked away. "I didn't have money to pay for the warranty. I barely managed to get the phone."

"Then it isn't my fault, is it? You should have been wise and purchased the warranty." Eadric leveled his gaze at her. There was something innocent and fragile about her, even though she was demanding.

"That's not the point! The point is that the phone broke after your company promised it would last a lifetime. I'll... I'll... I'll sue!" Even Amorette looked startled at the threat.

They stared at each other across the room, her gaze unwavering and Eadric's anger rising.

"Fine. Okay." Eadric folded his arms defiantly. His chin lifted for him to look down his nose at her. "You do that. Sue me. We'll see who wins. Your phone isn't my fault."

Amorette's eyes went wide again, making her seem more lost little girl than angry, confident woman. Moisture pooled in her eyes. Her chin quivered. "I need it for work, though. And I can't afford another one... It isn't my fault it broke. I didn't do anything to it."

"Bring my journal and I'll think about replacing it."

"I told you, I don't have it anymore." A single tear rolled down Amorette's cheek. "Do you have to be so cruel?"

"If you read that journal, you know I've been around long enough to recognize forced tears. I won't fall for the sympathy card you want me to fall for." Eadric arched a brow. He knew full well that women could manipulate with their tears. That they used them to get what they wanted.

Amorette wrinkled her nose and wiped the one tear from her cheek. "I'm not lying. I really do need this phone and I really can't afford a new one."

"Then you should have thought about that and acted responsibly when you bought it. Warranties are wise decisions. Having no backup plan is not."

Amorette snorted a humorless laugh. "You're a strange kind of person, you know that?"

"So I've been told. I did offer you a settlement. Bring my journal."

"And I told you I don't have it."

"I don't believe you."

"Obviously." Amorette folded her arms with a huff. "Replace my phone."

"Bring my journal."

"I don't have it! Stop talking in circles!"

Eadric watched her stubborn facade melt into desperation. As if her legs gave out from beneath her, Amorette sat down hard on the nearest surface. His coffee table. If not for constant practice of composure, he would have winced at the assault on one of his oldest and most favorite pieces of furniture.

"I really do need the phone..." Amorette swallowed, perhaps in an attempt not to cry. Perhaps a bit of feminine manipulation. "But... it's... it's okay. I'm okay. I'll... figure something out. Thank you for your time." She scrambled to her feet and shot for the door.

Eadric rolled his eyes at the obvious ploy for empathy. "If you find my journal, let me know. I'm sure we can work something out."

Amorette was already in the hall by the time he finished his sentence.

"Strange child," Eadric mused to himself as he picked up his tablet again. A few clicks opened the live feed from the camera out front. If that's how she came in, he had no doubt that's how she would go out.

Sure enough, he watched her sulk out of the front doors and straight toward a sleek-looking sports car. More surprisingly, toward the man standing next to it.

Eadric narrowed his eyes, trying to make out who awaited her. He didn't seem very familiar, but then again, Eadric had met a lot of people through the years. The man might be a boyfriend, but if that was the case he was doing a very poor job of it.

Whatever the case, the unidentified man wrapped Amorette up in his embrace. As if she needed comfort after what happened.

Eadric scoffed and reached for his phone. For a split second, he doubted that Amorette had lied to him. No more. She had the journal. He needed that journal.

"I literally just left! What's so urgent you couldn't wait until I come back with food, hm?" Doon sounded more annoyed than outraged when he answered his phone. Thank the heavens.

Eadric settled at his desk and set the tablet down, still on so he could keep an eye on the young woman. "I'm famished. Hurry back. And look into that bookstore. See what happened to my... I mean, *the* book."

"Pushy, pushy, pushy," Doon mumbled to himself, but Eadric heard it loud and clear.

He didn't mind. The episode with Amorette, both the night before and today, had his mind spinning. She was too young and naive. It was impossible. But then again, so was he.

Amorette dropped her head back against the seat and sighed. Just her luck that the same crazy person who wanted the old journal also ran the company she needed to replace her phone. She couldn't afford it on her own.

"Mi Amor?" Hunter's voice was soft, understanding. He didn't try to push or nudge her too far, but the concern in his voice forced Amorette's eyes open.

She turned her head to look at him. "I really needed that phone."

"If you think about it, it wasn't the best idea to start with. I'm surprised you managed to get in and see the CEO. How'd that happen?" He grinned at her, a look meant to encourage.

It grated some, that even Hunter believed she couldn't do anything about the broken phone.

"Am I a joke to you, too?" Amorette folded her hands together in her lap. She wouldn't cry any more today. She refused.

Hunter set a hand on her shoulder. "That's not what I meant. I know big companies, is all. They typically don't pay any mind to a girl complaining that her phone broke."

"They still don't. He said I was stupid." She rolled her eyes. "I'm not stupid. I'm just broke."

"I don't think you're stupid. I think you're very intelligent." Hunter let his hand fall away as he turned back to the wheel. "Don't listen to him. What does he know, anyway?"

Amorette shrugged. He ran a huge company. He had to be smart, on some level. She blew out another breath. "I don't even know his name."

"Does it matter? Will you ever see him again?" Hunter turned a corner and slouched back in his seat. "We should put this behind us."

"That doesn't change the fact that my phone is gone and I need a new one." Amorette sighed and leaned her head back again. "I didn't mean to drag you into this. Take me home. I'll figure out what to do."

"I don't know, Mi Amor. It doesn't feel right to let you go home without finding a solution." Hunter tapped his fingers on the steering wheel. "I'll replace your phone."

"You don't have to do that, Hunter. In fact, please don't. It's better if you don't get involved. But thank you." Amorette flashed a soft, wry smile.

Hunter clenched his fingers around the wheel again, clearly thinking about what he could do next to help. "Okay. Let me take you to lunch, then. You have to eat. We can pick something up from a drive-through if you would rather."

Amorette sighed. It would be rude to refuse him everything he suggested, and she was hungry, after all. She nodded her head. "Just a burger or something. I don't have much appetite after this morning."

"What was your plan, anyway? It's not like some stupid, rich CEO owes you a new phone. He didn't break it."

"Complaining to the company made sense at the time." Amorette twiddled her thumbs in her lap. "In hindsight, it was stupid and childish. I should know better."

"You've always been more emotional than rational, Mi Amor." Hunter chuckled as if recalling fond memories of times past. "If I thought I could have talked you out of it, I would have. We could have bought you a new phone. It's not like I can't afford it."

"Stop rubbing it in, Mr. Moneybags." Amorette wrinkled her

nose at him playfully. "Men with lots of money aren't high on my good list right now."

"In that case I'm as broke as you, trying to pay my way through college and pass all my courses to get scholarships." Hunter grinned. "Guess which half is a lie."

"Oh, please!" Amorette laughed despite the situation with her phone. Hunter had a boyish way about him. It was refreshing after fighting with a stuck-up snob. "I don't have to guess. I know you well enough to know what you made up."

"Oh, do you now?" Hunter pulled into the parking lot of a fast food chain.

"I do." Amorette leaned forward to read the large menu by the drive-through. "Just a meal, I guess. Burger, fries, drink."

Hunter nodded as he rolled his window down. He placed the order, plus his own, and thanked the employee on the other end of the radio. It took a bit of finagling for him to grab his wallet from his back pocket.

Amorette giggled at the way he twisted and turned his body.

Even in high school, he had been carefree and wild like this. Doing whatever he wanted with whoever he wanted to do it with. It hadn't been Amorette very often, but she cherished the moments he spent with her nonetheless. Perhaps more so, because Hunter didn't waste time on just anyone.

Hunter flashed her a smile as he held his credit card out the window to the cashier on the other side. "Everything good, Mi Amor?"

Amorette nodded, her smile splitting her face into the perfect mask of happiness. At least today wasn't a total let-down.

Part of her wanted to give in and let Hunter give her whatever he wanted, but her pride wouldn't let her accept more from him than a simple meal. It wasn't like she was dating him or anything. To accept too much would put her in debt to him for... ages. Knowing Hunter, he'd use that to his advantage.

No, she had to take control of her own life, no matter how hard it may be.

She didn't realize how hard she'd been thinking about things until Hunter poked her arm. Amorette jumped and looked over at him. "What was that for?"

"Food's up, daydreamer." He handed her a paper sack. His lips pressed together in a smile of understanding. As if he knew the crazy, whacked-out emotions racing through her head and strangling her heart.

"Sorry." Amorette pulled the bag open and snagged a fry from its packaging. "There's been a lot going on lately."

"It's okay, I'm just over here worried sick that you've had a brain aneurysm or something. Don't mind me. I'm just your food source and a friend who thought he was close to you." Hunter sighed dramatically, darting his eyes to look at her again.

Amorette punched his arm. "Stop it. This is your 'I'll be a goof so she cheers up' persona. Just be you."

"I'm sincerely worried, Mi Amor." Hunter's smile turned into a petulant frown. "You don't say it, but I know something happened at home. Something beyond the phone. You wouldn't have been crying on the street if it didn't. I don't want to see you hurt, no matter what you may think."

"You never cared this much during high school." Amorette winced at the words that left her own mouth.

She tried not to be mean or hurtful to others, but Hunter didn't act this way during school. They were from different worlds, despite the fact he spent time with her when the others didn't know.

Hunter grabbed a fry of his own as he pulled back onto the street. "What do you mean? Of course I cared. I wouldn't have spent my energy on you if I didn't care. Why do you think that?"

Amorette sighed and stuffed another fry into her mouth. "No reason."

"You always have a reason."

She couldn't argue with that. Hunter knew her well enough to know she hid her true feelings with the intent of sparing others' feelings. She didn't want to hide with him. He seemed genuinely interested. "You could have stopped the rumors if you cared."

"I didn't think you would want me to." Hunter pulled into a small park and stopped the car. "I thought you'd be angry if I stopped the rumors. You usually want to deal with things head-on."

Amorette nodded, pasting on a smile at his automatic response. That was Hunter, always the logical one. Following his head and not his heart. "True. I deal with my problems by looking them in the eye. You're a smart man for realizing that." She patted his shoulder before she went back to her lunch.

She and Hunter were silent while they ate, but the playful banter soon picked up again. How could it not, when Hunter was still attempting to cheer her up? Before either of them realized it, they had talked about nothing all afternoon.

They were so intent on their conversation, in fact, that they didn't notice the car parked on the street behind them. Nor the dark figure behind a distant tree.

[EPISODE 4]
UNFORTUNATE, REDEFINED

It was late when Amorette finally stepped out of Hunter's car and in front of her own home. At least, what she thought was her home.

A host of expensive-looking cars trailed down the street, all parked and empty. A heavy, bass thumping sound echoed from inside the walls of the abode before her.

"Looks like someone's having a party," Hunter commented through the open passenger window. "Be careful, you never know what kinds of people show up to these things."

"It's probably the neighbors two doors over. They're always inviting people over." Amorette shrugged. It wasn't the first time someone had thrown a midnight party around here.

Hunter frowned and shut his own car off. He stepped out and up onto the sidewalk. "Forget it, I know too many of these cars. I'll walk you in."

"You really don't have to do that." Amorette held up a hand to stop him.

Hunter was never one to be easily dissuaded. "I know you can take care of yourself. I know that better than anyone." He tucked his fingers around hers, tossing in a boyish grin for effect. "But humor me this time."

Amorette narrowed her eyes at him. Only Hunter would assume the position of protector so openly and suddenly. She didn't think anyone said no to him ever in his life. But she wasn't about to complain. Especially since she'd been crushing hard on him since sixth grade. Pretty much since the moment he acknowledged her existence. Besides, he'd been a good friend today.

"Fine," she finally gave in. "Let's go."

Amorette pried her fingers from his grasp and marched toward the building before them.

The music was ten times louder when they reached the door and a hundred times louder when Amorette pushed the door open. Lights flashed and bodies moved in tandem to the beat.

Amorette, slack-jawed, ventured farther into the room. It was difficult to side-step some of the people, easier for others. Either way, she recognized many of the strangers in her home. The ones who ignored her during school. The ones Leah and Lucas thought they befriended. All more masked than the one before.

Leah looked up from the group of girls around her. Her eyes widened. At first, Amorette thought it was because of something she did. Until she looked behind her and saw Hunter close by.

Leah's eyes narrowed in the petulant way Amorette knew well. She flipped her hair once and stepped away from her clique. "Well, well, well, if it isn't the little wanna-be. Did you come home so you can rat us out later?"

Amorette didn't flinch. Leah threw words like daggers. The surest way to avoid them was to hide behind a shield.

Leah tossed her hair again and pressed past Amorette to sidle up to Hunter. "Hunny..." she swayed her shoulders, her voice a sickeningly sweet timbre. "I didn't know you'd come. I would have waited."

"For what?" Hunter extracted his arm from Leah's grasp.

"To start the party. It's not a real party without you by my side." Leah pouted and moved to wrap her hands around his bicep again.

Hunter side-stepped her and shook his head. "I only came in to make sure Amorette got home safely."

Leah's jaw tightened and then released to allow her slimy smile back on her lips. "Oh. Amorette. I almost forgot." Leah snatched a glass of something alcoholic from a nearby table. "Even if you are a rat, might as well take a drink or two before you disappear."

Amorette didn't trust the look in Leah's eyes, but she wasn't about to back down. She took the glass with a single nod. She had never been much for drinking, but holding the glass wouldn't hurt anyone.

"Go on. Don't be a killjoy. Take a drink." Leah smiled sweetly and held her hands up. "Promise I won't try anything this time."

Amorette glanced around at the clique of beautiful, rich girls who began to gather around the trio. One drink wouldn't kill her. With a sigh, she lifted the glass to her lips.

Movement in her peripheral vision caught Amorette's attention a split second before she saw the cause. Lucas nonchalantly shoved Hunter sideways. Hunter stumbled and hit Amorette's arm.

The glass hit Amorette's nose first. It spilled half of its contents down her face and shirt before it slid out of her grasp.

The glass shattered against the floor.

"Mi Amor..." Hunter stared at her wide-eyed, as if even he couldn't believe what happened.

"You can't even drink properly?" Leah's laugh was a mere huff of indignation.

Something hit Amorette against the side of her head. She looked down to see some sort of hors d'oeuvre lying in the spilled alcohol.

Leah stalked in a half-circle behind Amorette. "You should clean up your own messes. You're not even good enough to hang out with us, so I don't know why you bother trying."

"Harsh..." Lucas clicked his tongue as he appeared out of the crowd, a girl on either arm. "Not untrue, but harsh. I suppose we should at least offer her the opportunity to make up for it." He tossed another hors d'oeuvre in Amorette's direction. "Clean it all up like the servant you are."

The tears brimmed in Amorette's eyes as she looked up at Hunter.

Hunter reached out a hand to steady her, but it was already too late. The damage was done. Amorette spun on her heel and raced back out the door.

She should have known better than to engage with Leah. She should have known better than to bring Hunter into the apartment. Leah and Lucas would never leave her alone. Not after that. She couldn't stay there with the ringing laughter and the curious stares. She wasn't a monkey in a zoo. She refused to let anyone treat her as such.

Amorette's steps moved faster and faster, until she was racing down the sidewalk in no particular direction. She had no plans, other than the one desire at the forefront of her mind. *Get away.*

9——

"Sir?" Collins bowed his head. "I'm sorry. We lost her."

Eadric studied the head of security who had, surprisingly, taken the initiative to show up at Eadric's door at this hour. He didn't have to ask who it was they lost. He only had them tailing one woman at this point and time.

"Lost her how? Where?"

"We didn't expect her to come flying out of the building so fast. Our response time wasn't up to par." Collins held out a tablet with the video already cued on it. "If you review the footage from the camera we installed, I think you'll see that there was an inciting incident."

Eadric wasn't quite sure what hidden meaning lay behind Collins' eyes, but he wouldn't question it. He snatched the tablet from Collins' hand and tapped it to start the recording.

They had chosen a good angle for the camera, at least. He could see the entirety of the living room, all the way down the hall to Amorette's bedroom door. His focus, however, quickly turned to the juvenile delinquent marching across the floor in too-high-heels.

The scene wasn't pleasant. Starting with some idiotic boy and ending with another who didn't even have the guts to follow Amorette out. Eadric paused the recording before he became any sicker to his stomach. He handed the tablet over again.

"It's unacceptable to lose her. Find her again and keep sending me reports. That girl... has the potential to be someone very special someday." Eadric straightened his shoulders.

He couldn't let sentiment wear him down now. She wasn't his and that wasn't why he was doing this anyway. That friend of hers annoyed him, that's all.

"It won't be so simple." Collins straightened his jacket. "I'm afraid, Sir, that we have no idea where she might have run to."

"Has that ever stopped you before?" Eadric rolled his eyes. "Listen, Collins, you're the best head of security I've had to date, but if you fail this mission I won't ever forgive you. Find the girl and keep an eye on her. Lives depend on it."

Collins shot Eadric a look that said he thought he was being far too melodramatic. However, he didn't hesitate to dip a bow. "Yes, sir."

"You don't sound so convinced." Eadric lifted his chin. He was already in a bad mood today. He didn't need any more reason to act out.

Collins shrugged his shoulders and offered a small, tight smile. "I don't understand what's so important about this particular girl, is all. In all the time I've known you, I've never known you to chase after a woman. Especially not one so insignificant."

"Then look again. Insignificant isn't exactly the word I would use to describe her. There's more at work here than you know." Eadric waved his hand dismissively. "Go on. Locate her. Do not return until you have."

This time, Collins dipped a bow and disappeared out the door. Right where Eadric wanted him.

Eadric let out a frustrated roar and kicked at a potted plant.

This girl shouldn't be so difficult to keep tabs on. As far as that went, if Codex knew about her or the book in her possession, they should have made a move by now.

Why did he have to be so noble? Why did he insist on keeping her under his protection? There were many better things he could do with his time.

Then again, it wasn't his time spent on her. Mostly. Only his resources. Eadric retreated toward his room, with a stop in the kitchen for a bottle of water.

He hadn't cued his monitor all day, but his tablet rested nearby. It only took a few clicks to bring up side-by-side screens. One, her home. The other, the bookstore. One still held a host of inebriated rich kids. The other sat dark and empty.

"All right, little mouse, where did you run to?" Eadric sighed and dropped the tablet onto his bed.

It wasn't a question that would be easily answered. Nor would its answer come in the timely manner Eadric hoped for.

⚷

"Hi! Welcome to The Nook!" Amorette blew a strand of hair out of her face and threw a smile over her shoulder. "Is there anything specific I can help you with?"

The man who stepped through the door was handsome. Dark hair framed bright eyes, his stature spoke of money. No one walked with such good posture if they didn't have to.

He spared Amorette a cursory glance before a smile curved over his lips. "I'm not here for books."

"Are you aware you walked into a bookstore, then?" Melodia's voice sounded detached.

Amorette spun her head to see Melodia buried nose-deep in a romance novel again.

"It's not the store that attracted me." The man turned to face the counter. "But rather its proprietor."

"That's a shame. Would have been nice to sell some books today." Melodia barely glanced up at him. She licked an index finger to turn the page before her. "Just my luck, I guess."

The man blinked as if flustered by her indifference. He shot that killer smile down at Amorette. "Would you excuse the two of us?"

"Don't bother, Amy." Melodia chimed in immediately. "He won't be here long. Just keep organizing."

The man stepped around Amorette and stalked closer to Melodia's perch. "It *is* a shame. That's the tackiest book I've ever seen a woman read."

"You're right. It is a shame." Melodia slammed her book down on the counter. "Those are the tackiest pick-up lines I've heard in my life."

"Compliments are tacky now?" He shook his head.

Amorette could feel the steam shooting from his ears. Melodia had, somehow, riled this customer in odd ways.

"I only wanted to treat a beautiful woman to lunch. Is that so bad?"

"There are plenty of beautiful women waiting for a Lothario like you." Melodia waved a hand at him. "It shouldn't take you long to find one."

"L-L... Lothario?" He looked so stunned, that Amorette thought he might pass out. "Are you... rejecting my offer?"

"Romeo and Juliet. Act one, scene one, line forty-one." Melodia sighed and snatched her book off the counter. "If you're not here to purchase a book, leave. We're very busy today."

The man looked around him as if customers might appear out of thin air. "You... it's not..." Speechless, he turned for the door. He only stopped to look down at Amorette. "I'll be back."

"Of course. We'll be happy to assist you at the next opportunity." Amorette shot him a brilliant smile, hoping to make up for Melodia's sharp refusal to serve him or date him.

The man smiled and offered a short nod before he marched through the door. Amorette watched him fume all the way to his vehicle.

She turned to look at Melodia. "You didn't have to be so mean. Or quote Shakespeare at him."

"I didn't quote. I referenced. He thought I was a stupid blonde." Melodia snapped her book shut and huffed. Her eyes wandered to the spot where the man stood moments before. "Do you know how annoying that is? Especially coming from someone attractive like him. Ugh! The nerve." She folded her arms defiantly.

Amorette grinned as she stood to her feet. "Mel... do you, by chance... like him?"

"I don't even know who he is. Don't be absurd." Melodia shook her head. Her gaze traveled back to Amorette. "What? Don't look at me like that. Get back to work. We have lots to do."

"Yes, ma'am." Amorette giggled.

She had known Melodia long enough to know that her acting out said more than her indifference. It was her personality. She couldn't admit things outright, yet she did all the time. One only had to be watchful.

"Do you think he'll come back? That would be the most annoying thing of all." Melodia wrinkled her nose.

Amorette focused on reorganizing the out-of-place tomes before her. "I don't know. He seemed pretty serious about it."

"I won't say yes. He didn't even ask properly." Melodia toyed with her book, running her thumb back and forth against the corner of the pages. "Did he really think I'm some dumb blonde? I know I'm pretty, but does that automatically make me dumb?"

Amorette only smiled. Melodia had her own way of seeing the world. This was one of those times she had to let her think out loud. It was refreshing, to not work in absolute silence. For the first time since she ran out of her own home, Amorette thought there might be something to smile about.

She didn't know who the man was, but she hoped he returned. It would be interesting to see how Melodia handled someone as hot-tempered and hard-headed as herself.

Amorette sighed. Would she ever find that special someone? It seemed to her that most people ran into their soulmates at the strangest times, in the strangest situations. But... she never had that epiphany moment. The only man who ever tried to take care of her was Hunter.

Her lips curled into a smile at the thought of him. He knew how to lighten her load, at the very least. Her once-dormant crush had blossomed and then curled in again when he didn't speak a word in her defense. He probably thought she would want to take care of it herself. Again. But, sometimes, it would be nice if someone would take the initiative to care for her.

"Here." Melodia dangled a sandwich in front of Amorette's face. "You've worked hard, way past lunchtime. Eat this. It's the least I can do."

"Thanks, Mel." Amorette grabbed the sandwich and stood to stretch her arms and back. She leaned against the shelf for support when her legs rebelled. "You didn't have to do this. You're already housing me."

"Hey. Shh." Melodia put a finger to her lips. "Let's not make that public knowledge, okay? You've had enough interesting days that I'm not trying to jinx the rest of your month."

"You couldn't if you tried."

"I could but I won't." Melodia laughed and shrugged a shoulder. "It's almost closing time. Will you shut down the store for me? I have an errand to run."

"Is there anyone in here right now?" Amorette opened her sandwich and bit into it.

"Some man called asking if we had a specific volume. I already pulled it for you, so when he gets here all you have to do is ring it up." Melodia smiled brightly and blew a kiss on her way toward the door. "*Ciao bella!* Have fun!"

Amorette laughed and rolled her eyes. Eccentric, beautiful Melodia. What did she ever do to deserve a friend like that woman? If she didn't have Hunter and Melodia, Amorette didn't know how she would survive life.

With that last depressing thought, she focused all her attention on the sandwich in her hands. Then she wouldn't have to worry until the final customer showed up.

Sadly, the bell rang just as Amorette made it halfway through the sub. She sighed and headed for the register, her smile fixed in place.

"Welcome to The Nook! How may I assist you today?" She stuffed her sandwich on a shelf below the register.

The middle-aged man eyed her with a sneer. He shook his head when his appraisal was done, obviously finding something lacking about her. "I called." He held out a slip of paper.

Amorette took the proffered note and smiled at it. "Melodia said you'd be coming. One second." She spun to scan the shelf behind her, finally grabbing the book he specified. She set it on the counter.

"That's not what I ordered." The man folded his arms.

"It is. I promise. Sometimes books differ from their online

listing, depending on lighting and publication year-"

"It's not what I ordered."

"It's exactly what's on this paper." Amorette held the note so he could see it. "If you changed your mind, you can leave. It isn't like you paid for it already. I'm sure we can find another buyer."

The man snarled and shoved the book back across the counter. "I want the book I ordered. It's a rare volume. You can't even get that right?"

"Sir, I'm going to have to ask you to calm down. This is the book you ordered. I can show you the emails asking for it, as well as the note that you literally handed me two minutes ago." Amorette took a breath.

It took everything in her power not to lash out at him. She hated customers like this. The kind that would tell you it was raining when the sun was at its brightest.

"No. I want the book I ordered now. No more excuses."

Amorette refrained from rolling her eyes, barely. She turned to walk away. It would be better to let him cool down.

The man reached out grabbed her arm, jerking Amorette to a stop and pulling her back toward the register. Her hip hit the counter with an audible clap.

Amorette hissed a breath when the pain shot through her thigh and up her side. "Let go."

"Not until I get my merchandise."

She opened her mouth to speak again as the tears built in her eyes. Nothing came out. *You will not cry, you will not cry, you will not cry...*

"The young lady asked to be released."

Amorette looked past the angry customer to see the source of the voice. The man was tall, in his thirties at most. His eyes were nearly black, his hair just as dark. She had never seen him before in her life, but she was more than thankful he showed up now.

The customer scoffed, but he let go of Amorette's arm. "Whatever. I'll deal with the owner lady when she comes back. This place isn't worth it."

"That's a matter of opinion." The newcomer watched the man storm out the door, then turned back to Amorette. "He seemed like a gem. Are you alright?"

"I'm fine. Thank you." Amorette tugged her sleeve back up onto her shoulder. "How can I help you today, Mister...?"

"Blakely. Imran Blakely." Imran produced a sheet of paper and held it out to her. "I thought you might have these titles."

Amorette scanned the list with a critical eye. "I think we have most of these. Give me a minute to run and check?" She glanced up with a soft smile.

Imran nodded his head. "Take your time."

Amorette took the list with her and began to pull titles he requested. "If you don't mind my asking, what are all these for? It's a... unique collection."

"A class I'm teaching."

"You teach?"

"I'm a professor of history," Imran answered.

Amorette peeked her head back out from around the bookshelf that hid her from view. "You're a professor?"

"That's what most of my students ask, too. Surprisingly, it's the truth." Imran nodded as if to reassure both of them.

Amorette arched a brow, surprised but not shocked. He carried the general aura of the professors she had known. Not that she knew many of them, but it fit somehow.

"You seem young to be a professor."

"I learn quickly." Imran grinned in her direction.

"There's something to be said for that." Amorette giggled. She pulled another book from the shelf and added it to the stack in her arms. "You must be very dedicated to your work."

"Oh, extremely." Imran agreed. "It's my life's passion."

Amorette returned to the counter with her arms full of books. She dumped them next to the register and held out the slip of paper to Imran. "We don't have the last three, but we can order them if you'd like."

"That would be very helpful, indeed." Imran accepted the list with a slight bow. It was a strange mannerism, but Imran seemed to be a strange person overall.

Amorette rang up the books in front of her and wrote the last three down. "We'll have those for you in the next few weeks, but if you leave a phone number we'll call to keep you updated in case something happens."

"That would be splendid." Imran took the offered sheet of paper with a grateful smile. He scribbled ten digits and handed it back with a flourish. "Can I escort you anywhere? He seemed serious about causing harm here."

"Thank you, but no. I'll be fine." Amorette set the bags of books in front of him. "Can I help you carry those to your car?"

"Thank you, but no. I'll be fine." Imran chuckled and extended a small, rectangle card toward her. "My business card. In case you need anything."

"That's very kind of you." Amorette set the card by the register. "Come again and I'll be sure to call when the books come in." She waved as Imran headed out the door. He seemed nice enough.

The clock chimed.

Amorette skipped to the door and locked it, tugging a few times to ensure it was secure. With that done, she retrieved her own book from behind the counter and pushed through the door into the back room.

A pile of pillows and blankets awaited her in the far corner. Amorette grinned and kicked her shoes off before she flopped down. It wasn't a mattress or a fancy hotel room, but it was hers for now. She had been more than overjoyed when Melodia told her she could stay back there. It wasn't much, but it was warm and dry. That's all she needed while she figured out what to do next.

Amorette laid her head back against the wall. Who could read when her thoughts raged so wildly in her head? She wanted to be peaceful, but she couldn't. Amorette blew out a frustrated breath. Running away from home didn't do much good, after all. She was more anxious now than she had been then.

"You have to sleep," she told herself. "You should do at least that much."

With a heavy sigh, Amorette cuddled down into the blankets and closed her eyes, hoping sleep would come.

"Sir, I think you should see this." Collins held out his tablet to Eadric.

Eadric glared at him. "Did you find the girl? Because we have nothing to talk about if you didn't."

"This pertains to her. She arrived safely at work this morning and stayed all day. This happened at closing time." He nudged the tablet closer to Eadric's face.

Eadric glared for another minute before he was satisfied that Collins was squirming. He snatched the tablet and tapped the play button aggressively. The footage rolled, and he didn't like what he saw. Neither of the visitors boded well, even if he couldn't see what went on inside. He could look that up later.

"Tighten security. I want to know where she's staying and with whom. Don't let her out of your sight for a moment." Eadric handed the tablet back. "If you lose her again, I won't forgive it."

[EPISODE 5]
ACTIONABLE CONSEQUENCES

Misty fog permeated the black night, making vision impossible. Only voices floated through the air. Voices of those who knew best.

"We can't tell them. You know what they'll do."

"We can't not tell them. If they discover we've lied and covered this up..."

"You know what they're capable of now. We never signed up for this."

"There's no going back. We know things now."

"Not this. Not her."

⊶

The shop phone rang early the next morning. Amorette groaned and wrinkled her nose. She hadn't planned on waking up so early. She couldn't even answer the phone, considering the shop wasn't open so anyone calling would question why she was answering at this hour.

The answering machine beeped, signaling the start of a new

message.

"For the love of everything holy, Amorette if you're there answer this stupid phone."

Amorette sat straight up, eyes wide as she stared at the store phone. Why would Hunter call here so early? How did he know she was here?

"Mi Amor, please..." his voice trailed off, like he wasn't sure he was doing any good.

Amorette sighed and stood. She grabbed the phone from its cradle. "Are you stalking me?"

"Oh, thank God. You're really at the shop?" The relief in his voice was palpable, as if he'd been worried something bad happened. It was a nice sentiment, even if it wasn't true.

Amorette ran a hand back through her hair. "Yeah, I'm here. So can you stop calling now? Do you know what time of the morning it is?"

"Yes. I've been searching all night. Come let me in."

Amorette's heart stopped for a split second. A convulsive gulp rang in the still morning air. "What?" He was here? Why would he come here? There was no reason for him to show up like this. Unless... unless her suspicions were correct. "You're... outside?"

"Mi Amor, can we discuss this inside? I look stupid standing at the door in front of a closed sign. Please?" Hunter didn't breathe between sentences, as if he meant every word. As if he was desperate to see her.

A war waged in Amorette's head. Hunter could be sincere, or he could be after something else. He had been nothing but a gentleman the other night. A nagging suspicion told her there was more to Hunter than met the eye. In a good way.

Amorette set the phone back in its cradle and marched for the front door, keys in hand.

As his phone call suggested, Hunter did indeed stand outside the door. She unlocked it. A swift tug on his jacket sleeve pulled Hunter into the shop. Amorette locked the door behind him.

"Why are you here so early?" Hunter turned to ask her, his eyes dark with concern.

Amorette folded her arms. "Why are you here at all?"

"I was worried. You ran out of your own house the other night and I couldn't reach you after."

"I don't have a cell phone, remember?"

"Exactly!" Hunter's hands landed on her shoulders. He held her at arm's length. Searching brown eyes scanned her face. "Where have you been? You didn't go home. I kept checking."

Amorette quickly thought of the only fib that he might buy. "I... stayed at a friend's house."

Hunter arched a brow at her. "Oh yeah? Which friend? Melodia?"

Hey, perfect excuse! Amorette smiled and nodded, lying the entire time. What Hunter didn't know wouldn't kill him. It was her life and she could make accurate, decent decisions without his interruption or opinion. Saying she spent the night with Melodia would get Hunter off her back.

Except, any semblance of a smile he used to carry slowly slipped from his features. "I called Melodia, Mi Amor. She said you weren't there."

Uh-oh. Unexpected obstacle. *Think, Amorette, think hard!* She swallowed and glanced up at her friend. "She... was lying?"

"Oh, give it up, already." Hunter snorted a derisive little laugh. "Mi Amor..." he trailed off. One eyebrow twitched, followed by a tick in his jaw. Amorette knew the look. He was thinking.

Processing. Realizing. "No. *Oh*, no." He shook his head.

The second he spun on his heel, Amorette knew she was in for it. Hunter was anything but dumb. He definitely put two and two together. Her fears and suspicions were only confirmed when he marched straight toward her backroom hideaway.

Hunter flung the door wide and sighed. "Mi Amor..."

"It's not what it looks like. Melodia let me stay here for a night. Or two. I'm not going to live here forever, I swear. And it's not that bad. If I put on enough blankets, I can't even feel the cold seeping through on the floor..." Amorette winced and let her rant end there.

She was making it worse. She knew Hunter too well. He may seem aloof, but he cared about people's safety. Including hers.

"Do you know how many things could go wrong with you living in the back of a bookstore?" Hunter turned back to her, but instead of the anger she expected, his gaze held only concern. "Mi Amor, did you stop to think that this isn't a livable area?"

Amorette clutched one hand around the opposite arm. She had disappointed him. She could hear it in his voice. "My house isn't very livable right now either."

A long pause probably meant that Hunter was processing that, but Amorette didn't dare look up. Not until he reached out and settled his hands on her shoulders.

"I know." Hunter sighed again. "And that's partially my fault. I'll fix it. Somehow. Just... don't stay here. Come stay at my place. You can have the bed, I'll take the couch."

"I'm not sure that's the greatest idea." Amorette took a step back, away from his fingers.

He was probably trying to make up for what he did the other night. Trying, somehow, to apologize for not sticking up for her when he had the chance. She didn't do well with pity.

"One night. That's all I ask. I'll find you somewhere else to stay."

Amorette looked past Hunter, to her pile of assorted pillows and blankets. The floor here was, admittedly, cold. Only one window held a place along the cement wall. It wasn't the best idea, but it got her through a few troublesome nights.

Amorette heaved a deep breath and looked up at him. "Okay. One night. But I'll take the couch."

"No way. Bed or nothing. I'll take the couch in case something wonky happens. Plus, then you can't sneak out on me." Hunter shrugged and tossed an arm around her shoulders. "I'm glad you see things my way. Now... what do you need to collect here before I take you to get a nice, warm breakfast?"

Hunter changed the subject so efficiently that he left no time for Amorette to get a word in edgewise. Which meant she also had no choice about going to his house or to breakfast. Thankfully, she knew how Hunter worked. He'd let it go if she let him spoil her for a few hours. In his book, money spoke loudest. He'd been that way since she met him. Amorette wagered it had something to do with how his parents raised him.

"Hurrying would be advised." Hunter rotated his finger in the universal gesture for "be quick about it."

Amorette ducked out from under his arm and dashed to grab her shoes and coat.

When she came right back to his side, Hunter gaped. "That's all you have?"

"Here? Yes." Amorette pulled her jacket over her arms. "I haven't had the guts to go home and grab my stuff yet. I'll work up the courage one day."

"Hopefully soon." Hunter wrapped his arm around hers and led her toward the front door. "Do you have your keys?"

"They haven't left my hand since I let you in." Amorette tossed him a tight, dry smile. "Why are you holding onto me?"

"In case you think you're going to be running anywhere." Hunter pouted at her. "I've dealt with enough of that over the past couple of days. Seriously, how could you not have called me? I thought we were closer than that."

"It's all about perception, Hunny Bun." Amorette took the moment of stunned silence to slip away from him and dart to the door. It opened easily enough. "Come on. We don't have all day."

⚿

Eadric traced a finger along a crack in the shattered phone screen. It was, indeed, broken beyond repair. He looked into it personally. He also confirmed her statement. She hadn't had the phone more than a few weeks. In this day and age, it was better to have a phone than be without one. Especially when one was a young woman.

It wasn't his fault the phone broke, but somehow he felt responsible for the girl. The men he sent to watch her seemed less competent by the day. She slipped away one way or another, at some point during the day. That shouldn't... No, it *couldn't* happen. She bore the mark, so she must be important. To someone.

Eadric blew out a breath. She wasn't his to protect, and he hadn't interfered in anyone's life in years. It went better for everyone if he didn't.

He glanced to the small black tracking device sitting nearby. He couldn't bring himself to plant it. Even if she was in danger, didn't she deserve some sort of privacy? He was infringing on the right he claimed every person deserved.

As quickly as he talked himself into the tracking device, Eadric talked himself out of it. Great. How was he supposed to keep an eye on her if he didn't know where she was?

"You idiot," he muttered. "She's not yours to be responsible for. She can take care of herself. She has that boy."

"Um, do I need to call the doctor?" Doon peered through the door to ask. "Grandfather did tell me that when you start talking out loud to yourself, it's time to reevaluate our decision-making paradigm."

"He would." Eadric leaned back in his chair and folded his arms over his chest. "I do not need the hospital, but many thanks for your concern."

Doon nodded and ventured a step into the room so he could close the door. "No problem. You summoned, Oh Great One?"

Eadric huffed a short laugh. His fingers toyed with the fragmented cellular phone. "I need you to deliver something for me. No one can know."

"Sounds like fun. Where am I going?" Doon grinned like he won the lottery.

Eadric snatched a small box from the end of his desk and rose. "Her bedroom." He held it out. "Leave this for her. I've already explained in the note."

Doon wrinkled his nose. "I was hoping for the shop," he mumbled. Unfortunately, Doon had never been especially talented at remaining quiet. Eadric heard every word.

There were a few reasons Doon could wish to enter the little bookshop again. Eadric didn't like any of them.

He scowled at his friend's grandson. "Whatever your

intentions, forget them now. It isn't your place."

"Hey, I'm a man, too. Not just a monkey." Doon stalked forward and snatched the box from Eadric's grip. "What I do on my own time is none of your business. Work and personal have a way of overlapping, but I promise I'll be the perfect gentleman while I'm on your dime."

Somehow, Eadric didn't quite believe that. Doon did what Doon wanted. Normally, it didn't matter. Doon got the job done, everyone was happy. For some reason, Doon's personality and vague designs grated on Eadric's nerves about this one. There was only one thing of interest at that bookshop. Doon would be a fool to overlook the young, naive Amorette.

The muscle in Eadric's jaw ticked. His lip curled up into a sneer. "I mean it, Doon."

"Alright, alright!" Doon backed away from the angry bear. He raised his hands in surrender. "I get the picture. I'll try to scale back. But I still think it's wrong for you to control my personal life. I'd think you would have learned that."

"Shut. Up." Eadric lifted a hand to rub the throbbing spot between his eyebrows. The insolence of young people these days. "Just deliver the package. That's all I need today."

"Yes, *your majesty*." Doon darted out the door before Eadric had time to throw anything.

Eadric growled at the closed door. There were other ways to relieve stress. He didn't need to throw anything at Doon's head, but it would have been the quickest way to make himself feel better.

Eadric grabbed his jacket off the back of his chair. He wouldn't get any more work done if he didn't do something physical. Which meant a quick trip to the basement was in order.

Everyone in the company called it *The Dungeons* when, in fact, it was the brightest area in the building.

For his employees' benefit, but also for his own, Eadric ensured the gym, studio, and pool areas stayed up to date and fully furnished. It was the studio he aimed for now. He shoved the door open and inhaled deeply.

A long, hand-whittled staff awaited Eadric against the nearest wall. He tossed his jacket to the ground and wrapped a hand around the blunt weapon. His fingers flexed against the smooth wood, remembering a time when it hadn't been as polished. When the wood bit into his fingers and reminded him how much he had to learn.

A simple twist of his wrist sent the staff whizzing in a circle through the air. The weight of it hadn't changed, nor had the minuscule force needed to wield it.

Eadric lifted his chin, meeting his own haunted eyes in the mirror. He didn't remember when he became this man. Cold-hearted and incompassionate. He never meant to shut everyone else out, but they didn't understand the things he'd been through.

Dozens of wars.

Hundreds of lost loved ones.

Centuries alone.

Eadric poised the staff in his palms and lunged. Imaginary attackers on every side, Eadric fought his demons with the strength and determination of a seasoned warrior. Each memory, each thought, each foe. Eadric whirled and lunged and slashed the air until his hair dripped with sweat and his lungs and limbs burned.

Only then did he allow the staff to clatter to the floor. For a brief moment, his mind was at ease. Blank.

And then a young face clamored to the surface, her eyes spitting fire and her tears wetting her cheeks.

Eadric growled at his own wayward imagination. Now wasn't the time to think about the young woman who turned his world upside-down. He thought he had himself under control. It appeared he needed to finish the job.

He bent and took up the staff once more.

⚷

"This is stupid." Amorette folded her arms under her chest and glared at Hunter. "I don't want to go back there."

Why would Hunter suggest she return to the ridiculous place she used to call a home? Sure, her things were there, but it was evening. Which meant her step-mother would be there. Which definitely didn't sound like a good idea after three and a half full days away. She would be in so much trouble.

Hunter rolled his eyes. "Mi Amor, you can't stay away forever. I lent you a sweatshirt but seriously, you need your own clothes. It'll make you feel better. I'm not saying stay there, I'm just saying enter and retrieve."

"What if she's home?" Amorette shivered, a bit dramatically, but Hunter would get the point. There was nothing worse than Amorette's step-mother, angry.

"I'll be on the lookout. She wouldn't hit you with me there, right?" Hunter's eyes went dark, a look Amorette knew well. His brain had gone into overdrive, or he was concerned.

She would like to think it was the latter, but she would wager on the former.

Amorette shook her head. "I'll run in and run out. It shouldn't

CODEX

be too hard, right? You don't have to come."

"You need a lookout," Hunter argued. "Besides, I know you and if I don't come you might chicken out."

"Hey! I am not a chicken, you jerk!" Amorette threw a couch pillow at his head.

How dare he insinuate that she had any scaredy-cat behind her tough, go-get-em demeanor. Amorette lifted her chin, offended by his allegation. She wasn't scared of anything. Except for dark rooms. Giant thugs. Spiders.

Whatever, she wasn't going to chicken out just because her step-family may be home. No way. No how. He could just... shove it.

Hunter caught the pillow before it hit his face. Pleasant wrinkles formed beside his eyes as he laughed.

Laughed?

Laughed!

Amorette stood to her feet and stomped toward the bedroom at the back of Hunter's small apartment. If he wanted to laugh, let him laugh alone. Like a hyena, his laugh could only mean he wanted to eat her. Or, in Hunter's case, spew insults and complements, intertwined.

"Wait!" Hunter's laughter stopped. "Mi Amor, I'm sorry! Come back."

"Absolutely not!"

Amorette slammed the bedroom door and huffed a breath. He wanted her to go pick up her things? He thought she was chicken? Fine. She would show him how wrong he was to think that. There was one option left to her, in order to prove her tenacity. She had to go alone.

The front door was no longer an option, considering she

would have to walk right past Hunter to get to it. He would undoubtedly follow her, and that defeated her purpose.

Amorette regarded the window with suspicion before she ventured over. It could work. She was small enough to slip out, but she would need something to help her down to the ground. This was the second floor, after all, she couldn't jump that far down.

Or she could try the fire escape outside the kitchen window. That might be tricky, but Amorette thought she could make it.

Awesome. One plan down.

Thankfully, the door didn't squeak or creak when Amorette cracked it open. Hunter was nowhere in sight. Knowing him, he was pouting in the living room. She would have to be careful.

Amorette tiptoed into the hall. It wasn't too far to the kitchen, but she had to pass the living room to make it that far. Drastic times called for drastic measures.

She wrinkled her nose and dropped to her hands and knees. The smaller she made herself, the less chance that Hunter would see or hear her. At least, that's what Amorette told herself.

On all fours, Amorette slowly made her way down the hall. It was harder to keep quiet this way, but Hunter would see her if she walked upright. Once she made it over the threshold, the high counter between the living room and kitchen hid her from his sight.

She let out a soft breath and scooted her way to the window.

"Hey, Mi Amor, if you come out we can watch a movie or something!" Hunter called toward the hall.

Amorette winced and curled into a ball between the microwave cart and the wall. She couldn't answer him. It would give away her position, something she would never do. Hiding seemed like the better idea.

"Mi Amor?" Hunter sounded concerned.

Amorette tried not to let that get to her.

A shuffle of clothes and footsteps told her Hunter got up from the couch. She counted the seconds it took him to walk down the hall. She wouldn't have much time to get out.

Hunter knocked on the bedroom door.

Amorette flew into action.

No longer worried about making noise, she dove out from beside the microwave and shoved open the window. From there, it was easy to crawl out onto the fire escape and hasten down. She rode the final ladder to the ground and jumped off. A quick jog took her around the corner and down the street.

If Hunter figured her out and followed, she doubted he would find her so quickly. Amorette tossed a look over her shoulder and grinned. No. Hunter would take a few minutes to start looking. Perfect.

Amorette headed down the sidewalk in the general direction of her neighborhood.

The streets were empty this evening, the wind too chilled for anyone in their right mind to want to be out in it. Amorette never claimed to be sane.

She was the type to daydream about the impossible. The one who watched for a love that would come snatch her from the nightmare of her own life. She had a weakness for White Knights and an affinity for finding herself in trouble. Two reasons why she came this far and endured so much. She didn't have a choice if she wanted to find the love she so desperately sought.

She should have thought to grab a coat, Amorette realized as the cold seeped through her sweatshirt, then her shirt beneath. A shiver wracked her spine. Amorette cupped her hands over her nose and mouth. It alleviated the cold somewhat, but not enough to satisfy her.

Only three blocks more to her house.

"Excuse me! Young lady!"

Amorette hesitated in her stride. That voice sounded familiar. Too familiar, really. She turned, only to see the old woman who usually set up camp close to Amorette's house. Amorette's fingers slowly slipped down from her face.

The old woman smiled. "Hello again."

"Why are you out here? It's so cold." Amorette tipped her head each direction, looking for anyone to help the woman for the night.

The lady waved a hand. "I have my coats and my scarves. But what do you have? You look positively frozen."

"I didn't really think before I headed out, but I'm almost home." Amorette smiled.

Somehow, this woman evoked a sense of camaraderie. Like she wanted all the best for Amorette and nothing more. Like there was more to her story than just an old woman who sat by the side of the road and sold sandwiches and pretty hand-made baubles.

"Come here, child." The woman crooked a finger to motion Amorette closer.

Amorette figured it couldn't hurt anything, so she squatted down near the old woman.

The woman smiled as she pulled a scarf from her pile and wrapped it around Amorette's neck. "Don't be so foolish as to be out in the cold without protection. Give me your hands." A pair of soft mittens were next on the list of things given to Amorette from the mountain of warmth.

"Thank you, ma'am." Amorette couldn't help but smile as she hunkered into the scarf. It helped, to have something that warmed her face. The evening chill didn't have quite the bite it once had.

"Ma'am seems so formal." The woman laughed, a soft, tinkling bell sound that lifted Amorette's spirits. "Instead, why don't you call me Nannie. It's been years since anyone called me Nannie."

"Nannie." Amorette smiled and nodded her head. "I hope we continue to run into each other."

"I'm sure we will. This is your neighborhood after all, isn't it?" A bright smile lit her face and made her look a hundred years younger. "If you ever need anything, don't hesitate to ask me. I'm rather resourceful."

"I can tell." Amorette laughed with her. "I think I want to be as resourceful as you when I grow up."

"No, child. You don't want to grow up at all." Nannie shrugged her shoulders. Her breath puffed a hazy gray in the air. "Don't. Refuse to grow up and live as if it's your first and last day on earth."

"I'll be sure to take your advice to heart." Amorette smiled once more before she stood. "I have to go now. I'll look for you on my way back."

"Then you aren't staying?"

"No. There's been some... family drama. I don't think I'll be staying there for the foreseeable future."

"A pity. I may have to move my shop."

Amorette laughed again. "If you do, I hope you find my new area of town."

"I'll do my best." Nannie made a shooing motion. "Go on. Go

on home and find your coat. Don't leave without it."

"Thank you, Nannie." Amorette waved again as she started down the road.

Somehow, seeing the older woman had cheered her. Who knew that the woman who once offered a sandwich would become such a light in her dark life? For the first time in a long time, Amorette was glad she met someone like Nannie. Someone who spoke freely and gave unconditionally. She needed those kinds of people in her life.

Amorette ventured the last few blocks with great trepidation.

Her house sat dark and looming at the end of the walkway. The good news was, the chances of her step-mother being awake and roaming around the house were pretty low. The bad news? There was a fifty-fifty chance of her step-mother being asleep inside. She would need to be quiet and stealthy.

Amorette pulled her key from her pocket and unlocked the door. The one perk of living here most of her life, she knew where all the squeaks and creaks were loudest.

One delicate step at a time, Amorette ventured down the hall and into her room. Surprisingly, it was as she'd left it. With a sigh, Amorette opened her closet and pulled out the one suitcase she owned. It would hold enough to get her through, at least.

Her dresser wasn't hard to empty out. She didn't exactly have the massive wardrobe her step-sister and step-mother favored. Amorette would rather spend her money on things that mattered. Like food.

She stood up from where she had bent to stuff clothes into the suitcase. Her eyes landed on her bed.

Amorette froze.

Blinked.

On the middle of her bed sat what appeared to be a present. Amorette ran through a mental checklist. Wrapping paper. Bow. Tape. No card, though. She ventured a step closer, then another, until she found the box in her hands. It had been wrapped so neatly, the tape clean and the ribbon perfectly centered. She almost felt bad about opening it. Almost.

Amorette untied the ribbon and let it fall to the bed. For the first time in her life, she took her time opening a gift.

It had been years since anyone offered her a present, and Amorette wanted to enjoy the thrill while she could. She took her time to open each fold, careful not to disrupt the paper as she made her way to the surprise inside.

When all was said and done, Amorette held a plain black box in her hands. At that point, she lost her self-control. She couldn't open the lid fast enough.

To her shock and utmost pleasure, a shiny new cell phone gleamed in the dim lamplight. An even better model than the one she broke.

Without a card, she couldn't be certain who left it for her. It couldn't have been her step-mother. It must have been Hunter. It made sense for him to do something like this. He did encourage her to return home and get her things. Did he plan this all along? It would explain a lot.

Amorette smiled softly at the phone in her hands. For once, she wanted to accept what he offered her. For once, she wanted to look after herself before anyone else. Amorette shoved the phone in her pocket before she could change her mind.

A few of her precious books completed the ensemble in her heavy bag. Amorette zipped it and rolled it behind her toward the front door.

The living room light flicked on.

Amorette froze.

Her step-mother folded her arms and sneered. "So, the prodigal finally returns. Where are you off to now?"

Amorette bristled at the high-and-mighty tone her step-mother used. As if Amorette had been in the wrong for staying away, even though she was a legal adult. A tone that said, in her step-mother's eyes, Amorette was still a child.

"I don't see how it's any of your business." Amorette took another step toward the door. Her arm wrenched backward, sending a shooting pain through her shoulder.

Her step-mother rolled the suitcase behind her and took a defensive stance between Amorette and the luggage. "It's absolutely my business if any daughter of mine is traipsing about at all hours of the day with God-knows-who."

"Then it's a good thing I'm not any daughter of yours." Amorette tried to side-step the woman but found herself once again face-to-face with her.

"Insolent, selfish child." Amorette's step-mother hissed. "You think I'll let you walk out so easily? After all you put me through?"

"All I put you through?" Amorette blinked in shock. How had she been the one to put her step-mother through anything? "I only stayed in case dad came back."

"You think he'd come back to take care of someone as careless as you?" A scoff turned into a shrill laugh as it spilled from her step-mother's lips. "He left because of you and your mother. He couldn't bear to look at you anymore. Don't you know that? I'm a saint for putting up with that woman's child. You should have been left to starve. I'm sure he's glad your mother died."

The anger boiled up so fast and hard inside Amorette that she didn't even realize she lost control until her palm connected with her step-mother's cheek. "If anyone is the cause for his leaving, it's you."

Her step-mother didn't waste a second retaliating. The back of her hand hit Amorette's cheek with enough force to make the younger girl stumble sideways. Something sharp sent a stinging sensation to Amorette's cheekbone, paired with the throbbing pain of knuckles hitting flesh.

"After all I've done for you, you repay me with slander and accusations. Perhaps I should let you go, after all."

Amorette fought tears as she darted around her step-mother and snatched the suitcase from her hold. "You only wanted me here because if father loves anyone enough to come back to them, it's me." She marched for the door. She couldn't get out fast enough. "If he ever comes back, tell him I won't be around. Give him my number if you want."

"How, when you don't have a phone anyway?"

Amorette shrugged. If she said much more, she would break down. Her face ached almost as badly as her heart.

The door slammed heavy behind her, the unsaid words weighing her down as she jogged down the sidewalk and around the corner. Anything to get as far away from her step-mother as she could.

[EPISODE 6]
AN INTERVENTION OF FATE

The incessant ringing of the phone made Eadric scowl, but no matter how many times he ignored it, someone called again.

With a growl, Eadric flipped the phone over and stared at the name that flashed across it. Collins. If that idiot buffoon had lost the girl again, Eadric couldn't be held responsible for anything he did to the man.

"*What* is it this time?" The volume of his voice rang through the house and echoed off the empty halls.

"It's about the girl, sir."

"You haven't found her yet?"

"No, sir. That's the thing. We found her, but..." Collins trailed off for a few long seconds. "I think it might be best if you check your inbox for our surveillance photos. We're keeping an eye on her right now."

Eadric scowled at the command. He didn't like anyone, especially Collins, telling him what to do or not to do. Still, now his curiosity wouldn't be satisfied until he knew what Collins referred to.

"One moment."

Eadric snatched his tablet and punched in the code.

The empty bookstore stared at him through the live feed. The second half of the screen still held the footage of Amorette's living room.

Eadric exited both and opened his inbox. A series of disturbing images flashed before his eyes. Tears and blood mingled on a shadowed face.

"What is this?" Eadric snapped at Collins. Their job was to protect the woman, not watch while someone beat her.

Collins sighed. "Should we observe and report? Or should we do something?"

Eadric couldn't imagine the incompetent simpleton would be of any help, but he couldn't leave this alone, either. "Where is she now?"

"She's sitting on a park bench. Hasn't moved in a while."

Of course. She must be frozen, even if the pictures showed a scarf and a coat. Eadric didn't trust Collins with this girl enough to send him in by himself. She was too intelligent to think the man a simple passer-by.

Eadric would go himself, but he refused to get into the middle of things. There was only one option left to him, and he didn't particularly like it.

"Send me the address."

"What?" Collins sounded more concerned than shocked.

"I said, send me the address. I'm sending someone to her, don't let her out of your sight. Not even for a moment." Eadric listened to Collins recite the information, then hung up the phone.

One more phone call would set things right again. At least, as right as they could be for now. In the morning, once Amorette was settled somewhere less dangerous than a park bench, he would work on righting everything for real. He owed her at least that much, for dragging her into this in the first place.

Eadric grabbed the keys to his car and dialed as he walked.

"What do you want now?" Considering it was only eight in the evening, it took Doon far too long to pick up his phone. Something they would have to work on.

Eadric slammed his front door behind himself. "Where are you?"

"I'm... home?"

Why Doon phrased it as a question instead of a statement completely eluded Eadric. He didn't have time to worry about it now. "Put on something warm, I'll be there in ten minutes."

"Why?" The never-ending cycle of questions wasn't unusual. Doon always asked questions. About everything. That didn't make it any less annoying when such infuriating circumstances loomed.

"I'll explain on the way." Eadric ended the call then and there. Doon would only ask more questions, which would lead to more aggravation.

Eadric had no intentions of throttling Doon this evening, but if the conversation went on he might change his mind. He had never been excellent at controlling his temper, least of all when it came to innocents.

The SUV ate up the road faster than Eadric intended. Still, when he arrived at Doon's residence, the younger man waited outside the front entrance. Eadric didn't even have to exit the vehicle or honk the horn to garner his attention. At least the boy took urgent instructions well.

Doon jogged himself to the passenger door and slid inside. "Okay, I cave. What's going on? You sounded upset."

Eadric shook his head. Doon guessed his current state of mind too easily. His emotions and temper must have gotten away from him again. Eadric strove to present a calm, cool front. If it faltered, people might see through him. Which was something he swore ages ago to never allow. He needed to be in control of his own life, such as it was.

"Hello? Earth to Eadric!" Doon snapped his fingers in his boss' general direction.

Eadric scowled at him. "What did you call me?"

"Hey, I was just trying to get your attention. What has your panties in a twist?"

"Watch your phraseology." Eadric glared harder at the crude expression.

Most of him wanted to give a long, arduous lecture about the finer points of good manners and common sense. He refrained only because he knew Doon wouldn't listen to a word of it. Doon, being Doon, would probably interrupt somewhere around the best part of the rant.

The duo rode in silence across town. Even during a brief stop at a convenience store for supplies, Doon didn't speak. It seemed suspicious to Eadric, but he wouldn't look a gift horse in the mouth.

He wouldn't admit to it, but Eadric breathed a sigh of relief when he saw his security team parked where they told him they would be.

Another part of him tensed. That meant the girl had been sitting out in the cold for nigh on an hour. He couldn't imagine how frozen she must be.

Doon folded his arms as best he could with the constricting slim jacket he wore. "Okay, I give up. Why are we at a park? Why is Collins here? What's in the shopping bag? What do you need me for?"

Eadric tossed the plastic bag into Doon's lap. "You'll find that girl sitting alone on a park bench. She's injured and needs help. Treat her wounds."

"Or... you could do it." Doon shrugged his shoulders.

Eadric wrinkled his nose, his lips turned up into a sneer. Doon had a knack for getting on people's nerves. Eadric's most of all. "I can't do it. We both know that. I shouldn't make my connection to her known."

"Ooh, a connection, you say?" Doon turned in his seat. "Do tell."

"I'll tell if you go give her treatment and hot packs."

"Or we could try the other way around."

"Doon. This is your only warning."

Doon sighed. "Fine, fine. I'm going." He reached for his door handle.

A snazzy red sports car zoomed past, almost skimming the side of the SUV.

"Hey! Idiot! Slow down!" Doon shouted, even though everyone in the vehicle would wager that the sports car didn't hear him.

Eadric frowned. That car looked familiar. Too familiar for comfort. "Doon. Go now." Eadric reached for his own door handle. "I think I have some business to attend."

"Here? Now?" Doon rolled his eyes and pushed his door open to step onto the frigid concrete below. His mumbling didn't stop. "How does he even get into these kinds of situations..."

Eadric couldn't hear any more after Doon slammed the door shut. He counted to ten before he opened his own door and marched for the sports car. He couldn't quite place where he knew it from, but he knew it nonetheless. It couldn't be a coincidence that it appeared here, now.

The boy that stepped from the driver's door didn't even look Eadric's direction. Instead, he took off running with a cry of, "Mi Amor!"

Eadric stopped in his tracks.

The plastic grocery bag rustled as this newcomer shot past Doon. Both Doon and Eadric watched the boy make a beeline to Amorette's side.

That's when Eadric remembered. The car. The boy. All things he saw only a few days ago. He didn't like it then. He didn't like them now.

Still, even at this distance, Eadric could see the relief on Amorette's face. She knew this boy, so he would keep his temper in check. For now. Even though the way the boy wrapped his arms around the girl was enough to make Eadric grind his teeth.

Doon shot a glance over his shoulder.

Eadric waved him on.

How? Doon mouthed the word over-dramatically. He motioned between the two young people at the bench.

Eadric shrugged and waved his hand again. He would wager money the young idiot didn't have anything to treat her wounds or warm her up. Body heat was out of the question.

Doon sighed and nodded his head. He really had no choice with Eadric looking on. So he marched forward, as instructed.

Amorette never expected Hunter to show up so quickly. After she ran away, she could only think to call him. Her only friend in the world and the man currently housing her and feeding her. In some ways, she needed his help anyway. He would see the aftereffects of her step-mother's anger once she went back to his place, so it didn't seem to matter too much if she called him to come get her.

She didn't expect the second man to show up. One who looked more familiar than she cared to let on.

Amorette frowned at the newcomer, pushing away Hunter's embrace to do so. "What are you doing here?"

The man waved a hand in an awkward gesture. "Long story."

"You know this guy?" Hunter hooked a thumb in the man's general direction.

"I wouldn't say we're best friends," Amorette shrugged. "But he came into the shop to hit on Melodia the other day."

"Hey, I was not hitting on her. I simply asked her out on a date." The man huffed his displeasure. "Can't believe she turned me down. How rude can one woman be? One date! That's all I asked. One measly date. She didn't even have any tact. Just shot me down. Rejected. Rude!"

Amorette and Hunter didn't move a muscle. Amorette was fairly certain that this guy forgot there were people next to him. He seemed lost in his own rant. Strangely, it sounded a lot like the rant from Melodia that Amorette endured.

Maybe they were better suited for each other than she originally thought. Pretty boy, pretty girl. He was right, one date wouldn't have hurt either of them. Still...

"What long story brings you here, right now?" Amorette tried not to wince. Talking hurt. Wincing hurt even more.

"Here."

At the rustling of plastic and paper, Amorette lowered her eyes from his face to his hand. The plastic grocery bag shouldn't have surprised her, but it did.

"What's that?" Hunter asked before Amorette had the chance to form words.

Amorette looked up in time to see the man's face contort in a flurry of emotions and inward conversations. "Antiseptic, bandages... things like that."

In a flash, Hunter somehow maneuvered himself between Amorette and the handsome man. "Who are you? Are you following her? How did you know she would need it?"

A heavy sigh from the older man spoke volumes more than any words. Still, he didn't seem the kind to remain speechless. Amorette counted to three before he, unsurprisingly, sprang into an explanation.

"I'll be brief. A friend of mine and myself got into a bit of a scuffle tonight. This was my apology gift. You need it more than he does." The man rested a hand against Hunter's shoulder and pushed him out of the way. "The name is Doon. You're not getting a last name so don't ask." Doon shot Hunter a knowing look. "Whatever happened to you, it was wrong. Sorry your face got hurt."

Doon didn't seem so bad. Despite Hunter's wary behavior, Amorette liked the flighty stranger standing before her. She usually had a pretty good instinct about people. Doon didn't seem like a threat. If anything, he seemed like an acquaintance she wanted to be closer friends with.

Amorette stood from the bench and held out an icy, bare hand to retrieve the sack. "Thank you, Doon. You didn't have to do this."

"Yes, I did. Trust me." Doon shot a look over his shoulder. "I can stay and help you dress the wound..."

"No, I've got that covered." Hunter moved closer to Amorette's side. The glance he gave Doon remained cautious, but he already seemed softer toward the man. "Thanks for being compassionate."

Doon nodded and turned to walk back the way he came.

"One more question," Hunter threw after him.

Doon stopped.

Amorette looked up at her friend. She had never heard that particular tone in his voice. He seemed curious, more than anything. Then his arm went around her waist in a protective gesture.

Amorette felt her eyes go wide. A mistake, since it only managed to tug at the bruise and swelling.

Doon glanced back over his shoulder. "Yeah?"

"If you were headed that way," Hunter tossed his head toward the park behind Amorette, "then why are you going the opposite direction now?"

A mischievous smirk lit Doon's features. He shrugged one shoulder. "Can't go back empty-handed." With that, he dismissed Amorette and Hunter in favor of returning to whence he came.

Hunter turned. His hands moved up to Amorette's jaw, gently cupping her swollen and bruised face. "Step-sister or evil witch?"

He would ask that. Amorette didn't mind answering, but it brought back all the emotions of the evening. She didn't quite know what to do about those. "My step-mother. She regrets raising me."

"She's an idiot." Hunter tugged the sack from Amorette's

fingers. He set it on the bench to rummage through its contents. "She should be proud someone like you ever stayed by her side."

"Don't say that." Amorette bowed her head. "She's horrible, but deep down I think she's lonely. Her own kids don't exactly get along with her, either, so she's all alone. All the time."

"That's not an excuse." Hunter opened some packaging and set about applying antiseptic to the cut across Amorette's cheekbone. "Her behavior isn't understandable, no matter how much you justify it. What did she hit you with, anyway?"

"Her hand." Amorette pulled away from the stinging sensation.

Hunter caught her chin between his fingers. "Stay still. It'll go faster that way."

Amorette sniffed. "Fine."

"That's my girl." Hunter winked at her, but it didn't seem as playful as his usual self.

Amorette watched his face, trying to determine what went on in that head of his. She didn't dare ask. She didn't think she'd want to hear the answer. At least not now.

Amorette's teeth nipped at her chapped lower lip. What would he say if she asked? Could she handle any confession about his behavior? There were too many variables. Too many strange ways he acted toward her lately. Surely he didn't... *like* her?

"What's wrong, Mi Amor?" Hunter smoothed a bandage over the gash in her cheek.

Amorette took a step back. "It's nothing. I'm just thinking."

"About what?"

"Behavior." Amorette stuffed her hands in her pockets. "If my step-mother's behavior is deplorable, then so is mine. I should go apologize."

Hunter glanced up at her from where he gathered the items into the sack. "To whom?"

"It wasn't the company's fault that my phone broke. It wasn't even their marketing at fault." Amorette shrugged her shoulders against the cold wind. "I should apologize for my behavior."

"That's different."

"No, it isn't." Amorette shook her head. "I blamed the CEO for something he never did. Just like my step-mother blames me. Personal responsibility is something I would like to pride myself on. So I need to make amends."

"I'm sure he's fine." Hunter grabbed the sack and reached for Amorette's hand.

She expertly dodged his grab and started for the warmth of the red sports car. "Thank you for the phone, by the way."

"What phone?"

"You don't have to play dumb. There aren't a lot of people who knew about that."

Hunter wrapped his fingers around her elbow. "I'm serious, Mi Amor. I don't know what you're talking about. What phone?"

"It wasn't you?" Amorette frowned. The theory fit so well. Who else would have purchased a new phone and programmed it with the same number she had on the broken one? "Then who gave me the new phone?"

Hunter shrugged. "Must have been your step-mother. Maybe the witch felt guilty."

That didn't add up correctly in Amorette's head, but there was little to no evidence for anyone else to have done it. Something nagged at her subconscious, but she couldn't quite place it. So, for now, she let it slide.

Amorette pulled her arm out of Hunter's grasp and walked

backward. "Let's go to your place, Hunter. Please? I'm frozen and in pain. I need ice cream. Do you have ice cream?"

Hunter smiled, albeit a weak impersonation of the boyish grin he usually offered. "Alright, alright. Let's go pig out on some ice cream."

⌐⊸━

"Hunter!"

"No."

Amorette wrinkled her nose out of pure disgust. "You promised."

"I did no such thing."

Hunter could be such a mule when he put his mind to it. Amorette didn't need his permission to do anything, but it would be a whole lot easier if he cooperated and gave her a ride.

"He was a jerk about the whole thing." Hunter poked his head out of the bathroom to arch a brow.

Amorette rolled her eyes at him. "I'm not asking for your opinion, I'm asking for a lift across town."

"I don't wanna." Hunter retreated behind the closed bathroom door once again.

"Okay, then, bye!" Amorette wasn't in a mood to argue this morning.

She may be staying at Hunter's place, but that didn't mean she had to cater to Hunter's whims. Especially not the childish tantrum he insisted on throwing about her apology to the electronics CEO.

Hunter didn't protest, but he didn't tell her goodbye either. As far as friends went, Amorette was learning that Hunter had more opinions than she thought possible.

On the other hand, Hunter underestimated Amorette's independent personality. She wasn't about to let his peer pressure deter her from what she knew was right. Never mind that it wouldn't be necessary if she didn't overreact in the first place. She was trying to be reasonable and make up for it now.

It took ten extra minutes on the bus. Minutes she could have saved had she convinced Hunter to drive her, himself. Seeing as how that was the past, Amorette graciously decided to forgive the imbecile for his inconsideration.

The closest bus stop to the company tower was only two blocks south. Not a difficult trek for Amorette, but she still took it slow.

She had never been very good at apologizing. Least of all after she did something as stupid as accusing a billionaire CEO of lying to his customers. The majority of people must be satisfied with the product, or he wouldn't make so much money.

Which brought Amorette to her next dilemma. She accused him of cheating her, and he didn't. How did she apologize for that?

Her fingers toyed with the clasp of her bag. Some deep, small voice told her the best apology would be the return of the black book. She hadn't had time to read it yet, so that was out of the question. Amorette refused to live her life wondering why she felt such a strange draw to the tome. That book was one mystery she intended to solve.

Amorette rolled her shoulders and steeled herself for anything. They probably wouldn't even let her in to see him. The first time had been a fluke anyway. So there was nothing to worry about.

With a new determination in her step, Amorette pushed through the glass doors into the lobby.

The receptionist looked up and, if Amorette wasn't mistaken, rolled her eyes. Despite the patronization, the woman pasted a smile on her face and sat up straighter. "How may I help you today?"

"I need to speak with the CEO, please." Even saying those words hurt. How would she ever manage to apologize?

The receptionist turned her nose up. "Do you have an appointment?"

"Uh... no." Amorette fiddled with the strap of her leather bag. "But I'm pretty sure it'll be okay."

"The CEO is a very busy man. I suggest you make an appointment or come back later." She waved her fingers as if flicking away an annoying fly.

The gesture made Amorette bristle. Who did the woman think she was? That was no way to treat a visitor to the company, no matter their identity.

"I won't take up much of his time."

"If you don't have an appointment, there's nothing I can do." Not even an insincere sorry passed from the woman's lips.

"Can I make an appointment, then?" Amorette could feel the heat rising to her face. Not from embarrassment, but from anger. Her temper picked the most ridiculous times to rear its ugly head.

The receptionist tapped a few keys on her computer keyboard. "I'm not the one who schedules those."

"Then who should I contact?"

"His secretary."

"Can I have his secretary's number?"

"He doesn't currently have a secretary."

Amorette slid her eyes closed. A deep breath did little to calm her frazzled nerves. "Then how am I supposed to make an appointment?" The bite in her tone should have tipped the woman off to the fury simmering below the surface.

It didn't seem to faze the receptionist in the least. "He's interviewing this week. I suggest you call back next Monday."

"But this is urgent."

"I suggest you get in touch next Monday." The receptionist returned to her computer as if Amorette never existed in the first place.

Amorette balled her fists by her side and shot a look to the high ceiling above her. This wasn't supposed to go this way. It should be a whole lot easier. Strange, how she expected them to keep her out, yet when it happened, it grated on her last nerve.

On second thought, though, there might be another way into the building. It couldn't hurt to look, right?

Without a glance to the receptionist, Amorette spun and stormed out the doors. If she had to wager money on a second entrance... Amorette rested her hands on her hips and looked around. The courtyard allowed too many wandering pedestrians to see everything, so this side of the building was out. However, there appeared to be some sort of alley or passageway beside the tower. Might as well start there.

Amorette jogged to the alley entrance. She cautiously stepped past the barrier between sunlight and shadow.

A *snick* behind her drew Amorette's full attention. She spun in time to see the blade and dodged aside. A screech leaped from her throat, loud and ringing.

The masked attacker cursed and lunged for her.

Amorette scrambled out of the way, but not fast enough. The knife sliced through her shirt and nicked her abdomen. Another squeal spilled out of Amorette's mouth.

The man grabbed at her bag, but Amorette yanked it away. Unfortunately, the force sent her sprawling against a stone wall. She gasped for breath, her lungs afire.

The attacker stalked toward her, the knife poised as he stooped to reach for the bag one more time.

Amorette cowered away.

A thick black dress boot connected with the attacker's shoulder. The masked man went flying sideways, but recovered quickly and shot to his feet.

Limbs tangled and fists flew. The attacker hardly got a hit in edgewise. Pure fury poured from the very air around Amorette's savior. Still, each punch was carefully calculated to take his opponent out with the least amount of effort.

It might have been seconds, it might have been hours. Amorette couldn't quite decide. In the time it took for her breath to return and her head to spin, her savior deftly dispatched the attacker.

The savior strode back to Amorette's side, his phone in hand.

Amorette looked up to meet the steely gaze she knew so well from their previous meetings. As much as she'd like to glare at him, she couldn't. No one ever looked more angelic than at that moment.

"Yes, I'd like to report a mugging." That steely gaze never wavered from Amorette's face. "Mm, yes. That's correct. Yes. He'll be detained by security. Yes. She appears all right. Thank you."

Only after he hung up the phone did Amorette let her eyes

close. The swimming in her head swirled around the backs of her eyes. She vaguely heard her name called out in the morning air.

Unconsciousness dragged her under.

[EPISODE 7]
A CHANGE OF SCENERY

"Amorette!" Eadric shook her shoulder gently. When she didn't stir, he cursed under his breath.

He never should have gotten involved in the first place. He meant to drive his car into the underground garage and let the problem sort itself out.

But she screamed.

Eadric couldn't ignore the desperate plea behind the wail. When he saw the knife and the harsh treatment, he couldn't sit back and let someone injure her again. Amorette had gone through enough. He didn't understand the rage, but he couldn't deny its presence.

Yet, here she lay, harmed once more.

Eadric dialed another number on his phone and waited far too long for an answer. "Collins. Come out back immediately."

"I'm in the middle of a security system update—"

"Did I ask?" Eadric bit out the sentence. "I need your men to detain a perpetrator. Come here. Now."

"I'll send someone out."

"You'll come yourself. This is too important. You have eighty seconds." Eadric hung up before Collins could protest. There was no time to wait for him. Eighty seconds could make the difference in the extent of Amorette's injuries.

He counted down slowly, stewing inside with every second that passed. At the count of sixty, one of the doors banged open. Eadric looked up to see Collins and two of the ex-marines he employed. Perfect.

Eadric scooped motionless Amorette into his arms and stood. "Detain the man at the end of the alley. The police are on their way to take him into custody."

Collins seemed shocked, but there was no time to explain the full story.

Eadric brushed past them and through the open door. He would have to send someone to park his car, but right now getting Amorette inside took precedence.

The fact she passed out didn't bode well, especially since she didn't seem the type to faint. Which meant a possible concussion. He was no doctor, much as he knew, which meant he would need a professional. In case.

Eadric carried the unconscious girl into the elevator and settled her on the floor. He knelt beside her, watching the rise and fall of her respiration. It seemed even. Good. Still, he wasn't taking any chances.

Eadric shot a text off to the infirmary, asking one of the doctors to meet him in his office.

High above the ground and under the tightest security, Eadric knew his office would be the best place for Amorette right now. Especially since he wasn't convinced that what she went through was any simple mugging. Eadric didn't believe in coincidence.

Amorette weighed next to nothing in his arms, even the second time he lifted her. Either his strength developed exponentially over the centuries, or she was much smaller than he thought.

She stirred some when Eadric placed her on one of the sofas in his office. A good sign, if you asked him. He would worry so much more if she remained still and silent.

"You imbecile." Eadric smacked a hand against his head. He shouldn't worry at all. She wasn't his to protect, no matter how much injustice had been done. Yet, here she was, unconscious in his office. As if he had a right to take care of her. "What are you thinking?"

The truth was, Eadric wasn't entirely sure what he was thinking when he carried her from the alley. He could have had one of the security officers do it for him, but he had been so enraged. Men these days had no courtesy toward women, and if Codex were involved, there was no telling what they might do beyond that.

Yes, of course. That's why he brought her to the second-most-secure location in the building. Because Codex may be involved.

Liar, his own mind taunted him.

A knock on the door brought him back around to reality. Eadric stood and turned. "Enter."

"You called for a doctor? Did something happen?" Stephanie Jacobs, one of the three physicians that Eadric's company employed, stepped inside and shut the door behind herself. She was a plucky woman, short and energetic, with wire-rim glasses. That, combined with her pouty lips, made her look more like a doll than a doctor.

Eadric motioned her toward the girl on the couch.

"Aw! Poor thing." Stephanie settled on her knees beside the sofa.

Eadric knew he lost all her attention the moment she saw Amorette. Stephanie was nothing if not focused on her patients. Sometimes even he wondered why she came to work as an infirmary physician instead of going on to a larger hospital. And he knew what he paid her.

A host of questions flew Eadric's way. Things that might play into any injuries Amorette might have acquired. He answered each with a calm tone, though internally he fretted like a madman.

What if, because of him, there was irreversible damage? Something had to be done. He had to protect her somehow and having his men watch her wasn't cutting it anymore.

A plan began to form in Eadric's mind. One he knew Amorette would object to, but one he needed to fulfill. To ensure everyone's safety, at least until she handed over that journal intact.

Stephanie pried Amorette's eye open to shine a penlight.

Amorette groaned and reached up to push at her hand. "Stop it..."

"Oh, good, you're awake!" Stephanie's frown finally broke into a smile. "You have a concussion and that bruise on your face is pretty nasty, but I think you're going to be fine."

Amorette's fingers fluttered up to her cheek. She sat up, fast enough that she almost collided with Stephanie's head.

Eadric's body tensed, ready to spring into action if she tried to fight or run.

Neither applied to Amorette. She winced and pulled her knees to her chest. Her free arm wrapped around them tightly. "The bruise isn't from today."

It was the first time Eadric heard her sound legitimately small and helpless. It sounded nothing like the feigned innocence from the last few times they met. This threatened to tear a hole in the wall around his heart. He couldn't have that.

Stephanie didn't pay any attention to the mental war raging behind her. She kept her focus on Amorette as she finished the rest of the check-up. "It's better that you're awake now. If you were unconscious for too long, I would have had to send you to the hospital. We're not equipped for things like brain bleeds." Her wry smile said she meant it as a joke, but Amorette's face paled nonetheless.

"Thank you, doctor. You've been very helpful."

Stephanie glanced at Eadric and stood. "I guess I'll be going, then. Do you have someone to stay with tonight? They'll need to wake you up every couple of hours."

"She'll stay with me."

Eadric couldn't believe he put himself in the middle of it again. Why couldn't he keep his mouth shut? What was it that forced his brain to short circuit when it came to the young woman on his couch?

"She will?" Stephanie's shocked question came out at the same time as Amorette's stunned "what?"

"Thank you, again, Stephanie. Amorette and I will discuss it from here." Eadric bowed his head in thanks. His eyes never left the shocked expression on Amorette's face.

"Call me if she starts throwing up or anything." Stephanie pushed her glasses farther onto her nose, tossed a smile in Amorette's direction, and skipped out the door.

Amorette's eyes lifted to stare at Eadric.

He couldn't quite decipher what she was thinking, but that glint of fire returned to her eyes. It smoldered hotter than he'd seen it before. Something he said must have enraged her again.

"I'm not going home with you." The words sounded civil, but Eadric detected the fury below them. She was trying to be cordial, probably since she owed him for saving her back in the alley.

Eadric leaned back against his desk, arms folded. "Oh, aren't you?"

"I'm not. I have a place to stay. I refuse to subject myself to your particular brand of torture."

"If saving your life counts as torture, perhaps you and I need to have a longer talk than I expected." He opened his mouth to insist she come to his home immediately. A notification on his tablet interrupted. Curious, Eadric opened the message. He flashed the picture at Amorette and sighed at the look of recognition on her face. "Looks like we have a visitor. We'll have to postpone this."

As much as it irked him to allow the man up, Eadric figured it would go a long way to convincing Amorette to be on his side.

If she weren't so stubborn, they could have been out of there ages ago. If she didn't walk straight into the middle of a war she knew nothing about, he wouldn't have to take her personal security into his own hands.

Eadric authorized the visitor and set the tablet down again. "It shouldn't take him long. Would you care to make introductions? After all, you are our mutual acquaintance, are you not?"

Amorette rolled her eyes, but she didn't say no.

In fact, she was much too quiet today. At their previous meetings, she had been nothing if not sass and snappy comebacks. Either the concussion had more effect than she let on, or the woman was plotting something. Eadric would bet money on the latter. Which meant he needed to keep an eye on her.

The knock on the door was harried this time. The man on the other side didn't wait for an answer before he pushed it open. The sheer relief on his face spoke volumes more than anything he could have said.

If Eadric learned anything in his many years of life, it was how to read a person like an open book. This man was no different from the others he met over the years. Still, Eadric knew his own fallibility, so he remained silent. For now.

"Mi Amor..." The man rushed to Amorette's side. "Are you okay? They told me something happened. Do you know who attacked you?" His fingers stroked her cheeks and shoulders, as if he had a claim to her.

Eadric didn't take time to examine why that rose his blood pressure.

Amorette shook her head. "I didn't get a good look at him."

"She isn't safe out in the open by herself." Eadric wanted desperately to put his desk between his person and the two across from him. His body begged for a defensive shield, but he wouldn't back down. "I've generously offered to house her at my home until such a time as it's safe again."

"What? Absolutely not." The man stood to his full height. "I strongly object. She's perfectly safe staying with me."

Eadric blinked once. So that's where she was staying. With the stupid friend with the sports car. Somehow, the prior evening made more sense once he knew that. No wonder this man came to her rescue like a knight in shining armor. "Fine. You can stay too." Eadric leveled his gaze at the younger man. "If it will make you feel better."

"It won't. She doesn't need to stay with some egotistical sociopath like you to be safe."

"Hunter." Amorette's voice broke on a squeak.

Eadric didn't recognize the tone since he hadn't heard it before, but it seemed like it might work in his favor. If he played his cards right.

"I don't think you have the power to speak on her behalf. Amorette is nothing if not independent." He didn't dare shoot a look in her direction, lest it ruin his chances.

"Well, I'm speaking for her. No thanks. She's not camping out at your place." Hunter folded his own arms in a weak impersonation of the imperious presence Eadric carried like a second skin.

"Um, excuse me?" Amorette shot to her feet and marched her way between the two men. Her eyes flashed with that fire Eadric was fast growing accustomed to. "First of all, much as I *loathe* to admit it, he's right and I am an independent woman. Which means I can make my own decisions. I don't need you telling me where to live or what's most beneficial for my safety." She spun sideways to face Eadric. "You want to take my protection into your own hands? Fine. I owe you for everything I accused you of. Let's try it. You did a pretty good job in the alley, so..." she shrugged.

If Eadric wasn't mistaken, that was a blush that rose in her cheeks. As if she remembered something specific and liked it a little too much. He smirked and shot a look over her head at Hunter.

A solid, steely glare met his gaze. "I guess she and I are

moving in. When do you want us?"

"You can bring your things this afternoon. I'll have someone meet you to assign rooms. He's moving in too. A kind of... friend." Eadric couldn't help but feel self-satisfied with this turn of events.

Better be careful, his mind warned him. He didn't know these people he was letting into his home. He didn't know who they worked for or what their destinies were. He would have to be cautious not to ruin everything he worked so hard to build. Which might be much easier said than done.

Still, for the sake of the marked girl, he would give it a try. Because she wasn't just marked. It appeared she was hunted. And, as even Eadric knew, it all boiled down to his fault.

⚷

"Is it true?" The eager young follower skipped a step to keep up with his senior.

The Benefactor dipped his head once. "I saw it myself."

"Then we should make preparations. Do something. She could be the one." The follower came to a stuttering halt beside a wide table. "We should take preemptive measures. Do we know where she lives? Works? Visits?"

A soft chuckle echoed against the wooden surface before them. The Benefactor rested his fingertips against the tabletop and leaned forward to study the images there. "Let's not get ahead of ourselves. We have eyes on her and everyone in her vicinity. Nothing will slip past us this time. We have the upper hand, yes?"

"Yes, sir." The follower glanced at the intel scattered miscellaneously across the tabletop. "Are you sure he's the one?

We've caught so many through our history. Is he...?"

"He is. Trust me." The Benefactor rolled his shoulders back.

It had been decades since he had the displeasure of seeing this face. Too long and yet not long enough. This face knew his, knew the pain of life and the harrow of time. Sadly, he didn't understand. But he would.

One mistake cost The Benefactor the only thing he ever wanted, and it would cost this face the same. It wasn't enough to find a way to finish him off. This pain went much deeper than that.

⚷

Amorette dragged one fingernail over another, a nervous habit she never did manage to break. It was a miracle Eadric let her come back to Hunter's apartment to gather her things. She half expected him to drag her back to his home and lock her away, but no. Eadric politely assured her someone would be there to show them to their rooms. It was almost too formal, too good to be true.

"You don't have to do this, you know," Hunter assured from beside her.

Amorette shot him a glare and shook her head. "I gave him my word. He seems nice enough. It won't hurt to stay here for a while, until my life calms down."

Eadric's home looked different in the daytime. Less menacing, but more imposing. Last time she was here, Amorette didn't take time to count the floors, but there were three. It was, in truth, a mansion, replete with a locked gate. In the distance, some large breed of dog barked loudly.

Even though she had all the codes to get in and out of the

property, something still felt cold and empty. Like a tower sealed from the elements. Like a prison sealed away from time.

Curiosity drove Amorette to open the car door and step onto the packed gravel. Despite its age and intimidating height, the manse was beautiful. The yard, too. Whoever looked after it maintained its natural beauty well. Amorette looked forward to exploring, given the time.

"Did he give you the code for the front door?" Hunter appeared beside her, his hands shoved into his pockets.

Amorette shook her head. "But there's another car here. So whoever our third housemate is, they're inside, right?" She shot Hunter a smile more confident than she felt.

Hunter sighed and reached forward to ring the doorbell, muttering all the while. Something about why Amorette was so stubborn, or something of the sort.

Amorette rolled her eyes and waited for someone to answer the door. She and Hunter would be talking later, for sure.

How did he think he had the right to boss her around like this? It wasn't like he stood up for her when it really mattered.

The door opened.

Amorette turned. "Y... You?"

Doon grinned and bowed with a flourish. "At your service. Please come in." He took a step back from the door.

Amorette stared at him. "I don't... understand."

"You don't need to, trust me. It's probably better if you don't. Oh, hey, grumpy." Doon waved a hand at Hunter. "I see your mood hasn't improved. Man. If I had known we'd always be meeting on these terms, I wouldn't have introduced myself in the first place."

"You still seem like an idiot to me." Hunter bumped his

shoulder into Doon's as he shoved past him.

Amorette sighed. "Sorry about him. I think you were really nice to give up the stuff you bought for your friend. Is he doing better?"

"What friend?" Doon scratched the back of his neck. "Oh. Uh... yeah." He grabbed Amorette's elbow to steer her inside, then closed the door. It locked with a click and a beep.

The inside of the house was as lavish as the outside, but in a different way. Some aspects remained classic, like dark wood and crown molding. Others were modern, like the open floor-plan and stainless steel accents. Somehow, it said more about its owner than Amorette thought possible.

"Oh, I've been meaning to ask!" Amorette spun to face Doon. "I never have caught his name."

"Who? Mister Hawkmore?"

"Oh. Is that what it is?" Amorette nodded and turned once more to study the main floor living and dining areas. "He has good taste. I've always wanted to live somewhere like this."

"He's not your best buddy or anything. Why are you so chatty?" Hunter muttered the complaint from his spot on one of the sofas.

"Ignore him. He's been in a bad mood all day." Amorette folded her hands behind her back. "So where do I go?"

Doon laughed and offered an arm to her. "Well, my lady, let me give you the map to your new paradise. Seriously, you won't regret moving in once you see this room. I mean... I knew he'd set it up nicely but he really outdid himself this time."

"Who did?" Amorette slid her arm through Doon's. At this point, he was better company than the man moping on the couch. If that's all Hunter could do right now, she didn't want to be around him. "Mr. Hawkmore?"

Doon nodded. "Of course. He has a lot of hobbies. I'm telling you, even I can't keep up with the man and I'm... younger." He cleared his throat as they started up the stairs. "So, obviously I talk a lot. If you ever need anything, don't hesitate to ask. You can usually find me in the kitchen, I like to eat all his food."

Amorette laughed at the sheer absurdity of it. If she didn't know better, she would think Mr. Hawkmore was Doon's guardian or something. They certainly seemed like family.

"It's so coincidental that you ventured into the Nook and then the park. Isn't it such a small world?"

"Small world? Uh... yes." Doon raised his eyes heavenward as he took a breath. "Anyway, this room... it's one of his best works, I'm positive." Doon led her down the third-floor hall and shoved open a thick wooden door.

Amorette's eyes went wide. There was no way. The room was larger than all the bedrooms at her old house, combined. A king-sized bed sat against the opposite wall, covered in a blanket that held all kinds of bright colors. Yellow drapes adorned windows that let in plenty of light. A desk sat against one wall, floor-to-ceiling bookshelves on the other. It was almost perfect, in every way that counted.

"There's no way he did this in two hours!" Amorette spun on Doon. "What's going on here?"

"Trust me, he did it in an hour and a half. I've had people coming in and out of here like ants at a farm." Doon shrugged his shoulders and looked around the room. "Oh, which reminds me. He had them leave a gift on the desk. It's for the door."

Amorette tipped her head, sizing up the man beside her. These guys didn't seem normal, but who was she to define normal? It seemed a bit much, but she wasn't going to object to yet another gift in the span of a week.

Amorette skipped to the desk and ran her fingers over the box lid, inscribed with her name.

This present, she didn't have to unwrap. She lifted the lid.

"Jingle bells!" Amorette reached into the box and snatched the bells to inspect them. The very top held a plaque with her name, the bells descending from it in a cascade of chimes. "I love them!"

She looked back just in time to see Doon's pleased smile. It seemed to her that there was something deeper and more meaningful behind the expression, but she didn't want to hurt her brain trying to figure it out. If she played her cards right, Doon would tell her on his own. Just like he'd tell her why he had really been at the park that night.

"I'll let you get settled. Don't worry about your things. I'll bring them up." Doon stepped back into the hallway. "Oh, and your friend is down the hall. As soon as I can convince him to come up, I will. Don't worry, I'll take good care of him. If you hear shouting, ignore it."

"Shouting?" Amorette turned to tell him not to do anything too harsh, but Doon had already left.

She shook her head at the crazy man. He would be a handful, she could tell.

Usually, people thought Amorette was juvenile. She had nothing on Doon. Amorette somehow knew she and Doon would be great friends. He spoke to the free spirit inside her. Besides, she had some sleuthing to do on Melodia's behalf.

Amorette hung the bells on the door and closed it. They jingled merrily along their way.

There was so much to see and explore in this room. Amorette considered what she wanted to do first and finally settled on the most obvious. She took a running start and leaped onto the bed.

"It's so soft!" Amorette squealed and burrowed under the blankets against the sheets and mattress.

How Mr. Hawkmore knew what kind of mattress to buy or what kind of colors to use, Amorette may never know. At this point, she didn't care. Everything was too good to be true. If this was a dream, she never wanted to wake from it.

"They arrived?" Eadric shot up from his chair. He couldn't remember the last time he felt so nervous about... well... anything. Some part of him needed the girl to be safe, even if he couldn't stand her little friend.

Doon sighed. "Yeah, they're here. The girl's in her room and the other kid is moping. You know, I don't think I like him."

Strange, how Doon's sentiments echoed his own. Eadric couldn't quite place what irked him so much about Amorette's friend. He'd been trying to identify it since the moment he laid eyes on him.

"Keep an eye on him. Where did we put him again?"

"He's down the hall from her."

Oh, yes. Now Eadric remembered. It was a wise decision to let them remain close, but he still didn't like it. There was a look in that boy's eyes that said he thought he had a claim on her. Considering what Eadric knew, there was little to no chance of that.

"What should I feed the kids for dinner?" Doon asked with a chuckle.

Eadric rolled his eyes and settled back in his chair again. "We can order something if you've cleaned the refrigerator again."

"Of course I cleaned the refrigerator. Who keeps mincemeat pies and leg of lamb in their fridge? You're not exactly subtle."

"There hasn't been need to be subtle. I rarely have visitors."

"Yeah, we're going to talk about that one too. I cannot... no. I *refuse* to work for a hermit such as yourself. It's called growth and you need it. To grow up. Wow, I'm really not making sense. This is your fault."

"How is this my fault?" Eadric scrubbed his palm against his forehead. He never asked for this kind of stress. What had he done to deserve this situation?

"Look, I'm not saying I know *how* it's your fault, I'm just saying it is." A pause on the other end of the line. "Seriously? Who keeps a tanker of ale? Where did you even get this? Why is it labeled? Did you need to be reminded?"

"Does it matter?" Eadric snapped back.

Doon sighed again. "And once again I've become the parent. I swear, Mr. Hawkmore, you're worse than my grandfather. Don't tell him I said that."

"Excuse me, I have a phone call to make." Eadric smirked, even though he knew Doon couldn't see him. Telling on Doon to Otto would be so much more fun than taking care of the kid himself.

"Don't you dare! Mister Hawkmore! No! Please. Please, I beg of you don't—"

Eadric hung up before the boy had any time to argue further. He had no intentions of calling Otto just yet, but it sounded pleasant, the idea of making Doon squirm. A little payback for all the things Doon put him through on a daily basis. The small things had a way of making a large impact on one's happiness. Besides, Eadric needed the distraction for a bit. Until he finally managed to muster up the courage to go home.

In hindsight, though the security on his land was the best money could buy, inviting Amorette and Hunter into his home hadn't been especially well thought through. For the first time in over a century, he had acted on impulse. Eadric couldn't even say when or why he made the decision, just that he needed to have her where he could keep an eye on her.

It wasn't often he met someone with the mark. In fact, he'd only met three in his lifetime. All were long gone. Even Codex, as he knew them, had gone years without sign of another. Eadric often thought the marked no longer existed. It wasn't until he met the woman with fire in her eyes and warmth in her heart that he started to believe in their existence once more.

Amorette was a rare specimen, which might explain many of the incidents going on in her life. There were too many unanswered questions when it came to her. Eadric knew he needed to go home and have a chat with her, but part of him didn't want to get too close. Not now. Not ever. He couldn't afford what it might cost.

It was that fear that kept him out late into the night.

[EPISODE 8]
TOO MANY CHIEFS

Morning dawned on the Hawkmore estate with bright sun and clear skies. Amorette sprang from her new bed with a smile, energized and ready to explore. Her stomach had other plans.

The smell of bacon and sausage floated from somewhere far away. Amorette imagined it came from the kitchen, logical as she was.

There were a lot of halls here, but she was ninety-eight percent certain she remembered the way downstairs.

With a happy hum, Amorette threw open the drapes over her windows.

She gasped. Even the backyard was beautiful. There were extensive English gardens, complete with a labyrinth. From the angle, she could tell only a few windows overlooked it well enough to see the way out. It might be fun to explore that later. After work, of course. Melodia was still counting on her.

Amorette changed into a long-sleeved shirt and a pair of jeans. She could retrieve her jacket later. Barefoot, she ventured into the hall and looked both ways.

Hunter was just making his way out of his room. He looked up and grinned at her. "Morning, Mi Amor."

"Hi!" Amorette waved a hand. "You smelled breakfast too, huh?"

Hunter nodded. "I didn't realize anyone in this house actually cooked. That is definitely not a freezer meal."

Amorette grinned and walked backward toward the staircase. "I know, right? I'm really excited. Don't ask why, because I don't know. It's been like this since I got to my room last night. I want to know everything and explore everywhere but I kind of feel like Belle because I'm pretty sure at least part of this house is off limits—" A loud cry interrupted her own thoughts as her foot hit the top stair. Amorette lost her balance and flailed to recenter herself.

Hunter snatched her wrist and tugged her forward. It was enough to right her. "You should watch where you're going."

"Sorry." Amorette twisted her wrist out of his grasp. She took a breath to calm her racing heart and prayed the adrenaline receded soon. Carefully this time, Amorette started down the stairs.

Hunter followed right beside her. "Did you sleep okay?"

"Don't be a weirdo." Amorette stuck her tongue out at him. "You've never asked that before so don't start now."

"You're still angry at me."

"Yes, but I'll get over it. I always do." Amorette flashed a grin at him this time, more mischief than gladness. "It's become a habit to forgive you after that crush I had on you in high school."

"You had a crush on me in high school?" Hunter opened his mouth to ask another question, but Amorette had already raced away down the steps. He had no choice but to follow.

Amorette made it to the dining room first. Her eyes went wide at the spread set before her. She had never seen so much food for breakfast before. Even pie, which she had to admit sounded the best out of the lot.

"This is for three people?"

Mr. Hawkmore looked up from the dish he had just placed at the center of the long table. "Did you sleep well?"

"Yes. Thank you." Amorette ventured toward the table. "We're going to eat all this?"

Mr. Hawkmore nodded. He glanced up again at the sound of a second set of footsteps.

Hunter didn't stop at the door. He raised one eyebrow and shoved his hands in his pockets. He claimed the chair at the head of the table immediately.

Mr. Hawkmore shot him a glare. "Move."

"Why? Am I not allowed to eat?" Hunter's haughty attitude immediately put Amorette on edge.

He should at least be thankful that Mr. Hawkmore allowed him to stay, even though he had a perfectly good apartment not fifteen minutes away.

Mr. Hawkmore sneered at the younger man. "It's my seat, my house, and my rules. Move." He stabbed a finger toward the chair to the right of Hunter's current position.

"Hunter..." Amorette shot him a look, silently begging him to do one thing right this morning.

The last thing she needed was two guys getting into a fist fight over a chair. She had other things to stress over. Like if and when she was ever going to give Mr. Hawkmore's book back to him.

She should have done so already, but he acted so condescending when he asked for it. Every time, she meant to acquiesce, but then he said or did something that made her feel like a child and all logical thought fled.

This was why she always ended up apologizing. Amorette knew she needed to get a hold of her temper, but she didn't know how to do that. Yet.

Hunter huffed a breath and stood to his feet. Instead of taking the indicated seat, he marched to Amorette's side and flopped into the chair there.

"Not there." Mr. Hawkmore frowned. His dark eyes studied Hunter with such intensity that Amorette feared one or the other might burst into flames.

"Why not? I moved." Hunter flashed a smile more patronizing than happy.

Mr. Hawkmore sneered. "It's uneven now."

"Wow. OCD much?" Hunter reached for his silverware.

His fork was just headed for the largest piece of sausage when a knife embedded itself into the wood beside Hunter's wrist. Hunter froze.

Mr. Hawkmore narrowed his eyes at the man. "Ladies first."

Hunter retracted his hands. The look he shot Amorette didn't bode well for the rest of this meal.

Amorette attempted a smile in Mr. Hawkmore's direction.

She would admit, the knife was a little unexpected. She might have thought he would kill her that first time, but he didn't seem homicidal any of the other times their paths crossed. The knife stuck in the hard oak table said otherwise. Amorette made a mental note to avoid angering Mr. Hawkmore in the future.

For now, there was a ton of food calling her name. Amorette made an effort to ignore the idiots on either side of her. Instead, she focused solely on the sausage and steak and eggs and... pie.

So much pie. Amorette had never seen pie offered for breakfast, but she wouldn't complain about it. Especially not when she could smell the sweet apple goodness begging for her attention.

By the time Amorette came back to her senses, her plate was loaded down and both men were staring at her like she had lost her mind.

"I really like breakfast food." Amorette shrugged, playing innocent as best she could.

Hunter snorted.

If she wasn't mistaken, Mr. Hawkmore's lips tilted into an amused smile. That was a new one.

Amorette couldn't remember seeing him amused. Angry, annoyed, proud... yeah, all those. But never amused. She made a mental note what that looked like.

"Can I eat without losing a hand now?" Hunter shot Mr. Hawkmore a glare.

Mr. Hawkmore motioned a hand toward the food before them. "Be my guest."

Amorette dug her fork through the pie and settled the bite in her mouth.

Her eyes darted between the two men. Both seemed far too silent. They might both be planning the other's death. She couldn't have that mess on her hands.

"My room is beautiful," Amorette blurted.

Mr. Hawkmore didn't look away from the steak on his plate. "I know."

Okay, so much for that. As chatty as Doon seemed, Mr. Hawkmore seemed the silent, stoic type. It didn't help that her benefactor and her best friend appeared to hate each other's guts. If only she could figure that one out.

"How did you know what colors are my favorite?" Amorette asked, directing the question once more to Mr. Hawkmore.

He paused his cutting for a second, a hesitation so brief that Amorette almost missed it. "I didn't."

"Oh." Amorette dug into her pie again. Strange. For not knowing, he decorated the room almost exactly as she would have if she had a choice. "Still, you must have put a lot of thought into it. Thank you."

Mr. Hawkmore didn't answer this time. His focus stayed on his plate.

Amorette rolled her lips together. Apparently, that line of questioning wouldn't get her anywhere. Fine, then. Next thought.

She turned to Hunter and flashed a smile. "Is it tasty?"

"I've had better." Hunter shot a look over Amorette's head. She didn't have to ask to know he was glaring at Mr. Hawkmore again.

"But it's good, right?"

Hunter shrugged.

Amorette had never, in her life, gotten such a shallow and indifferent answer from Hunter. Effectively shut down, Amorette turned back to her food and sank lower in her chair. Weapons might start flying any time now. She didn't want to get caught in the middle of the war.

The room rang with silence, broken only by the scrape of a knife or the clink of a fork. Daggers in the form of sneers and glowers shot from one end of the table to the other.

Just when Amorette was sure someone would launch across the silent room, a new set of footsteps made their way toward the dining room. She blew out a breath. Only one person left, and he might be her savior this morning.

Amorette spun in her chair to greet him. "Doon!"

"Good morning. What's..." he studied the scene before him.

Amorette jerked her head toward Mr. Hawkmore and glanced toward Hunter. If Doon had any brains, he'd see she was trying to plead for his assistance.

In case Doon was stupider than he looked, she mouthed a single word. *Help.*

Doon stared at her blankly for what felt like centuries. Finally, the sight of food broke the passive look on his face.

"Ooh, steak!" Doon jogged to the other side of the table and started to load a plate.

Amorette took a sharp breath to compose herself. "So, Doon, I've been wondering... who came in to wake me up every two hours last night? I guess I was groggy since I don't remember."

"Wake you up?" Doon cut into his steak with gusto, pausing only to think. "Oh, your concussion. Uh... I did. I woke you up."

He shot her a smile she didn't quite believe, but that could just be Doon's face in general. So far, he hadn't proven himself the most honest, upright person.

"I could have done it," Hunter grumbled.

Amorette elbowed his ribcage. "Be nice," she hissed at him.

Hunter shrugged at her. "He's not giving me many reasons to be congenial." He wrinkled his nose in Mr. Hawkmore's general direction. "I didn't want to come in the first place."

"Don't you have to go to work?"

When Amorette looked up, Doon grinned at her and nodded his head. As if he could fix all her problems if she left the house. For the first time, Amorette wanted to trust him. If her idiot step-brother had been less of a fool, she could have had a brother like Doon.

Amorette stood from her chair and scooped one last bite of pie into her mouth. "Hunter, we have to talk when I get home."

"Yeah, we do." Hunter looked up at her. "Be careful."

"One of my cars will drive you." Mr. Hawkmore peeled an orange as he spoke this time. "Both ways. Please don't argue. It's for the better good."

"Okay, wow. No need to be so dramatic." Hunter spat back.

"I'm going to go change and head out. Thanks for the food!" Amorette fled the room quicker than a skittish doe could flee a predator.

As long as she made it out of the house, this day might progress in an orderly manner. Somewhat. Amorette didn't have much hope for what she might find when she came back.

Eadric couldn't believe the nerve of the young twit trying to usurp his position in this house. He didn't like Hunter before, but now Eadric thought his ill feelings might have turned into full-on hatred. Eadric wasn't sure why he hated Hunter so much, aside from the power play. Maybe because he saw the softness when the boy looked at Amorette.

"Gentlemen, I think it's time for a chat." Doon spread his hands on the table.

Hunter and Eadric barely turned to look at him.

Doon didn't give up so easily. He stood to his feet and acknowledged first one, then the other. "Let me begin with the little staring contest I walked in on this morning. I'll tell you how it looked from the outside in." Doon cleared his throat and began. "There were lasers. Lots of lasers, and an unfortunate victim caught between the two of you. Seriously, I've never seen her so scared for her life. You should both be ashamed of yourselves."

"It's not my fault." Eadric scowled at Doon. How dare the man take sides in this? "He enraged me right off the bat."

"I didn't do anything," Hunter shrugged.

Eadric pointed a finger at him. "See? This right here. That's what irks me most. He won't take personal responsibility."

"I don't think his lack of personal responsibility is the real problem here." Doon shot a look at Eadric. One that Eadric knew too well. Doon meant to expose everything he thought about this situation.

Fantastic. They'd be there for ages longer.

"Why are you taking his side?" Hunter piped up. "I'm plenty responsible."

"He pays the bills, sorry." Doon shrugged and settled back in his seat. "I do have a point here, if either of you are interested."

Hunter and Eadric exchanged another look, but both turned back to Doon. "We're interested."

"That's the problem."

Eadric sighed. He would talk in riddles when they needed him to speak with the most clarity. "What's the problem?"

"You're both interested." Doon grinned at them. "In a pretty little woman named Amorette."

"That's absolutely ridiculous," Eadric spat. Why would Doon even think that? Clearly, he was taking care of her like he might... a little sister.

Hunter shrugged his shoulders. "I won't deny it."

"Of course you won't." Eadric rolled his eyes. "You've been on her like... Doon, what is the saying?"

"White on rice."

Eadric nodded. "Yes. That. Ever since I first met her. You cannot have her, little boy. She isn't yours."

"Not yet." Hunter's lip turned up in a half-smirk that made Eadric's stomach twist. "I made some mistakes with her, but I have no intention of letting Amorette slip past my fingers. I like her too much to let her get away."

"I think we should get back on topic here—"

Eadric held up a hand to silence Doon. "This is the topic you steered us toward. Wouldn't you rather we discuss this like gentlemen now?"

"I'd rather you put aside your differences and try to get along for Amorette's sake. She's gone through enough."

"Which is why it would be better if you just let her come to me like she was already doing." Hunter ignored Doon and leaned forward to stare Eadric down.

Eadric sneered. This child thought he could give orders around here? Not likely. Not when Eadric had centuries of experience on him. "You aren't a part of that woman's destiny."

"What do you know about her destiny?"

"More than you."

"Guys, I think you're missing the point again..." Doon tried to interject, but even he knew they were both too far gone.

Hunter stood first. His chair scraped the floor like nails against a chalkboard. "If you know so much about her destiny, then try me. If I'm not her destiny, I'll change her fate."

"Is that a challenge?" Eadric didn't need to stand to sound intimidating. A single raised eyebrow and a cold stare did the job.

"Take it as you will. I'm not backing down." Hunter huffed a laugh. "Good luck winning." He stormed out of the room, back up the stairs he descended from earlier.

Eadric bolted from his chair. His fingers raked back through his hair, disheveling it. "That insolent, arrogant airhead!" He stormed in the opposite direction, toward the garage.

No one remembered that they left Doon all alone. No one cared, either.

⚷

"Okay, so let me get this straight." Melodia folded her arms on the counter and leaned closer to her employee. "You got mugged, but the handsome billionaire saved you? And now you're staying at his house? Because he wants to protect you?"

It took most of the morning, but Amorette had finally managed to spill the whole story. No details excluded. Melodia wasn't exactly the understanding type sometimes, but she seemed pretty with it today.

Amorette nodded. "It sounds stupid and fake."

"Lucky!" Melodia tapped a hand on Amorette's arm. "Most girls would kill for an opportunity like this. Ditch the Malibu Ken and go for the CEO. More stable job."

"Mel!" Amorette buried her face in her arms. "Stop! That's not the kind of advice I need right now."

"Why? You like both of them, don't you?"

Amorette glared at Melodia from the very top of her eyes. "No. I don't understand Mr. Hawkmore. At all. He's all nice one minute and Mr. Freeze the next. Hunter messed up his chance, too. I'm not ready to forgive him."

"Which is why you should dump him and date the CEO."

"Melodia Morris!"

Melodia shrugged her shoulders. "Tell me I'm wrong."

"You're wrong." Amorette had no trouble spitting out the words.

She wasn't looking for a relationship. She was barely looking for someone to be her friend. She never asked to move into the CEO's house or have his driver chauffeur her to and from work. None of it made sense.

The bells over the door jingled.

Amorette turned and smiled woefully at the newcomer. "Hey, Doon."

"You know him?" Melodia stood straighter, her spine stiff in a defensive posture that Amorette knew too well. "Whatever you're doing here, forget it. Turn around and walk away."

"Relax, princess, I'm not here for you. Today." Doon smirked at Melodia, followed by a wink. "I tried to talk to them. They're both stubborn."

Amorette sighed. Of course they were. She didn't expect anything different, especially after this morning's breakfast fiasco. "How stubborn?"

"I think the gauntlet has been thrown down. I don't foresee friendship any time soon." Doon brushed an invisible piece of lint from his coat sleeve. "I'd like to make up for it. Are you hungry?"

"Why are you asking her out for lunch?" Melodia interrupted. "Didn't you try that on me like three days ago?"

"I owe her an apology. I couldn't bring peace back to her new home." Doon turned his intelligent gaze to Melodia. "You're welcome to join us if you want."

"Why would I want that?" Melodia snapped. Her arms folded under her chest, but Amorette saw the indecisiveness on her face.

"Although... I don't know you. I can't let my friend walk away with a stranger."

"It's settled then." Doon breezed past Amorette to retrieve her coat from behind the counter. He held it out, open so she could slip into it. "Let's go."

"Hey, what about me?" Melodia's mouth fell open in astonishment.

Amorette looked up at Doon. Interesting, how quickly he figured Melodia out. The woman was used to being the center of attention. The fact that Doon was using that to his advantage impressed Amorette.

Doon offered his arm and kept his gaze forward, not once looking back at Melodia.

Amorette wrapped her arm through his and patted a palm over his bicep. "Good plan."

"I thought so." He shot an indifferent look to the woman struggling to pull her coat over her sweater. "We'll see you at the car then." Doon pulled Amorette out the door before she could say anything else.

"You should do something more exciting than lunch for your first date." Amorette tossed a mischievous grin in Doon's direction.

"First... what?" Doon spluttered. "N-no... No. That's not what this is. I rejected her." He yanked open the passenger side door and released Amorette's arm. "Don't get the wrong idea."

"She rejected you," Amorette reminded him. "And I don't think I'm wrong at all."

"No, of course not. That's why you suit him."

"What?"

"Huh?" Doon shook his head, a trickster's smile tugging at the corners of his lips. "Nothing. It's nothing. What would you like for lunch?"

"I have a better idea than lunch." Amorette reached for the door handle.

Doon gently tugged her hand away. "A better idea than food? What's wrong with you? Are you sick?"

"No." Amorette flashed her most innocent smile. She needed a project like this after the morning she went through. "Trust me. Let's pick up sandwiches and eat them on the way."

"To where?" Doon shot her a look.

Amorette read it loud and clear. He didn't trust her farther than he could throw her. He knew she thought of something grand and unexpected.

Amorette shrugged. "A shortcut to Melodia's heart."

"What?" Doon released the door for a fraction of a second.

That was all it took for Amorette to pull it shut and lock it. Melodia wasn't the most perceptive when it came to relationships. Amorette liked Doon. She wasn't about to let two of her favorite people to pass by each other. Not when she could do something about it.

Doon marched around the front of the car at the same time Melodia appeared. Both crawled in and slammed their doors in unison.

Amorette waited for Doon to start the car, then tapped the GPS button. She entered their final destination into the system. "Let's go here."

"That's a park," Melodia intoned from the back seat.

Amorette spun to smile brightly. "I know. We're going to get sandwiches and picnic."

"It's freezing outside," Doon argued.

Amorette shot him a glare. "You said whatever I wanted. Besides, the sun is out. It'll be okay."

Doon and Melodia shut up, but the atmosphere in the car remained charged and tense. So tense, in fact, that Amorette had to feed Doon the order when they pulled up at the drive-through. He gritted out the instructions. Thankfully, he didn't have to talk to pay the tab.

Even if they both thought Amorette was crazy, Doon and Melodia listened well. Doon followed the directions as the girls sorted sandwiches.

Amorette didn't dare suggest they eat in the car. After thinking through that original plan, it might have been rash. Melodia would never buy the park picnic story if they ate before they arrived.

Doon pulled into a parking spot. "Why are there so many people here?"

"It's a park." Amorette shrugged and grabbed the sandwich bags. "Come on! We still have to scope out a good picnic spot." She was out of the car before anyone could protest.

That lasted all of five seconds. Melodia sprang from the vehicle and clamped a hand around Amorette's arm. "Not so fast, Tricky McTrickerson. What are we really doing here?" She lowered her voice. "How do you know that guy? Did he do something? Is he a criminal? Was he one of the ones who broke into your house?"

"Don't be ridiculous." Amorette yanked her arm out of Melodia's hold. "Just enjoy lunch. We didn't have to buy it and we got out of the shop."

"I happen to like the shop..." Melodia muttered. Still, she didn't argue with Amorette. They both knew it was futile.

If she didn't lead the way, Amorette knew the other two would back out. So she took the lead without another word. Amorette figured Doon had orders to keep her safe, which meant as long as she was in the open he couldn't go anywhere. Melodia would follow on her false pretenses. It was a perfect plan. The other two just didn't realize it yet.

Amorette followed the crowds down the pathways, until she spotted what she had been looking for all along.

Amorette grinned in Doon's direction, then put on her best acting face. "Oh my gosh! Puppies!" She took off jogging toward the animal adoption van, leaving the others no choice but to follow her.

Amorette went to her knees beside the corral of puppies.

Doon was the first to join her. He reached over the metal fencing to retrieve a tiny pup and settled it between his hands in his lap. "Puppies?"

"Wait for it." Amorette set the sandwiches down to retrieve one of the other puppies. She cradled the tiny brown fur-ball in her arms. "What would Mr. Hawkmore think if we adopted one of these guys?"

"No. He doesn't do loss well and the dog will inevitably pass away." Doon shot her an apologetic look. His attention went back to stroking the pup in his hands.

Melodia sank to the ground, cross-legged between Doon and Amorette. "You picked a good one. Good eye."

The way Melodia stared at Doon's hands in awe and respect convinced Amorette that she made the right decision.

Melodia may play hardball on the outside, but give her a puppy and she was a goner. It was how her last two failed relationships started.

Amorette wasn't usually one to tempt fate, but she doubted Doon would be as callous as the last men. Somewhere between his first visit to the shop and their reunion last night, Amorette developed a trust for him.

A flash of red and purple near the sidewalk caught Amorette's eye. She did a double-take before a smile broke on her face.

"I'll be right back." Amorette shoved her puppy into Melodia's arms.

Melodia arched a brow but accepted the puppy. "Hurry back. You know I'll end up with five dogs if you don't."

"Five? You've improved since last time." Amorette laughed as she sprang to her feet.

It was the scarves that initially caught her eye. She would know them anywhere. She didn't think this was close enough to be Nannie's stomping grounds, but apparently Amorette guessed wrong. She couldn't pass by without saying hello.

There were too many people between them. Amorette tried to dodge the crowd, but she overestimated her aversion abilities. The crowd around the adoption van swallowed her, blocking her from both returning to her spot beside Melodia and moving toward Nannie. Amorette tried to push her way past people, but they were stronger than she assumed.

Her feet tangled, sending her sprawling sideways.

A firm hand gripped her arm and pulled her upright.

Amorette looked up into a semi-familiar face. Recognition took a second, but it came.

"Professor!"

"Fancy seeing you here." Imran chuckled and dragged Amorette past the thickest part of the crowd. "You shouldn't try to be a salmon. It doesn't work well for mammals."

"I saw someone I knew. I was trying to say hello." Amorette bent to look past Imran's shoulder. Where she had definitely seen Nannie earlier, the sidewalk sat suspiciously empty. Amorette sighed. "Looks like I missed her. What are you doing here?"

Imran released Amorette's arm. "What is everyone else doing here?"

"Oh." Amorette looked over her shoulder at the adoption station. "That's fair."

"Is this what brings you out today? I should think you would be working." Imran drew her attention with the question, but Amorette's brain still scattered a thousand directions.

She shrugged her shoulders. "Lunch break. My boss came with me." She didn't know what caused her to exclude Doon from her answer, but it felt right. "She has a soft spot for puppies."

"Who doesn't? I'm sure they've been a distraction for centuries." Imran chuckled. "I could probably find enough information to write a thesis on it."

Amorette laughed, but it was more nervous than sincere. Something about Imran drew her in and yet... he was strange. A part of her that felt thankful to him for standing up for her now felt uncomfortable around him.

"I should... get back." Amorette jabbed a thumb over her shoulder.

Imran gave a slight bow. "Of course. Forgive me for taking up your time. I sincerely hope we meet again soon."

"Okay." Amorette waved. This time, she bypassed the crowd altogether.

Melodia noticed her first when she returned. "What's wrong?"

"Nothing. I'm okay." Amorette snatched the sandwich bag.

"You're pale." Doon dumped the sleeping puppy back into the corral. His face was too serious when he turned to inspect the area around them. "I'm cold. Let's eat in the car." He reached down a hand for Melodia.

The woman set her puppy back in the corral, as well, and actually accepted Doon's help to stand. "I agree." She leaned to whisper something in his ear.

Amorette couldn't hear a word of it.

Doon nodded and wrapped a hand around Amorette's arm. "Let's go."

Amorette didn't fight him. How could she, when she felt cold and confused? If she could pinpoint the source of the emotions, she could at least make sense of it. Instead, Amorette found herself following like an obedient robot. What was wrong with her?

[EPISODE 9]
THE FLOWER THAT'S WATERED, BLOSSOMS

"Mr. Hawkmore!" The call rang through the manse with deafening panic.

Eadric sprang from his chair and snatched his tablet. Just in case. He recognized Doon's voice immediately, of course. It was the tone behind the usually carefree exterior that bothered him.

Eadric hadn't been able to bring himself to go in to work. Not when he had far too many people to worry about.

After the incident the prior day, he didn't think it such a good idea to leave Amorette unattended. She was too independent to broach that subject without preparation. He refused to be held responsible for anything that happened to her. Which meant he needed to keep a closer eye on her.

Eadric had just stepped into the hall when Doon appeared beside him.

Without another word, Doon put a hand against Eadric's chest and pushed him back into the bedroom.

"What do you think you're doing?" Eadric intoned.

Doon slammed the door behind him. "I think we have a problem. A major problem."

Every instinct and internal alarm that Eadric learned through the years went into high alert. Doon didn't say things like that unless he had proof or a pretty solid hunch. "What's wrong?"

"Codex definitely found her." Doon leaned back against the door.

Eadric arched a brow. "How do you know about Codex? You and I haven't had that conversation."

"I'm smarter than I look." Doon shrugged. "Grandpa told me some things and I figured out the rest by myself. You're a really interesting guy. Oh, I've been meaning to ask, how'd you survive the Great Depression? Didn't it hit you too?"

"I'm good at restarting." Eadric folded his arms. "You mean to tell me that you've known this whole time? And you've still been acting like this?"

"Should I have acted differently?"

Incompetent child. Eadric sneered at the only real friend he had. "You should have let me know. I could have been telling you things. I've had my eye on Codex for years. I could have told you the real reason I need the woman close."

"Because you like her."

"Because I need my journal back. It's the only way to protect us. Our only bargaining chip."

"Keep telling yourself that."

Eadric huffed. Leave it to Doon to pick out something inconsequential and make it into a giant ordeal. Of course, he didn't like the girl in that manner. He only needed her safe for the sake of his journal.

"What makes you so sure they have eyes on her?"

"Professor Blakely was at the park today."

"What park?" Eadric frowned. He didn't hear anything about a park from the driver.

Doon waved a hand. "I took Amorette and Melodia out to lunch. Amorette insisted on the park so we went."

"Why am I just hearing this now?"

They should have had security measures in place. He couldn't be everywhere all the time. He couldn't magically tell if one of those closest to him was in trouble. Security was as much for Doon's protection as it was for Amorette's.

For the first time since their conversation started, Doon looked afraid. "It was lunch. I was with them the whole time."

"The *whole* time?" It wasn't that he didn't trust Doon, but the man had a propensity for half-truths. This wouldn't be the first time, nor would it be the last.

"Okay, so she walked off to say hi to someone for like two minutes. Nothing happened. She came back." Doon shrugged.

Eadric couldn't deny the anger that rolled through him. Two minutes was a lifetime around Codex. Anything could have happened, even if she did come back this time.

"Don't let it happen again."

"Why don't you watch her yourself?" Doon shot back. "I was, for all intents and purposes, on a date. You can't expect me to ditch my date to run off with another woman."

"I can when it's your job to ensure her safety."

"But it isn't. Not really."

If Doon didn't provide such invaluable help, Eadric would have sliced him in two. Instead, he grabbed the man's collar and yanked him close. "I don't care if you have blooming feelings for Amorette's employer. Deal with them on your own time, not when you're on my dime."

Doon snorted, then broke out laughing. A strange reaction, indeed, to being in Eadric's clutches. "Knew it. I knew it! You do like her. This is priceless. Admit it already."

"You're a fool." Eadric didn't know why he put up with this idiot, especially when he kept insisting things that weren't true. He dropped Doon's shirt as quickly as he snatched it. He wouldn't admit to anything of the sort. Not now. Amorette wasn't for him. She couldn't be for him. He would destroy her like he destroyed everything else. "What of Imran? Did he see you? Her?"

"I don't think so. But... you do realize he was in their shop a few days ago, don't you?"

"I am aware." Eadric rubbed a finger along his lips. He needed a plan, one that hadn't, as yet, caught up to him. They couldn't leave the girl in the open, exposed to Imran and Codex. "I'll think of something. Until then, no one let the girl out of their sight. Where is she now?"

"Her room. She seemed a little shaken."

Eadric balled a fist at his side. That could only mean one thing. "He contacted her."

Doon opened his mouth to say something else, but a knock on the door interrupted him. It came again. Then again, more frantic.

Eadric frowned and pushed Doon aside. He swung the door open.

Hunter didn't flinch. Instead, his eyes went wider, his chest heaved like he had run a marathon.

"What's wrong?"

As if Eadric needed something else to worry about this evening. He had enough on his plate without something else going terribly, irreversibly awry.

Hunter glanced between the two men and sighed like it hurt him to utter the words. "Amorette isn't in her room."

"Did she go to the kitchen for a snack? She didn't eat much today." Doon took a step in front of Eadric.

Hunter shook his head. "I've checked everywhere. She isn't in the house. I tried calling her, too. Her phone is still in her room."

Eadric's internal alarm rang loud and clear. She couldn't have gone far. "Doon, lock down the front gate. Hunter, check all the rooms again. I'll sweep the grounds."

"I'll come with you."

"No, you won't." Eadric left no room for argument. He knew what he was doing. Chances were that Amorette either tried to run home or strayed into some obscure corner of the manse. "Check the rooms again. All of them. If you find a locked door, contact Doon. You have his number. I'll search the grounds."

"But—"

"Do as you're told. It's more efficient if we all split up." Eadric nodded at Doon but refused to acknowledge Hunter.

The boy cost too much time and effort already. If EAdric hadn't offered his home to the wayward snob, he would kick him out immediately. Since he was most likely the only reason Amorette submitted to the security measures in place, Eadric knew he couldn't do that.

For now, he had a young woman to find.

Eadric didn't bother to grab a weapon. This turf belonged to him. Besides, he never had anything to worry over when it came to injuries.

The evening breeze was cool and fast. It swirled in indecisive spirals around the yard, blowing this and that through the darkening sky. Of all the times for the girl to disappear, it had to be in the dusk.

There were few places to hide on the grounds, save the trees. She wouldn't have gotten that far if she hadn't made it to the gate, either. Amorette seemed more the type to run far, far away if she were to run at all. Chances were, she lost her way somewhere along the expansive property. She must have gone out the back.

With only a hunch to light his way, Eadric jogged around the side of the house. Here, things sounded different. The wind didn't blow quite as harshly. Leaves rustled from bushes and trees.

A low rumble vibrated across the gravel pathway.

"Cronus..." Eadric groaned and closed his eyes to better pinpoint the sound. If he had to wager, he would bet all his money that Cronus found the woman first.

A second rumbling noise, similar to the first, alerted Eadric that Kratos had tagged along.

Eadric took off running. If he heard correctly, they were somewhere in the maze.

That architectural beauty took years to grow as tall as it currently was. If he had known then that she would get lost in it, Eadric might have reconsidered.

His knowledge of the maze and the menacing growls of the dogs led him to a dead-end corner. He hesitated but a second at the sight before him.

Amorette sat huddled in the corner, her entire body pulled up and as far away from the dogs as she could get. Kratos watched her every move, but it was Cronus that worried Eadric the most.

The dog drooled at the sight of the fresh meat before him. Eadric had only seen him like this once before. It hadn't ended well for the man on the other end of Cronus' focus.

The shift in Cronus' stance alerted Eadric to the danger. Eadric lunged forward, vaulting over his dog and into the path of the sharp canines headed for Amorette's throat.

Cronus' teeth latched onto Eadric's arm, instead.

Eadric growled and shook the dog off. "Bad boy." He hit at Cronus' muzzle with his fist, just hard enough to dislodge him and remind the Doberman who ran things around here.

Cronus backed off with a whine. Kratos, always the gentler of the two, sat back on his haunches and let his tongue loll. His tail wagged, expecting treats from his master, no doubt.

Eadric turned his attention to the trembling girl in front of him. "Are you alright?"

"Are they your dogs?" Amorette didn't move an inch, as if she didn't think the dogs would back off.

Eadric couldn't say he blamed her. "They are."

"Good. You take care of them. I'm going back inside." Amorette braced her hands against the shrubbery and clamored to her feet.

Eadric watched her, sure she wanted nothing more than to get away from him. She shouldn't have winced if that was the case. He didn't overlook anything when it came to the safety of his friends and guests.

"You're injured. What happened?"

"I'm not injured. I'm fine." Amorette somehow refrained from sticking her tongue out this time. Pity. Eadric had been looking forward to her childish tantrum. "You didn't have to come looking for me."

"You'd rather I let Cronus have his desired dinner?" Eadric looked up at her, maintaining eye contact even when he wanted to look away.

Amorette tugged her lip between her teeth. "His desired dinner?"

"You." No sense beating around the bush.

She couldn't possibly be dense enough to believe that Cronus wouldn't harm her. Cronus and Kratos were guard dogs, trained to take out any intruder. Really, it was Eadric's own fault for not introducing them to Amorette the moment she moved in.

"Oh." Amorette nodded.

If their previous encounters were any indication, she took everything in stride. Eadric had to admire that in a woman. "How long have you been out here?"

"Long enough to get chased and cornered." Amorette wrinkled her nose. "Are you okay?"

"Me?" Eadric looked down at his arm, where blood soaked the material of his jacket. "Oh. I'll be fine. I think you're the main concern here." He didn't admit that the wound was deep. She didn't need to know. It wouldn't matter in the long run.

Amorette turned her nose up. "I told you, I'm fine. I'm a little cold, so I'll head out now." She took a step forward. Her legs gave out beneath her.

Eadric wrapped an arm around her waist as she fell. Deftly, he swung her up into his arms, bridal style. "You aren't fine."

"So what if I'm not? I'm thankful you saved me and all, but seriously, how bad could it be?"

"You couldn't even walk. Did you hurt your ankle?" Eadric

turned his head to look down at her.

Amorette's face was closer than he anticipated. It had been years since he carried a woman. He forgot how close it put him.

Amorette curled her arms against her chest. Her shivering fingers clenched above her heart. "Maybe..."

"We'll check it inside." Eadric cleared his throat and looked over his shoulder at the dogs. Only one thing to do with them now. "Cronus. Kratos. Heel."

Even Amorette jumped at the command, but that was none of Eadric's concern. For now. He needed to get her inside. Her skin was cold and clammy, every inch of her shaking. Because of chill or because of fear, he couldn't say.

The dogs fell in line behind him, docile now that their master had the situation in hand.

"I can walk, you know." Amorette didn't struggle physically, but her words sounded desperate to Eadric.

He glanced down at her again. If he could spend a while studying that pretty, ever-changing expression of hers, he would. But he shouldn't. So he wouldn't. "You cannot. We established that in the maze. Stop arguing."

For the first time since he met her, Amorette listened to instruction.

Of course, it didn't take long to heft her through the back door and set her on the kitchen island. The sooner she was out of his arms, the better. Eadric refused to admit the stirring of conscience he had around her. Why did this have to happen now, of all times?

Amorette settled her palms on the counter and made to push off.

Eadric reacted without thinking. His fingers wrapped around

her wrists. He pressed his legs against hers. Effectively, the grip he had on her kept Amorette from going anywhere. "Stop."

"You don't scare me." Amorette lifted her eyes to glare.

Eadric allowed his lips to bend into a wry smile. "I'm not attempting to frighten you. If you don't hold still, I can't assess your injury."

Amorette wrinkled her nose. "I'll be okay. It's not even that bad."

"Amorette."

"You carried me all the way in here. I'm sure I can find my way around the house. It's much easier than navigating out there with the dogs—"

"—Please shut up."

"To be honest, I'm more concerned about you. I mean, look at you! You're still bleeding. Are you sure it's not a deep wound? Because you've been known to placate me before. Oh, wait, I didn't mean it like that, I'm sorry, I—"

Eadric released one of Amorette's wrists to clamp a hand over her mouth. "I am quite alright. Thank you. Are you going to calm down now?"

Amorette's head bobbed, Eadric's hand following its movement.

"If I let go, you won't try to talk or run your way out of this?"

Another nod. Innocent doe eyes stared up at him, but Eadric knew better than to believe them.

"Hold still. Let me examine your injuries. No arguments." Eadric tipped his head and shot her a firm look, brooking no more disagreement.

Amorette didn't open her mouth to protest. She held perfectly still, like a child who had been scolded one too many times.

Eadric tried not to pay attention to the petty way she stared him down. Instead, he dropped to one knee and gently lifted her ankle in his hands. It had already turned purple and blue. Not a great sign, but not terrible. Eadric rolled the joint and listened to Amorette's reactions.

"Ow," she complained on a whine.

Eadric glanced up at her. "It's not popping and the joint seems fine."

"Mi Amor!"

Eadric winced at the term of endearment shouted from the doorway.

Hunter dashed into the room. His fingers roamed Amorette's face and arms, presumably searching for an injury. "Are you okay? Where did you go? What happened?"

"I'm okay." Amorette's voice sounded a lot stronger talking to Hunter than it had speaking with Eadric.

"She's not." Eadric figured he might as well tell Hunter the truth. Amorette wouldn't be able to hide it for long, anyway. "She sprained her ankle. It will need elevation and ice."

"Are you a doctor now?" Hunter spat in Eadric's general direction.

Cronus and Kratos, who had followed their master inside, both growled.

Eadric grinned as Hunter shrank back from the Dobermans. Thank the heavens for such loyal companions as canines. "I've seen enough injuries to know how to treat them." Eadric released Amorette's ankle and rose to his feet. "Rest, elevation, and cold compresses. That's all she needs."

"Oh, so you can tell her what she needs, but I can't?" Hunter scoffed. His arms slid around Amorette as if to lift her.

The dogs growled again. Cronus barked.

Eadric bit back his grin and leveled a stare at Hunter. "Easy, boys," he commanded the dogs. He didn't like Hunter touching Amorette any more than they did, but it wasn't his job to say that out loud.

"I'm taking her up to her room," Hunter announced.

Amorette rolled her eyes. "I can walk."

"No." Eadric and Hunter shot the word her direction in perfect unison.

"Why not?" Her pout did nothing to help her case, but Eadric would admit to its cuteness.

"Your ankle." Eadric folded his arms. "No walking for the next few days. There are three capable men here. We can help you get around if you absolutely have to move."

"Yeah, where is Doon?" Amorette perked up.

Hunter reached to lift her again. "He's on his way back from the gate. I'm sure he'll be relieved that you're okay. Let's get you up to your room."

Cronus and Kratos growled again.

This time, Eadric couldn't help the chuckle. Apparently, his dogs disliked Hunter even more than Eadric did. "I'll take her."

"No, you won't." Hunter shoved Eadric out of the way.

Cronus and Kratos both leaped to their feet.

"Down." Eadric held out a hand to calm them.

He didn't appreciate Hunter's use of force, but he could play the better man. If need be, he could challenge Hunter to a duel. The younger man hadn't used a broadsword before.

"It's okay, Mr. Hawkmore." Amorette offered a tired smile. "Hunter can take me up. You should bandage your arm. Thank you. For everything."

He didn't want to let her out of his sight again, but Eadric knew he didn't have a choice. Pushing Amorette too far too fast meant risking another runaway situation. Caution must come first.

"You're welcome. But, please, call me Eadric."

"Eadric." Amorette's smile lit her eyes this time. "I can do that. Thanks for calling off the dogs, too."

"They won't bother you from now on," Eadric assured. "Now that they know you're my friend, they'll expect your presence."

Of course, the explanation was unnecessary, but Eadric found he liked Amorette's company. He could never quite be sure what she would say or do next. She kept him on his toes.

"Okay, awesome, we're all buddies." Hunter didn't try to pick Amorette up this time. Instead, he turned his back and looped her arms around his neck. "Hang on tight."

A distinct twinge of sadness overtook Eadric as he watched the duo disappear. If he had courage, he could have taken her, himself. Instead, Eadric yanked the freezer open and rummaged through the ice packs.

"Is she okay?" Doon's voice floated into the kitchen this time.

Eadric spared a glance over his shoulder. "She sprained her ankle, but I don't have the whole story yet. Take Cronus and Kratos back outside, will you?"

"Sure." Doon bent and clapped his hands at the Dobermans. "Come on, gents. Time to patrol again. I'll bring treats."

Like moths to a flame, the Dobermans perked up at the word. They raced to Doon's side and followed when he jogged out the back door.

Eadric sighed and rested his head against the refrigerator

door. What had he gotten himself into? Why did he suddenly have feelings, of all things? He didn't interfere in the lives of mortal beings. Yet, here he was, desperate to protect a girl he knew little about. Wouldn't his friends laugh if they could see him now?

Idiot, Amorette berated herself. Why did she go outside? She knew about the dogs; she heard them when they first arrived. Why didn't she think that they were guard dogs, set to devour anyone they didn't know? Laying in bed with a sprained ankle gave Amorette too much time to think.

Eadric appeared in her thoughts way too much.

Oh, sure, he was handsome and rich and mysterious, but seriously? How cliche could one girl get? Eadric wanted to protect her from something, but Amorette didn't have a clue what that something was.

On one hand, it was nice to finally have someone taking care of her. On the other, this whole situation seemed too peculiar to be a coincidence.

Which reminded her...

Amorette contorted her body until she could reach her bag beneath the edge of the bed. While she was down and out, she might as well read the book... journal... novel... whatever it really was. She intended to find out before anyone knew she still had it in her possession. Might as well start now.

The leather felt familiar by now, old but supple between her fingers. Amorette carefully unwound the bindings and opened the journal.

A knock on the door made her jump. The journal fell off her

lap and under the blanket. Perfect. It could stay there while she dealt with this.

"Who is it?" Amorette called in her most pleasant voice.

Instead of an answer, the door opened. Eadric strode into the room, followed closely by Doon.

"I see he elevated your ankle." Eadric lifted an ice pack wrapped in a towel. "He overlooked the cold compress part of the instructions."

Amorette giggled. Eadric already knew Hunter too well. Hunter wasn't one to listen to instructions, especially when he wasn't the one giving them.

"What's Doon doing here?"

"He brought your dinner." Eadric waved a hand, beckoning Doon across the room.

Doon set the tray on the bed with a flourish. "Mademoiselle..." he gave a dramatic bow.

Amorette laughed again. Doon had a calming way about him, as if he knew she needed to be reassured after the day she had. "Okay, if injuring myself means I get to see Doon in an extra good mood, I'm all in."

"No more injuring yourself," Eadric intoned.

Amorette rolled her eyes at him. "I can't really control that, now can I. To be fair, this is the first time it's my own fault that I'm injured."

"Yes. About that..." Eadric locked eyes with her. "Won't you tell us what happened?"

Oh no. Amorette pulled her lip between her teeth and chewed on it. "Well, you see... it's nothing spectacular. I wouldn't know where to start."

"How about the beginning?" Doon suggested.

Amorette snapped her head his direction. Leave it to the one she thought she could trust to take the other side. She should have known he would be curious. Doon didn't let things go, and she would know. He hadn't given up on Melodia yet, despite the woman's cool brush-off.

"What if I don't want to?"

"Doon..." Eadric motioned to the other side of the room. "Does that sofa not look particularly comfortable?"

Amorette jerked her head the other direction. "Is that... a threat? Are you threatening to stay in here indefinitely?"

"I said no such thing, but make your assumptions as you will." Eadric rearranged the ice pack around Amorette's swollen ankle.

Sly man. Amorette underestimated him, her first mistake. If she weren't injured and unable to move around properly, she would kick him in the nose. He deserved it. "Fine. I'll tell you the abbreviated version."

"Start with why you left the house in the first place."

"Personal reasons." Amorette stuck her tongue out in a childish fit of temper. "Play nice or I won't tell you anything at all."

To be completely honest, she didn't think the ultimatum would work. From everything she knew about Eadric Hawkmore, he didn't give up so easily. Yet, despite that, he merely nodded.

Amorette sighed. Now she had no choice but to tell the story. "I went for a walk in the back. I was going to avoid the maze because it looked so difficult to navigate, so I picked a random path instead. Unfortunately, a couple of large canine terrorists decided I was dinner. I ran, they chased me into the maze, I tripped over my own two feet and sprained my ankle."

A sudden thought occurred. Amorette snatched Eadric's wrist and shoved his sleeve up his arm. Where there was once a large, gaping wound, now only a small incision remained.

"How...?"

"I told you it wasn't deep." Eadric wrapped his larger fingers around Amorette's wrist and dislodged her hold. "I am well. Thank you for your concern."

"Let me see it again." Amorette reached out for his arm. Even in shock, she knew he bled profusely. It couldn't have healed that far in a matter of an hour or less. Ridiculous. "How do you heal so fast?"

Eadric blocked her grab by standing. The look on his face settled somewhere between shock and amusement. "I told you it wasn't deep. Just a flesh wound."

"I didn't believe you for a second." Amorette pasted on her prettiest smile.

This man, whoever he was, frustrated her beyond belief. She didn't want to be a snob or a jerk around him, but he made it hard to be on her best behavior.

"Think about it this way." Eadric folded his arms behind his back. "If I was so mortally wounded, would I have been able to carry you inside like I did?"

Okay, so he had a point there. Amorette thought back to the maze. Unbidden, her cheeks flamed. She pressed her hands against them to stop the embarrassing redness.

So, he carried her. That didn't mean anything. Anyone would have carried her with the way she collapsed after trying to walk. It was the close proximity of his face that had her embarrassed. She would admit to being momentarily distracted by the pretty tilt of his lips, but she got over it fast enough. Chalk it all up to shock or stress. That solved everything.

"I see you remember it quite well." Was that a smirk she saw starting?

Amorette narrowed her eyes at him and stuck her tongue out again.

Eadric chuckled, a deep, dark sound that spoke more than any words. "Rest well, Amorette. No getting up for a few days. Call one of us if you need something." He tapped a finger on the ice pack. "Keep this on until it thaws. Doon or I will switch it out in the morning."

"I don't need babysitters."

"You do need babysitters, apparently. This week, alone, you've been mugged, lost in the park, and almost eaten by my dogs. I think we should keep a keen eye on you, don't you agree?"

"I was not lost!" Amorette bristled at Eadric's sarcasm. Did he think her a child? She could handle herself in a lot of situations. Growing up around her step-mother meant learning to survive. Amorette could be scrappy if she needed to be, and she was more intelligent than she let on. "Doon told you that, didn't he?"

"He said you went to the park together." Eadric arched a brow. "You seemed... unlike yourself when you arrived home."

"This isn't home."

"And your last house was?"

With a snap, Amorette closed her jaw. He had a point. Even when she had her own room, tuition, and food, Amorette never thought of her father's house as a home. Not since her mom left. Not since her dad stayed away for the majority of the year. Definitely not when her step-mother used her as a live-in housemaid.

Amorette didn't understand the trepidation she felt around

Professor Blakely, either. He was a nice person, but a small part of her brain seemed to recognize him. Impossible, she knew, but something about him bothered her.

"I think I'd like to be alone now." Amorette pulled the blanket over her good leg and nestled a pillow to her chest.

She had a journal to read. One that apparently belonged to the man who took her in. One that would, hopefully, provide answers to questions she couldn't voice out loud. She had to know. She wanted to know now.

A soft sigh floated from the other side of the room. Amorette didn't have to look to know whose lips it fell from.

She looked sideways to Doon instead. "I'll eat alone, but thank you for the company. And for the food."

Doon grinned as if he knew she wouldn't send the food back just because she was upset. "I'll come back for the tray."

"You don't have to. Grab it in the morning when you switch out ice packs." Amorette shrugged.

Doon laughed and stood to his feet. "I'll be back for the tray," he repeated. Doon hustled Eadric out of the room before Amorette could protest.

Amorette leaned her head back and blew out the breath she'd been holding. Why did Eadric's presence unravel her and anger her all at once? It made no sense.

Eadric closed his bedroom door and leaned his head back against it. It made his head ache, trying to figure out why she decided to leave the house in the first place. Amorette had a free soul, a wild spirit, but she was no idiot. With the exception of her friendship with Hunter.

No matter how he tried, Eadric couldn't like the younger man. Something in his eyes or behind his too-perfect smile twisted Eadric's gut in knots. Being near Amorette seemed to ease the new-found anxiety, but she sent him away. Again. Probably for the better, before she figured out his secret.

If only he had anticipated her inspection of the dog bite. He would have prepared better. Bandaged it. Done something to mask its healing process.

Footfalls above his head broke the mental boxing match Eadric found himself in. He closed his eyes to listen better.

They didn't belong to Amorette. They would stumble more if they did. Doon definitely said he would be in the kitchen. Which left...

Eadric's eyes flew open. "That sneaky punk." He spun, his hand on the doorknob before he took a minute to think.

It sounded like the footsteps were pacing. Four toward Amorette's door, four away. Four toward, four away. As if the kid couldn't make up his mind what to do.

"Don't overreact, Eadric." Eadric blew out a breath and held still.

Hunter must be nervous about something, or unsure what to say.

Eadric would never understand why Doon put them on the same floor. He said the boy could stay in the house, not two doors down from Amorette. No telling what mess the two of them could get into alone on the third floor.

Minutes ticked by like hours. Hunter's stuttered steps paced a while longer, hesitated once more, and then retreated. Whatever he meant to say to Amorette, he must have decided it could wait.

Eadric's heart slowed to a normal beat, a rhythm that settled undetected in his chest. Why did he ever invite that kid into his house? If this desperation and confusion kept up, Eadric would have a premature heart attack.

If only death were that easy.

Because he wouldn't deal with these tormenting thoughts any longer that night, Eadric grabbed his tablet and set to work on the newest game launch. A mindless activity would erase the inhabitants of his home from his mind.

Or so one would think.

[EPISODE 10]
MOVING DAY

Amorette woke with a stiff neck and shoulders. She groaned and pried her fingers from around the book in her arms.

Things seemed a little clearer after reading a few entries, but the puzzle pieces remained scattered in her mind.

Why did she never remember what she read the next morning? Did she fall asleep that easily?

The bells on her door jingled along with the knock.

Amorette shoved the journal under her pillows and pressed up onto her elbow. "Come in."

Doon opened the door with a grin on his face. "Good morning, princess. I came to retrieve the tray and switch out ice packs. Is it still swollen?"

Amorette shrugged. Why would he ask her something like that? She didn't know. How did he expect her to know anything when she woke up not five minutes ago?

"Okay, so you're not a morning person." Doon stooped beside her bed to lift her discarded tray. "What do you want for breakfast?"

"Can I go downstairs for breakfast?" The words croaked in her throat. That's what she got for not keeping water beside her bed. Morning throat.

"I'll help her." Hunter's voice came from the doorway.

Amorette looked up with a brief smile. Even if she was still angry at Hunter for a number of things, she liked knowing her friend was still around. She relied on him more than she liked to let on. He helped her out in a tough spot, took her in when she had nowhere else to go.

Then again, so did Eadric. Except Eadric was far more annoying than Hunter, for the most part.

"You can help me instead." Doon held out the tray toward Hunter.

Hunter rolled his eyes. "Your hands are already full. Just let me help her downstairs. No one's going to die because of that."

"You don't know that." Doon pouted. "Mr. Hawkmore may kill me if I let you carry her or assist her or touch her in general."

"I'll attend your funeral." Hunter jogged into the room and settled on the side of Amorette's bed. "Come on, Mi Amor. Hop on." He patted a hand against the back of his shoulder.

Amorette didn't have the strength to argue. She wanted food and television. In that order. If attaching herself to Hunter's back could get her downstairs faster, so be it.

She wrapped her arms around his neck and finagled her legs around his torso.

Hunter stood up and hiked her higher. "Come on, Doon. Let's go get her some breakfast."

"Mm. Food." Amorette smiled and laid her cheek against the back of Hunter's head.

"We're all going to die." Doon sighed heavily as he trailed the duo out of the room. "Rest in peace. May the world forget we all existed and never repeat this travesty."

"Shut up, you're so dramatic," Hunter called over his shoulder.

Amorette slapped a hand against his chest. "You shut up. You're louder right now. No one talk. Just take me downstairs and feed me. I need nutrition."

"You seem awake enough to me." Hunter started down the stairs. "That was a lot of words."

"Humor me, I'm injured."

"Injured, my foot."

"Actually, it's *my* foot. Now shh." Amorette cuddled against him again and closed her eyes.

This whole not having to walk thing was nice, she'd admit that much. It was the bickering that she hated.

Doon popped up by Hunter's free shoulder. "Are we sure it's a good idea to carry her down the stairs like this? You could fall. Something could happen. Mr. Hawkmore could see."

"Why are you so concerned about him seeing? We already talked about this. It isn't as if she belongs to him or anything."

"Technicalities..." Doon muttered, so quietly Amorette almost missed it.

She turned her head to study the man she almost trusted. "What does that mean? Technicalities of what?"

"It's a long story. Let's get you fed first." As quickly as he appeared, Doon sprinted down the last flight of stairs and disappeared toward the kitchen.

"He's weird." Amorette yawned and laid her head back down.

Of all the times for Doon to bring up something important, it had to be right now. In Hunter's presence. Somehow, Amorette felt it was something she should hear about alone, not with Hunter looking over her shoulder.

Hunter chuckled as they made it to the ground floor. "He is strange, but I can't say I dislike him. I just don't agree with him sometimes."

"About what?" Any desire to fall back asleep fled in the wake of Amorette's aroused curiosity.

Hunter glanced over his shoulder at her. "It's nothing. Where are we going? The living room?"

"Yes, please." She kicked her good foot lightly, finally coming awake.

If the guys had things to do today, she could watch whatever she wanted. One perk of being injured, Amorette supposed. Besides that, if they left her alone—though not likely—she could raid the refrigerator without supervision. That sounded fun.

A deep, irritated voice interrupted her visions of peace. "What are you doing?"

Hunter spun so fast he almost lost his grip on Amorette.

Amorette squealed and gripped Hunter's neck tighter. Her eyes squeezed shut in fear of being dropped, but she didn't fall as expected.

Hunter managed to save his grip and hike her higher on his back again.

Amorette peeked one eye open.

Eadric scowled from his place on the bottom step. This time his gaze focused on Hunter instead of Amorette.

Relief flooded her.

Hunter took a step backward. "What's it look like we're doing? Mi Amor wanted to come down for breakfast and television."

"Set her on the couch, then." Eadric's gaze narrowed dangerously.

Amorette had seen the look last night, too. Once before he jumped in front of his dog, and once when Hunter tried to take her upstairs. She didn't understand the expression, but she wanted to explore it. To learn more about how Eadric's mind worked. If she watched closely, she could figure out why he seemed so aloof all the time.

Hunter obeyed Eadric's command with little resistance. Who would resist, with the way Eadric growled and glared? He must have spent years perfecting his angry exterior.

Amorette found she couldn't quite look away. Eadric was too fascinating, too hard to figure out. Amorette had never been good at resisting puzzles or mysteries. Eadric and that journal he claimed belonged to him both qualified as such.

Hunter took extra care settling Amorette on the couch, going so far as to gather the throw pillows and tuck them around her.

Eadric lifted Amorette's foot onto an ottoman and marched to the kitchen. Seconds later, he returned with an ice pack, which he settled under her ankle.

Hunter wrinkled his nose and brushed Eadric's hand aside. "I've got this. I can take care of her, too, you know. I was doing it long before you even thought about it."

"Oh, really?" Eadric shrugged a shoulder. "Then I'll be off, I suppose."

Off? Amorette jerked her chin up, meeting his gaze. In a quick turnaround, she narrowed her gaze in suspicion. Eadric hadn't done anything by accident so far. So why did he give up so easily this morning?

"Someone around here has to work. Besides, I have an

important meeting in..." Eadric consulted his watch, "...twenty minutes. I'll be back later. Doon!" He waited until Doon's head peeked around the kitchen doorway. "It will be you and Amorette here, so take care of her for me."

Doon saluted and disappeared again. The sizzle and pop of bacon filled the awkward silence.

"Where are you going?" Amorette queried.

Hunter shook his head at her. "He has an appointment, Mi Amor. Let him go."

Amorette wrinkled her nose at Hunter, but she couldn't argue with the logic. Appointments were important. She should honor the fact that this man had a job to do. No matter if she was injured or not.

"Yes. Well." Eadric nodded once to Amorette. Before she could ask a single question, he retreated.

Amorette watched his back with a new-found interest. Strange, that he wouldn't tell her what was going on when he seemed to want to linger. She would investigate this further. Right after breakfast.

At least, that's what she told herself. For now.

Hunter tapped a finger against her temple. "Hello? Earth to Amorette. Good morning, sleepyhead."

Amorette moved just her eyes to look at him, a soft pout formed on her lips.

Hunter knew better than to interrupt her thinking time. She could have figured out something important, but no. Hunter decided it was time to be an attention hog again.

"What?"

Hunter arched a brow. "Okay, ouch, first of all." He draped his arm over his knee. "Secondly, I have to go to class today. Will you be okay here with Doon? I won't be long."

Amorette nodded once. If the guys left, she could sort some things out. She needed that desperately.

⚷—

The store smelled as musty as Eadric remembered. The scent of ink and ancient parchment. He inhaled deeply.

"Welcome to The Nook, how may I help..." Melodia glanced up from her novel and scowled. "Oh. It's you."

"Did I make such a terrible impression the first time?"

Who was this woman that she thought she could get by with treating her customers in such a degrading way? Eadric straightened his shoulders, prepared to do war for what he wanted. A strategy would be nice.

Melodia shrugged a shoulder. Her book snapped shut. "Not really a bad first impression. More like... too mule-headed? Sometimes you have to take no for an answer, big guy."

Big guy? Eadric resisted the urge to wince or rub his aching head. Instead, he took a moment to step back and evaluate the situation.

To Melodia, he was nothing more than a customer. She didn't know his connection to Amorette. She didn't know his connection to the entire situation. Ideally, he would keep her in the dark, but he needed her help this time.

"Is there a specific book you're looking for today? I still don't have that journal you asked about last time." Melodia slammed her book on the counter. "Hurry and tell me. My employee is missing. I don't have time for this."

"About that." Eadric stepped up to the counter beside Melodia. "She won't be coming in today. She injured her ankle and is on a strict resting regimen."

"And how would you know this?" Melodia arched a brow.

Eadric grinned at her. This was the strategy he needed. The opportunity knocked, and he would be a fool not to answer. "Because Amorette is staying at my home."

Realization dawned in Melodia's eyes, far more intelligent than Eadric originally thought.

Melodia turned to prop her hip against the counter behind them. "Oh, so you're the CEO benefactor. Interesting."

"Is it?"

"Of course. The man Amorette described doesn't seem a thing like you."

"How did she describe me, then?"

"Mysterious. Aloof. Lonely." Melodia smiled. "But really, you're not that hard to figure out."

Either Melodia had incredible skills of perception, or she had a completely different view of the world. Eadric didn't know how to respond to the news that he was, in her eyes, simple.

Many people had used many colorful words to describe him, but he never heard the word simple before. He made a great effort to remain complicated. The average mortal being didn't want to waste their time trying to deconstruct a thick-skinned and mysterious man. It was safer for all if people stayed away from Eadric.

Yet, somehow, a whole flock of them seemed to congregate around him recently. It would be better not to delve into details.

Eadric set his jaw grimly. "I have a proposition."

"For me? Oh, how exciting." Melodia sounded anything but excited.

"Move your store into Hawkmore Tower."

Best to come right out and say it.

Leaving Amorette alone and without security, halfway across town, didn't suit Eadric. He would do anything to contain this situation before it got out of hand.

Eadric straightened his shoulders. "Name your price. I'll buy out the store if I have to."

"Let's start at the beginning. First of all, you're offering me space in Hawkmore Tower? The most sought-after sub-contracting space in the city?"

Eadric nodded. "We have an empty space on the tenth floor and we don't have a bookstore. It's not like the company is hurting for money."

"What's the rent?"

"For you... I think we could work out a deal."

Truth be told, Eadric would let her move in for free if it meant Amorette would be safe inside his building. No one came in or out of Hawkmore Tower without his knowledge.

Besides, his employees would undoubtedly find the bookstore intriguing. Most of the other shops inside the building were cafes or coffee shops.

Melodia nibbled at her lip. "This has a lot more motive behind it than the goodness of your heart, doesn't it?"

"It's safer for everyone if this store moves into my building. Security is tight there."

"You're going to have to give me a little more to go on."

"You have to learn to take no as an answer." Eadric folded his arms across his chest. "You can move the store into my building or I can offer Amorette a full-time secretarial position. I'm positive it pays more than what she makes here. She stays out of loyalty, nothing else."

"What makes you so sure that money will outweigh her loyalty to this shop?"

Eadric chuckled. "Melodia Morris, you and I both know that Amorette currently has nowhere to go except my house. You don't want her to stay there indefinitely, do you?"

"If I'm honest, I can't say I completely oppose the idea. I think I like you better than Malibu Ken."

Finally, someone on Eadric's side. He couldn't suppress a smirk at the news that Amorette's most trusted friend preferred him over the boy. "Then move the bookstore. I can have people here to help in a matter of hours. It should be done before Amorette recovers. She won't have a say if she doesn't know until then."

"You think she would refuse you?"

"Absolutely." Eadric pushed off the counter and ventured to the nearest bookshelf. "She opposes me every chance she gets. This would be no different."

"So you're saying I shouldn't tell her it was your idea that we move."

"You're an intelligent woman." Eadric grinned over his shoulder. "How much will your silence cost me?"

"Free coffee anytime I want it from one of the shops in your building. None of this paying for coffee business for me."

"Done. I'll tell them to put it on my tab. Anything you like." Eadric plucked a novel from the shelf and held it out to Melodia. "I'll take this, as well. And something for Amorette to read while she's indisposed."

"I like a man who knows how to negotiate." Melodia snatched a classic from a nearby shelf. It took less than thirty seconds to ring up both purchases.

Eadric paid the tab and reached for the small paper sack.

Melodia's fingers folded over his. She waited until he looked up at her to say anything.

Even then, Melodia's request startled Eadric. "Take good care of my girl. Don't make her cry. She's had enough of that."

"Tell me what makes her cry." The request was out before Eadric had time to think about it.

He heard, once, that what a person truly thought in his heart would come out when he had nothing else to say. Eadric didn't want to believe its truth now.

Melodia grinned. "Ask her yourself. I think it's part of your job to figure out what hurts lie in her heart. If she doesn't tell you anything, I have a list of names. I'm sure we can come to an agreement."

The more this woman spoke, the more Eadric liked her. He knew some of the circumstances around Amorette's unhappiness, but he had so many to discover. Asking and getting an answer immediately would be anticlimactic. Melodia was right in her assessment of the situation. Eadric had work to do.

"We will speak again." Eadric tucked the books under his arm and nodded his head in a respectful bow.

Melodia waved and reached for her own book. "Send some people this afternoon. We'll start the move immediately."

"Consider it done."

Eadric exited The Nook with a spring in his step. He hadn't felt so alive and content in years. Things were going his way, for once in his life. It appeared this situation could be diffused before any real tragedy occurred. That was what he hoped for the most.

———

"Doon!" Amorette knocked furiously on the man's door. "Did you steal my shoe? I can't find it and since it didn't have my leg in it I assume it didn't walk off by itself."

"I've been told not to let you out of the house yet." Doon's voice sounded muffled through the solid wood. "I'm sorry, but it's the only thing I could think of."

"I have other pairs of shoes."

"And yet here you are at my door instead of changing them."

Okay, so he had a point there.

Amorette had about four pairs of shoes, but she liked these the best. They were both cute and comfortable, a hard balance to find. If Doon didn't steal it, she would be well on her way to work by now. Melodia needed her, whether she admitted it or not.

"Doon, give me my shoe!" Amorette slammed a hand against the door. Hard enough to rattle it.

Something crashed on the other side. "Good gravy, woman, do you have to be so violent about it?"

From the outburst, Amorette deduced that the noise she heard was Doon tripping over his own two feet. He had a tendency to do that when someone freaked him out.

"What's wrong over here, Mi Amor?" Hunter asked from the end of the hallway.

"Doon won't give me my shoes." Amorette ran her fingers back through her hair. "I need to go to work! The car is waiting, you inconsistent lunatic!"

The door shot open. "Hey, be nice!" Doon pouted at her. "Do you have to go? I don't have anything to do today and Melodia isn't answering my calls. Again."

"She's never answered your calls." Amorette held out a hand and wiggled her fingers. "Shoe."

"No."

"Doon," Hunter gave a warning glare.

Doon stuck his tongue out. "You don't scare me, pretty boy. Get a life, get a job, and get out."

"It's not your house, so that's not your decision."

"And here I thought we were friends." Doon sighed dramatically.

"Guys, my shoe!" Amorette slapped the back of her hand against Doon's chest. "Give it!"

A chime sounded from Doon's pocket. He held up a finger and pulled out his phone to check the notification.

Finally, with a smile, he held out Amorette's shoe. "Thank you for your patience."

"You're insane." Amorette snatched her shoe and slid it onto her foot. "Really, you should think about getting someone to look into it."

"I second that motion." Hunter raised a hand.

"No one asked you." Doon slammed his door in their faces.

"Rude," Hunter mumbled.

Amorette raked her hair back from her face and breezed past Hunter. She had places to be and the fight with Doon wrecked her timetable. How would she ever get to work on time now?

"I'll drive you," Hunter offered.

Amorette flicked her fingers through the air. "Doon has a car waiting for me. I'll see you tonight!"

She didn't wait for his answer. She could finally leave the house without a herd of boys around her, trying to convince her to rest. No way would she give up her free time for a ride with Hunter.

As promised, a familiar SUV sat idling outside the front doors. Amorette climbed into the passenger seat and turned to smile at the driver.

Her jaw fell slack.

Eadric lifted one corner of his lips in the closest thing to a smile Amorette had seen from him. "Surprised?"

"That's one word for it." Amorette reached for the door handle, fully intending to exit the vehicle.

The lock clicked shut.

"Hey!" Amorette shot a glare Eadric's direction.

Eadric put the car in drive. "I'll drive you to work this morning. Please buckle your seat-belt."

"This is kidnapping."

"This is kindness. Buckle."

"I don't want to." Amorette sat back in her seat, arms folded.

Eadric sighed.

Before Amorette registered his movement, his arm was around her, snatching the belt. Eadric clicked it into place across her arms and torso.

"Safety first. Then you can argue all you want."

Great. Close proximity. Just what she needed to deal with this morning. The walk from outside into the kitchen still confused her. She didn't need another reason for her brain to go blank.

After what felt like ages, Eadric chuckled and settled in his own seat. "Breathe, Amorette. You don't have to go so still any time I'm near. I won't hurt you."

"I don't think I'm worried about that."

Amorette pulled the corner of her lip between her teeth. She didn't mean to say that out loud. She didn't mean to say a lot of things out loud around Eadric, but somehow they slipped out.

Eadric stopped at the gate to allow it to open. "If you aren't worried I'll hurt you, why do you look so frightened?"

"Good question." Amorette shook her head in hopes of kick-starting her brain again. She had to keep her wits about her. Eadric pulled out onto the road and stopped to watch the gate close. "You've never found issue with setting me straight before. Are you concerned I'll put you out on the street?"

"No." Amorette dug her phone out of her pocket.

Maybe if she had something to do, he would stop talking. She needed to sort her thoughts before she tried to engage with him. On cue, the device chimed.

Amorette glanced sideways at Eadric, but he didn't take his eyes from the road. Good. She didn't want him to pay attention to her, anyway. A quick flick of her thumbs opened the screen. A single text jump-started Amorette's brain again.

Your father is coming. Friday.

Leave it to her step-mother to fill Amorette in now that they didn't live together. The woman never cared before, but apparently she cared now.

Amorette exited the message and slid her phone back into her pocket.

If her step-mother thought she would come at any beck and call, she was mistaken. Amorette was through being bullied and pushed around. She had somewhere else to go now, outside of her father's home.

Amorette leaned her head back and watched out the window. For about three seconds.

"This isn't the way to The Nook."

Eadric finally tore his eyes from the road to spare Amorette a glance. "Yes, it is. Trust me."

"Um, no. This is definitely not the way we should be going. This is going to take you downtown, and the traffic will slow you down. Besides, The Nook is in the other direction." Amorette jabbed a thumb in the general direction they should be going.

"Trust me." Eadric turned his full attention back to the road.

Amorette wrinkled her nose. As if she didn't know how to get to her own workplace. She wasn't an infidel. Melodia would rip her a new one when she arrived over thirty minutes late.

But, hey, that wasn't her problem. It was her idiot driver who needed to open his eyes to the situation.

"I can feel your anger from here."

"Good." Amorette shifted to face away from him.

Eadric's fingers wrapped around her arm and turned her back. "If you have something to say, say it."

"You're a jerk and terrible at listening."

"I probably deserve that, but it isn't true."

"Yeah, you keep telling yourself that."

A heavy sigh came from Eadric's side of the car. His fingers slipped away from Amorette's arm. "You'll see, just trust me for thirty minutes."

"Ten."

"Twenty."

Amorette tipped her head, considering. "Okay. Twenty minutes, but you explain to Melodia why we're late."

"Of course." Eadric grinned at her.

Actually *grinned*, as if he didn't have the most unreadable face of all time.

Why? Why would he do something so trivial but send Amorette's mind to racing like it was the craziest thing? She had to get a hold of herself before she completely lost her mind.

Eadric passed sights that seemed far too familiar for Amorette's liking. Around the time he pulled into an underground parking garage, she caught on. Somewhat. This garage seemed empty, but Amorette recognized the entrance.

She debated the benefits of bringing it up. Right up to the moment Eadric opened the console and held out a lanyard.

"You'll need this."

"This isn't The Nook." Amorette narrowed her eyes suspiciously.

Eadric wrapped a hand around the back of Amorette's hand and pressed the lanyard into her palm. "You'll need this." He grabbed the keys and stepped out of the car.

"Hey!" Amorette fumbled with her seat-belt, then the door. She reached back in for her bag. "Hey, this isn't The Nook!"

Eadric pressed the elevator button and turned to look over his shoulder. "Come along, then."

"But this isn't The Nook." Amorette jogged to his side and wrapped a hand around his wrist. "You have to take me to work, Eadric. I can't skip. I'm an employee, not a CEO."

"You think I skip work?" Eadric chuckled again. "You don't know much, do you? I work harder for this company than anyone else."

"That's nice, but can we talk about it while you drive me to work?" Amorette gave his arm a gentle tug. "Or give me the keys. I know how to drive."

"No."

The elevator doors opened.

This time, Amorette's hold on Eadric worked to her disadvantage. He was taller and stronger than she was, so he merely pulled her into the elevator after him.

She stumbled to a stop by his side. "Mr. Hawkmore—"

"I don't answer to that from you anymore."

Amorette sighed. "Eadric. Please? I really need to get to work."

Eadric tugged his arm out of her grip and flicked a wrist. He stared at his watch, then looked up at Amorette. His fingers were gentle as they pried the lanyard from her hand.

Eadric looped the strap around Amorette's neck. "I still have two minutes. Trust me for two more minutes."

Two minutes. Could she trust him for those precious two minutes? On the one hand, she needed to get to work. On the other, Eadric seemed to have something planned. She couldn't place what it was, but those dark eyes pleaded with her to understand.

"Fine. Two minutes."

Eadric smiled.

In all honesty, Amorette wished he would stop smiling. It took years off his face and sucked her into whatever scheme he crafted. Yes, she would admit to being soft for his smile, but only because he looked so grumpy the majority of the time. Everyone deserved to be happy sometimes.

The elevator doors dinged.

Eadric motioned to the hall outside and waited for Amorette to precede him.

Amorette studied his smile. Why now? Did he have something big planned? This was definitely Hawkmore Tower, but why did he bring her here?

If he planned to hold her in his office, he had another thing coming. She didn't even have the journal with her, so he couldn't make her hand it over. She had half of it left to read. Then he could have it.

"Sixty seconds." Eadric pressed a hand against the elevator door to keep it from closing.

"Oh. Right." Amorette tried not to trip over her own two feet as she hustled out of the elevator and into the hall.

Eadric stepped out after her. "This is the fifteenth floor."

"Okay..."

He reached out to flick a finger against the card on Amorette's lanyard. "This allows you access to the gates in the lobby and the elevator we exited."

"I still don't get why you're telling me all of this."

"Follow me." Eadric gripped her elbow to steer her down the hall.

Amorette tilted her head to look up at him again. How did she ever think he was scary? Eadric had the softest touch and the most intriguing words. Had she known, she wouldn't have been so harsh at the beginning.

Right now, Eadric seemed to be the only person who always spoke honestly with her. She could admire that.

A slight tug on her arm signaled a stop. Amorette stumbled to a halt and fixed her eyes on the floor instead of the man beside her. She needed to get a hold of herself. Butterflies and obsession weren't her things.

"We're here." Eadric let his fingers slip away.

Amorette rolled her tongue over her lips to wet them, then looked up. "What in the world?" This wasn't possible. No way this happened in the last three days. Right? "How is this here?"

"Aren't you late for work?" Eadric consulted his phone this time instead of his watch.

All thoughts of fascination fled Amorette's head. How did she think he had something wonderful planned? Clearly, this was all a ruse so she didn't get angry with him earlier.

"This is low. You could have told me."

"It appears Melodia is waiting on you." Eadric pointed in a direction over Amorette's shoulder.

"We'll talk when I get home."

Amorette spun on her heel, sure to flip her hair defiantly. She meant to put it up this morning, but Doon's theft of her shoe postponed that idea. She sincerely hoped she hit Eadric in the eye. Not likely, but a nice thought.

The store-front was entirely glass, which afforded Amorette the opportunity to see Melodia smiling and interacting with a customer. A *customer*. A weird, and rare, experience.

Maybe moving here wouldn't be so bad, but the secrecy behind it all scared Amorette to no end. Why would they hide this from her? Aside from the obvious temper tantrum, but that was bound to happen anyway.

Might as well get it over with.

Amorette shoved the door open and marched inside the brightly lit space. Yes, okay, it felt more open and much nicer than the hole-in-the-wall she was used to. They still should have told her.

Melodia tossed a look toward the door. A smile was quick to follow. "Amy, you're here!"

"Yeah. I am." Amorette stalked to the counter and tossed her bag behind it. "But what are you and the store doing here?"

"We moved." Melodia shrugged.

It was going to be one of those days. Apparently, Melodia didn't want to tell her the reason.

Amorette sighed. "I noticed. A text would have been nice."

"You figured it out. Ooh!" Melodia spun to plant her elbows on the counter. She rested her chin in her hands. "I hear our handsome CEO drove you here."

"So?"

"So! Spill the details. Are you two official? Has he confessed his undying devotion?" Melodia's eyes sparkled with curiosity.

Amorette rolled her eyes at her boss. "We can barely be in the same room without arguing. I'd say your hopes and dreams for me are a little far-fetched."

"Mm, I don't think so." Melodia wrinkled her nose. One hand slipped away from her chin to reached out and grab her current romance novel. "There's definitely something there. I'm just not sure what kind of destiny it is yet."

"Stop saying things that don't make sense."

Melodia arched a brow, but not another word fell from her lips. She didn't need to speak. What she said already sent Amorette's brain into overload.

There were too many questions and unknowns. Amorette made a silent vow to discover everything she needed to know. Soon.

[EPISODE 11]
WHAT HAPPENS ON FRIDAY...

Eadric's eyes didn't leave the computer screen. The girls were working hard today, making friends with various employees. Amorette's smile remained bright and cheery. If only she showed that bubbly side of herself more often instead of fighting him.

Things seemed too easy this week. Conversations with Hunter didn't result in a fight. Melodia agreed to his terms without much of an argument. Even Doon seemed to be behaving himself. This house of cards sat precariously balanced. Any small breeze might blow it over. Eadric needed to avoid that catastrophe at all costs.

His phone vibrated against the desk.

Eadric reached for it blindly and lifted it to his ear. "Yes?"

"He's at school today," Doon answered without preamble.

"Good. Keep an eye on him." Eadric tossed the phone back on the desk. One less thing to worry about. If Hunter went to his college classes, that meant he wouldn't seek out Amorette here.

Eadric didn't know why Hunter's presence bothered him so much. Perhaps because Amorette trusted the hooligan implicitly.

She needed someone like that, but he wished it could be himself or Doon.

Hunter's attention wasn't welcome toward Amorette. Eadric could read his intentions like an open book. Besides, Hunter himself said he was after Amorette's heart. It wasn't fair, this head-start that Hunter had on her affections.

Eadric shot from his chair.

No, no, no. He couldn't think like that. The mark meant she belonged to an immortal, but it didn't mean she was his. He swore long ago never to bring anyone into his fight. He couldn't chance it. Not with the devil himself hovering so close.

The buzz of his phone brought him back to attention. Eadric picked it up and slid the green icon. "What now?"

"Is that any way to greet an old friend?"

Eadric's heart dropped to his stomach. He knew this voice all too well. Had heard it far too many times. "How did you get this number?"

"Is there anything I can't find?"

"Only a handful of people know about this number. I don't give it out freely."

How did he find out? Did he have someone on the inside here? What kind of technology had he advanced to use? Did he place bugs or trackers somewhere? There were too many questions and not enough solid evidence.

"It wasn't free, believe me." The voice on the other end laughed. "Oh, Eadric, it has been ages since we last spoke. How are you these days? Still living?"

"If you can call this existence a life." Eadric kept his tone even. Anything to hide the trepidation welling in his gut. "I assume you have a reason to call me during office hours."

"I heard there's a lovely little flower growing at your humble abode." A click of his tongue. "I thought to myself, why would he take someone in like that? It's not in his nature to be so kind or forgiving."

"Well, people do change. Mature."

"Not you. Not this much. Which made me think that perhaps there's more to this than he's letting on."

"You instigated this whole ordeal. If you had kept your distance, I would have kept mine." Eadric barely kept his voice steady this time. "Call off your dogs and let's leave the woman out of this."

"It's too late for that." The voice on the other end of the line went ice cold. "An eye for an eye, a tooth for a tooth. The Eadric I know would agree to such a thing. I never intended to go this far, but... you need to know how it feels."

Eadric's eyes shut tightly. Of course. The entire reason for this whole ordeal. "She has nothing to do with me."

"We'll see about that." The voice chuckled again. "I believe it was you who took her in, in the first place. The Tower. Even before that, with the phone. A nice touch, if you ask me."

"How do you know about that?"

"You're full of questions, aren't you?"

"How else am I to discern your true motives?"

"You don't know them already? I'm not doing my job well enough."

Eadric winced. He knew the ease of his plans was too good to be true.

"No comeback for that? Interesting." The voice sighed. "Don't think moving her into your territory will stop me from fulfilling my plans, Eadric. She's no safer there than she was in her father's home. Walls and locks aren't things that can stop the true destiny of a person."

Eadric's gaze traveled back to his computer screen, to the live feed of the bookstore. If only she knew the danger that lurked, would she still smile so brightly? "Why must you bring her into this?"

"To make you understand."

"I did the right thing."

"As I'm doing the right thing now. We'll speak again." The line clicked and went dead.

Eadric dropped his hand to his side. His phone shook in his grip and clattered to the floor. All this effort, for nothing. He thought holding her close would make it easier to survive this, but it hadn't. He only opened the door for hate and revenge.

If only he had never brought her into this in the first place. If only he knew what to do now that she was the center of everything.

Yet... he couldn't push her away, and he couldn't pull her closer. What exactly was he to do?

⚿

Patience had never been Amorette's thing, but sometimes she found it absolutely necessary. Like when she needed to sneak out of the mansion undetected.

Her door didn't squeak, thank goodness, but the bells on the outside were a nuisance. Thus, Amorette moved slowly, careful not to yank too hard or jerk at all. If those little bells stayed quiet, she could sneak through the rest of the house.

Eadric hadn't come back from work yet, either, which made life a whole lot simpler. One less guy to fool.

With the door open, Amorette poked her head into the hall. So far, so good. No sign of the ever-present Hunter.

Amorette tip-toed her way to the stairs.

This was where things got tricky. The house may be in good condition, but even she could tell how old it was. The stairs creaked; nothing she could do about it except pick and choose carefully.

A single toe reached out to test the first stair.

"Where are you going?"

"Oh my—" Amorette clasped a hand over her heart. Over her shoulder, she shot Hunter one of her best glares. "Don't sneak up on people like that."

Hunter grinned. "Sorry. Where are you off to so stealthily?"

Amorette turned her lips up into an innocent smile. "I'm going to go retrieve the rest of my stuff from my room. No need to panic, I'll be back in a couple hours."

"I'll drive you."

"No!" Amorette tried not to wince. She'd never been the best at lying. Maybe she should have learned. "That is, one of the drivers is taking me, so I'll be okay. It shouldn't be long."

"Are you sure?" Hunter stepped closer. "We haven't had much time together this week. Not since your store moved into the Tower."

Amorette shrugged her shoulders. "Let's hang out all day tomorrow. Saturdays should be lazy, right? Movie marathon?"

The idea seemed to pacify Hunter. He backed up a step and shoved his hands into his pockets. "Alright. I'm going to hold you to that, though."

"Two hours. Don't tell anyone okay?" Amorette flashed one more smile before she dashed down the stairs. Silence had become a moot point the second Hunter spotted her.

She paused at the bottom of the stairs to look around for Doon, but she didn't see him. All the better. He would pester until he got the real information. She didn't lie, exactly. She simply omitted some of the facts.

Whatever. Every girl deserved a night off.

Amorette hastened out the front doors and breathed a sigh of relief. Almost home-free.

A sharp bark to her left startled her again.

Cronus and Kratos came bounding toward her from the side of the house.

Amorette's first instinct was to cower against the door. The dogs had other ideas.

Kratos nuzzled his head under Amorette's hand, begging her to pet him. Cronus immediately set to work nuzzling against her opposite hip. His rough tongue found her fingers and licked.

Amorette took it as an apology and ran her hands over each of their heads. "You were just doing your job."

Satisfied they wouldn't hurt her today, Amorette set off down the driveway.

Yes, she told Hunter someone would drive her, but all the drivers reported everything back to Eadric. Tonight, she needed to do this alone. It was personal, and she had too many questions to ask.

The dogs trailed her all the way to the gate.

Amorette stopped to stroke each of their heads again. "Stay here."

Of course, the dogs merely looked up at her with big, soulful eyes. Hard to resist, but Amorette knew the hard and fast rule that the Dobermans stayed on the property at all times. She was pretty sure Eadric hadn't been joking when he said: "under penalty of death."

Tempted as she was to bring the dogs along, Amorette slipped through the gate without them. Their frenzied barking served to distract the guard for the brief moment Amorette needed to escape down the road.

There was a bus stop not too far from the house, which required less extra cash than a taxi. Amorette liked the anonymity of it, too. Bus drivers rarely remembered a face when they saw so many in the course of one day. She didn't need a bus to take her all the way home, just close enough she could walk.

The evening wind blew brisk around her, making Amorette wish she had brought a thicker jacket. She pulled the windbreaker tighter around her neck and shoulders.

The bus arrived shortly, and Amorette climbed aboard with a shiver. Approximately thirty minutes later, Amorette stepped off in her old neighborhood.

Familiar sights and smells enveloped her like a warm blanket. Amorette breathed deeply and turned down the street toward her house.

She hadn't lied, entirely. She intended to go home this evening, but she didn't want to tell Hunter the real reason. She didn't want to admit that her step-mother's text piqued her curiosity.

"Young lady!"

Amorette smiled at the voice that floated from across the street. She turned to wave at the woman. "Nannie!"

The woman waved a hand, beckoning Amorette to her side of the street.

Amorette didn't mind the detour. She glanced both ways and

jogged to Nannie's side. "Were you at a park on the other side of town a few days ago?"

Nannie sighed. "Child, child. Always running about without scarves, mittens, or a coat." She crooked a finger. "Come here."

Amorette hunched in front of Nannie and wrapped her arms around her legs. "I've missed talking to you. I feel like we're kindred spirits, somehow."

"You're a fanciful girl." Nannie looped a scarf around Amorette's neck.

Her wrinkles didn't look quite as pronounced in the dim evening light. Amorette could see the remains of a beautiful woman in their place. Even at this old age, Nannie seemed prettier than Amorette expected.

"I may be fanciful, but it makes life more interesting, don't you think?" Amorette laughed.

Nannie patted a hand against Amorette's shoulder. "How so? Tell me a bit about your interesting life."

Amorette glanced down the road. She would rather tell Nannie than anyone inside her old home. "I don't live in this neighborhood anymore. A rich CEO took me in and I stay at his house now."

"Alone?" Nannie arched a brow.

Amorette shook her head. "No. My friend Hunter stays there, too. And my new friend Doon. It's not like we all see each other that much anyway. Doon and Eadric and I have work, and Hunter has school, so most of the time we're not all together in the house, anyway."

"But it is fanciful, isn't it? My, my, you're going up in the world. A CEO benefactor? Why, in my day, such a thing wasn't heard of except in scandals." Nannie clucked her tongue.

Amorette laughed again. "The thing is, I'm confused. I thought I liked Hunter, but... the more time I spend around... someone else... the more I think I might like them too. I'm coming to depend on him. Is that bad?"

"That's how relationships often start." Nannie plucked at the scarf around Amorette's neck. "You began as friends?"

"Not exactly." Amorette wrinkled her nose.

"Then what, exactly, did you begin as?"

"Um... bitter enemies? We argue a lot. He's so stubborn about things and sometimes I need some space, you know?"

"Ah, so there's passion brewing in your relationship."

"Nannie!" Amorette pressed her hands to her face. "I think this is where this conversation needs to end."

"Don't misunderstand me." Nannie laughed this time, a sound like the bells on Amorette's door. "People always misunderstand the word passion. In this case, it's two people who burn hot with conviction and a sense of justice. It isn't a bad thing. Try to find the good in each other, to see how similar you are. Destiny will run its course, one way or another."

"Thank you." Amorette breathed a sigh of relief.

Nannie's words meant more than she knew. To Amorette, they meant another day she didn't have to worry too hard. Worry over relationships was the last thing she needed tonight. Especially when there were other things to worry about.

"I have to go now. If I don't leave after a few hours and someone comes looking for me, will you point them toward my house?"

Nannie nodded. "Go on. You're shaking from the cold. Get yourself inside."

Amorette blew a kiss and stood. Home wasn't so far away now, just a short jog. She raced toward her front door and, upon arriving, found it unlocked.

She pushed inside.

Four people sat around the coffee table, laughing as if they were the picture perfect family. Only, Amorette knew the difference.

She wrapped her fingers around the long scarf Nannie had given her. "D-dad?"

Her step-siblings both stopped to send a glare her way. Her step-mother wasn't much better.

Her father, of course, didn't see any of the looks they gave her. His attention snapped to Amorette immediately. His smile faltered, then fell. "Amorette."

"Have you eaten yet?" Her step-mother pasted on a bubbly personality. "We already ordered takeout but you're welcome to join us."

"That... would be nice." Amorette couldn't tear her gaze from her father's eyes.

Why did he look so disappointed? Why were his eyes so sad and remorseful? She didn't understand. Didn't he want to see her? It had been years. Why show up now?

All these questions, but none managed to force their way past her heart.

Her father didn't look away, but his expression didn't change either. Amorette remembered, briefly, how deep his eyes went. In the oldest vestiges of her childhood, she remembered wondering how her father's eyes always told a story. Today was no different, except she couldn't discern what the story meant.

"O-on second thought... maybe I... should just get my things and go." Amorette spun toward her room.

"Stay." Her father's voice was quiet but firm, like always.

Amorette looked over her shoulder at him. "Are you sure?"

He nodded. His fingers splayed over the couch cushion beside him. "Sit here. I think we have a lot to discuss. It's been a while."

None of this made sense, but Amorette wouldn't pass up a chance to spend even a few minutes with her dad. She missed him. It frustrated her, not seeing him around for the years her step-mother raised her. It angered her that he would abandon them like that.

He would never know any of that if she didn't say something. If only she could get her words to work.

"If she's busy, we should let her go." Amorette's step-mother tried to paste a smile on her face, but it fell flat.

Amorette's father shook his head. "Are you telling me to send away my daughter, who has grown into the living image of her mother? Are you telling me to let her walk away without even taking the time to memorize her face again?"

"I look like mom?" Amorette's stomach quivered. Her mother, whom she remembered as beautiful. Did she really look like her?

Her dad nodded. "So much it startled me."

Amorette relaxed into the couch. She looked like her mom. She always hoped, but there was no one to tell her if she resembled the woman. At least one good thing came from her father's reappearance.

"We ordered Chinese food. Is that okay?"

The question snapped Amorette out of her haze. She nodded her head in the affirmative. "I like Chinese food."

"Good." Her dad reached out a hand and patted her shoulder twice. "I like Chinese food, too."

Amorette forced a smile for his sake. Whoever said time and

distance didn't matter with family, they had never met her family. "Can I ask a question?"

"Of course." Her dad's fingers returned to his lap. For the first time, Amorette noticed his fingers fidgeting with his phone. A nervous tick, perhaps.

She took a breath. "Why did you leave? Did I do something wrong?"

Silence hung thick in the air. Leah and Lucas sent matching glares toward Amorette. She could imagine what they were thinking. Amorette was always the culprit in their eyes. Leah leaned over to her brother and whispered something in his ear. Lucas snorted and nodded his head.

"You didn't do anything wrong," Amorette's father answered. "You wouldn't believe me if I told you the reason."

"There are a lot of things I didn't think I would believe, but... sometimes the unbelievable is the only thing that makes sense."

If she didn't believe a few impossible things, Amorette knew her current situation would overwhelm and incapacitate her. The impossible became probable when she saw it with her own eyes.

Her father sighed. "Why did it have to be my daughter, of all people?"

Amorette almost missed his mumbled question. He said it so low that, had she not been listening, Amorette wouldn't have understood. The comment still made no sense, but she was bound and determined to figure it out now.

"Why did what have to be me?"

"It's better if you don't know." Her father shook his head. "Maybe you shouldn't have appeared here tonight. Your mother would be ashamed of my actions."

"What actions?" On impulse, Amorette reached out to wrap

her fingers around her father's hands. "Please, daddy? Please tell me why you left me here all alone. Why couldn't you stay?"

Her father's eyes met hers, and this time she read the agony in their depths. "Because you're not safe if I'm near you."

§—⚷

Eadric looked from one side of the table to the other. He didn't like eating with these two buffoons as it was, but especially not when neither would make eye contact with him. And not when the most important resident of the mansion, beside Eadric himself, was nowhere to be seen.

With a huff, Eadric folded his arms. "Where is she?"

"Out." Hunter mimicked Eadric's posture.

A nice attempt, but he didn't have the experiences and natural presence Eadric carried. On the other hand, Eadric knew he was less likely to receive any information from Hunter.

Eadric turned his attention to Doon instead. "Out? Where? With whom?"

"Well, you see, I don't exactly know... that..." Doon winced and reached for his water. "She took a driver."

"That's a lie." Eadric arched a brow at Doon. "None of the cars are gone. Try again. Where is she and how did she escape the house?"

"Okay, in my defense she's sneaky." Doon folded his hands on the table in a pleading motion. "Also in my defense, I was legitimately working when she left the house. Hunter was the one who saw her go."

"Hey, you can't throw me under the bus like that!" Hunter gaped at Doon.

"Too late, already did." Doon shrugged. "It's not like he's

going to throw you out. You're one of the only things keeping her here in the first place. He's not gonna chance her running away again."

"And yet, here we are, discussing her escape." Eadric lifted his eyes heavenward. If he had known these two would let her go so easily, he would have kept her closer to himself. A mistake he wouldn't repeat in the future. "Perhaps one of you has an idea where she went?"

Doon shook his head.

Hunter shrugged his shoulders.

Eadric stood to his feet and planted his fingertips against the tabletop. "One of you is going to tell me what you saw and heard."

"But I didn't see or hear anything!" Doon pouted.

Hunter remained silent.

"Fine." Eadric lifted his chin in preparation to change the subject, but a chime on his phone interrupted him. He slid the device from his pocket and frowned at the unfamiliar number on the text.

Upon opening it, he found one picture and a simple message, neither of which warmed his heart.

The picture featured Amorette, all alone walking down a sidewalk.

The message stated one word. *Sloppy*.

"You're both fools." Eadric pushed away from the table and searched his phone for a seldom-used application. "Doon, call Collins. I'll text him an address when I have it. Hunter... next time, don't interfere and keep the woman inside."

"What's wrong?" Hunter shot to his own feet.

Eadric shook his head. "Stay out of it and don't go anywhere.

I'll be back soon."

As far as Eadric was concerned, the app couldn't load fast enough. He was inside his vehicle before it beeped at him.

Eadric zoomed in on the area marked on the map. At least he had a general idea of her location now.

He tapped a finger to the screen as if she could hear his scolding. "Don't move."

The fool woman didn't even know the danger that lurked behind her. How could she run off like that? How could the dogs allow her out of the yard? They nearly killed her before. Why did they suddenly love her?

A thousand reasons she should have known to stay put all spiraled through Eadric's already crowded mind.

A drive that should have taken him thirty minutes lasted only fifteen.

Eadric parked his SUV at the end of the block and climbed out. The app on his phone dinged again, alerting him to Amorette's close proximity. Good. There was no time to waste. Not when Codex had eyes on her. Eadric jogged a few paces down the sidewalk, consulting his phone every few steps.

"You're looking for the girl, then?"

Eadric stopped and glanced sideways.

An old woman, covered in scarves with her head down, pointed a long finger to a house down the street. "She's there. Asked me to send you her way."

Well, at least Amorette wasn't a complete idiot. He didn't understand why she chose an old scarf woman, of all people. Did it really matter?

Eadric shoved his phone into the inside pocket of his coat. His feet ate up the pavement.

If Codex already had eyes on her, it was a matter of time before they made a move. He needed to be faster. She wasn't safe here. They knew where she lived. Besides, last time she came home, she left with injuries.

As much as he wanted to barge through the front door unannounced, Eadric didn't. Manners had been instilled in him since birth. He couldn't break down a door without definite proof that she was in danger. So, despite his panic, Eadric knocked.

A thin woman who clearly cared too much about her appearance answered the door. Eadric recognized her from surveillance pictures and video. The step-mother. He didn't spare her a word or another glance.

With a single brush of his arm, Eadric stepped past her and flicked a glance around the room. If this was the living room, Amorette's room must be... He turned left and started down the hall.

"You can't barge in here! I'll call the police!" The step-mother screeched.

Eadric didn't particularly care what she did, as long as Amorette was somewhere in this house. He flung open her bedroom door and breathed a sigh of relief.

The step-siblings looked over their shoulders from where they had the poor woman cornered on the other side of the bed.

Eadric clenched his teeth and stormed into the room. He shoved them aside.

His fingers wrapped around Amorette's wrist and tugged. "Let's go."

Amorette allowed him to lead her past the step-siblings before she tugged back. "Just a second."

Eadric stopped, but only to face her. Amorette's big eyes stared up at him from where she stood a fraction of an inch away from his chest.

"You don't understand what's going on here. We have to leave."

"I need to grab the end of my stuff." She jerked her chin toward the bed.

Eadric inhaled through his nose and let her snake out of his grasp. "Quickly."

Amorette rushed to the bed. Her fingers flew over the zipper of the suitcase. All the while, the step-siblings stared open-mouthed from the corner. Eadric spared them one glare before he returned his attention to Amorette.

The suitcase clunked against the floor. Amorette wheeled it to his side.

Eadric tucked her hand in his and herded her toward the door.

"Wait!"

"What's going on? Who is he anyway?"

The step-siblings' outbursts tumbled over each other in an attempt to be heard first. None of their questions mattered to Eadric. He pulled the door open again, only to stop dead in his tracks.

Amorette stumbled to a stop beside him. "Dad?"

"Is this him?" A man, almost as tall as Eadric, ran an assessing gaze over the couple. He paid special attention to Eadric.

Eadric narrowed his eyes at Amorette. "How much did you tell him?"

Amorette shook her head, her eyes wide as if she didn't have a clue what her dad meant either.

"Why did it have to be you?" Her father scrubbed a hand over his face. "It could have been anyone but you. You should give them what they want, don't drag my daughter into this."

"How do you know about what we're in the middle of?"

It seemed too coincidental to Eadric. Why would Amorette's father have any idea what was going on? What was all this, that he reacted in such a way?

"She was safe!" Amorette's father shoved his fingers back through his hair. "She was safe and oblivious and content. Why did you drag her down into this mess?"

Eadric took a single step in front of Amorette. He didn't think her father would hurt her, but the man seemed volatile. The conversation turned in a strange direction, too. Almost as if Amorette's father knew more than he let on.

Eadric knew, more than most, that danger could come from anywhere, in any form. Even from beloved or trusted friends.

"From what I've heard," Eadric chose his words carefully, enunciated each one, "you haven't been near your daughter for most of her life. Why would you choose to interfere now?"

"Because she's my daughter!" The man spat. "Because my absence kept her safe, but your undue entrance into her life put her in harm's way." Amorette's father reached out to wrap his fingers around the lapels of Eadric's coat. "Let her go. Let her go now, while you still can. It isn't too late to save her."

"What do you mean by that?" Eadric knit his brow in sheer confusion.

Amorette peeked around his shoulder. "Dad?"

"I'm begging you. Save her." Amorette's father tugged on Eadric's coat.

Eadric narrowed his gaze. This wasn't a delusional man. His

eyes remained clear and focused. Only his fingers shook. So why did he beg for mercy for his daughter?

Eadric blinked as realization set in. "Did you call them?"

"Just let her go. Go on living the way you are. Don't pull her into this."

"Did you call them?" Eadric raised his free hand to shake the man's shoulder. "How long ago? Are they here? How much time do we have?"

The man's face went stark white. "I'm sorry." His head dropped against Eadric's chest. "I'm so sorry. I didn't have a choice. It's the only way to save her."

No. No way. In all the realms of possibilities, Eadric never expected something like this.

What a cruel twist of fate to put an immortal's love into a Codex family. He could only imagine the living Hell they went through.

"What's going on?" Amorette's innocent question snapped Eadric back to reality.

Eadric brushed her father aside and wrapped his fingers tight around Amorette's.

"Get out of this house before they find you," he ordered Amorette's father.

Eadric didn't give Amorette the option to say no. If her dad already called Codex, and they had eyes on Amorette before that, then they were out of time.

"Where are we going?" Amorette used her shoulder to support her suitcase as she hiked it off the ground.

Eadric reached out to grab it himself. "Is there a back door? There must be, right? All houses have one."

"In the kitchen."

Eadric took her surprisingly heavy suitcase out of her hand. They needed speed, and burdening her with the object wouldn't help them.

The step-mother spewed insults and threats as they passed. Eadric ignored them all.

First things first, he had to get Amorette out of there.

He dove through the kitchen and out the back door. A street lamp flickered in the dark evening.

"This way." Eadric tugged Amorette behind him down the alleyway. Everything seemed too quiet, right down to the buzz of insects crawling along short stone walls.

Either he managed to render Amorette speechless, or she sensed the gravity of the situation. She hardly made a sound, save for the tap of her shoes against the ground.

A blinding light from behind them cast their shadows before them like ghouls.

Eadric tightened his grip on her hand.

Amorette threaded her fingers through his.

Eadric looked down at her to find her looking back at him, trust shining in her expressive eyes. There existed only one option.

"Run."

Eadric's boots and Amorette's sneakers pounded against the pavement. Their fingers locked together, neither willing to let go lest they lose their balance or fall behind.

The alley exit raced toward them. Eadric yanked Amorette around the corner. Stone erupted from the fence-line beside them. A loud crack echoed in the air.

Amorette screamed at the same time Eadric turned his body to cover her.

Stinging needles prickled Eadric's face and shoulder. He lifted his head to gauge their destination. If they could get to his vehicle, they had a chance. Just a few measly blocks. He tightened his grip once more around Amorette's hand.

Each step forward presented its own risk. Each alley or doorway they passed could hold any number of insurgents.

Eadric kept Amorette close to his side, using his own body as a shield against more bullets or attacks of other kinds. He could take it, survive it. Amorette had less chance to live.

For the first time in his life, Eadric saw his cursed existence as a blessing instead.

The duo reached the SUV to the tune of another loud crack. The back window on the passenger side splintered around the slug.

Eadric opened the driver's side and hefted Amorette inside. Her suitcase followed, tossed into the backseat. Eadric slammed his door shut and fired the engine.

Whap! A pair of palms hit the driver's side window.

Amorette screamed again and cowered in her seat.

"Help me too! Take me with you!" Amorette's father tapped his hands against the window again. "Please! They'll think I know something. Take me too."

Another bullet hit the side of the SUV, narrowly missing the man's abdomen.

Eadric glanced back at the woman in his passenger seat.

He knew very well what Codex would do to a failed member. He heard the stories for centuries. His cold heart could leave the man behind to die, but Amorette would never forgive him if he did.

Eadric unlocked the doors. "Get in. Hurry."

In the split second that the back door opened, a shot sailed through the door and buried itself in the opposite window.

Eadric pealed away from the curb before Amorette's father closed the door. He had questions, that man had answers. If he were to keep Amorette safe, he needed all of them.

First, they needed to get to safety.

[EPISODE 12]
TWO PATHS DIVERGED

"Who are they?" Amorette turned to look out the back window for the fourteenth time. "Are they following us?" She didn't need to know who they were to know they most certainly meant harm.

"Even if they are, they won't catch us." Eadric reached a hand into the middle console.

"You're bleeding."

Amorette reached shaking fingers to his cheek. Rough granite scratched her fingers beneath the sheen of crimson blood.

Eadric gently pushed her wrist away from his face. "We can deal with it later." He tucked a blue-tooth headset over his ear and tapped the middle button. "Call Collins."

Amorette pulled her knees to her chest and wrapped her arms around them. So many questions presented themselves, especially after her father's non-answer earlier. How did his presence put her in danger?

Amorette shot a look over her shoulder, but her father didn't notice. His gaze focused out the window.

What happened to make him so fearful? Why did Eadric bring him along when they didn't like each other? Her brain hurt from trying to deduce.

"Collins." Eadric's voice broke the silence. "I need the team at my house ASAP. No. No, it's fine. We're ten minutes out. Yes, lock-down. I'll tell him when we get there. Put someone on the boy, too." He pulled the blue-tooth away from his ear and tossed it back in the console.

Amorette waited a second before she asked. "Is someone trying to kill me?"

"It's more likely that they're trying to kill me." The tick in Eadric's jaw alerted Amorette to the fact that he may be lying. On the other hand, she saw the same tick when he got angry or annoyed.

"Am I going to die?" It made no sense, but neither did most of the things happening these days.

"Absolutely not."

"Are you going to die?" Amorette didn't know why the thought made her heart stop.

Eadric shook his head. "No."

She could ask so many more questions but now didn't seem like a good time. Amorette looked forward. If she didn't look back, she wouldn't think about the people chasing them. If she looked forward, she could worry instead about the speed with which Eadric drove.

Her father didn't utter a word the entire ride. Even when they rolled through Eadric's front gates, he didn't question it. As if he expected it all.

Eadric flew up the drive and came to a screeching halt outside the front doors.

Men in black suits and earpieces scurried out from the front door. One of them tore open Amorette's door and took her hand to help her down to the gravel. With a single hand on her shoulder, the guard ushered Amorette inside and up the stairs.

"What's going on?" Amorette looked over her shoulder to catch a glimpse of Eadric or her dad. "We're safe here, right?"

The guard ushered her up the second flight of stairs and toward her room. Not a word left his mouth until he had her safely inside the door.

Then, and only then, did the guard press a finger to his earpiece. "She's secured." To Amorette, he offered a tight smile. "Please stay here." He shut the door.

Amorette wasn't sure if it was to keep her in or to give her privacy.

So much happened. Flashes of memory played on repeat through her mind.

Bullets.

Shattered glass.

You're not safe if I'm near you.

Amorette's legs gave out, sending her down to the edge of the bed. She pressed her palms against her eyes.

Somehow, everything connected. How did everything fit together? Was someone after her, or were the bullets aimed at a different target? Two other options made sense, but then why did Eadric drag her out of the house so quickly?

Her door burst open, the bells jangling. Amorette looked up.

Eadric crossed her floor in two strides. His palms cupped her face to tilt her head up, his thumbs brushed once against her cheekbones. "Are you alright? You aren't hurt are you?"

Amorette shook her head. She reached her fingers up to

Eadric's cheek again, where blood still oozed from his wounds. "You're hurt though. You should get someone to treat that."

"It will heal soon enough." Eadric knelt beside Amorette. His fingers ran over her arms and legs, as if he didn't believe she was really okay. "Nothing happened? They didn't hit you?"

"Who are they? What am I missing?"

Eadric looked up.

Amorette held his gaze. Speaking without words wasn't possible with Eadric. Yet, somehow, she knew there was a whole host of things he hadn't divulged to her.

Eadric brushed Amorette's hair away from her face one last time. His fingers lingered to brush down the back of her head. "We will talk once I have the answers I seek. For now, stay here. Collins and Bryant will stay outside your door."

"Why?" Amorette pouted. "This is home. Why do I have to stay here?"

A soft smile spread across Eadric's lips. He shook his head once. "Until we're sure they didn't follow us. The boys will tell you when you can roam around again. I'll send Doon to keep you company in the meantime."

"Where are you going?"

"To get answers." Eadric backed away and stormed out the door.

The guard from before, either Collins or Bryant according to Eadric, reached for the doorknob and gave Amorette an encouraging nod.

Amorette sighed and flopped backward onto her bed.

Why couldn't she go get answers too? Why did she have to stay in her room with guards outside the door? That didn't seem fair. Not one iota. Did she do something wrong? Or, as EAdric said, was it to ensure her safety? Eadric didn't treat her like a criminal, so he probably told the truth on that one.

She pressed a hand over her cheek where Eadric held her. What did she do with the soft way he touched her? How did she process that?

The bells jingled as the door swung open again.

"Mi Amor!"

Amorette propped up on one elbow and knit her brow. "Hunter?"

"Are you alright? I finally got information out of one of the penguins." Hunter dropped to the bed beside her and pulled her to a sitting position. "You're not shot or anything, right? You're okay?"

"Do you really think I'd be here if I were injured?" Amorette giggled. "Eadric would have me in some top secret VIP wing in the hospital. Trust me. I'm okay."

"You're laughing about this?" Hunter frowned. "You were almost killed! How are you okay with that?"

"I'm not okay with it." Amorette tucked her hair behind her ears. "If I don't laugh, I'll cry. Do you get how hyped on adrenaline I am right now?" She held out a quivering hand. "I don't know what on God's green earth is going on and I sure don't know when I'll get answers. I'm currently locked in my room with guards outside because someone might have followed us. Who? I don't know. All I know is they want to kill someone in that vehicle we drove. That narrows the target down to three."

Hunter's brow furrowed even deeper.

Amorette licked her lips, then rolled them together. "So if it's not me, why the others? Did dad do something wrong while he was away? Or did Eadric tick someone off? He runs a very successful business so it could be an angry rival, but I wasn't getting that kind of vibe."

"Mi Amor." Hunter clasped his hands around Amorette's. "Look at me. Calm down."

"Oh, like I have a choice in that matter." Amorette yanked her hands away and pushed them back through her hair. "I can't calm down. Someone tried to kill one of us, don't you understand that?"

"I do. I get that. But being hysterical isn't going to help anyone, least of all you."

"Good grief, that's a lot of goons." Doon's voice echoed from the hall. He pushed past all three of the guards outside Amorette's door, but stopped when he saw Hunter. "Oh. That explains the uneven number of Collins' guys."

Hunter glared.

Amorette stood and paced to her desk. "Hi."

"Hey." Doon waved a hand. "You doing okay, kiddo?"

"Oh, please, don't call me that." Amorette winced. The word *kiddo* sounded weird coming from Doon's lips. Sure, he was older than her, but not by that much. "And of course I'm not okay."

"She refuses to calm down," Hunter supplied.

Doon rolled his eyes. "And when in the history of ever has a woman calmed down by being told to calm down?"

"Thank you!" Amorette pointed a finger toward Doon. "See? At least he knows not to tell me useless things." She paced toward the bookshelves on the other side of the room. "Where'd Eadric go? Is he okay?"

"He had some... things to do." Doon kicked the door shut. "I'm supposed to keep you company. Probably because he knew Hunter would be here."

Amorette looked between the two guys. She didn't mind their company, but she would rather have answers right now. Maybe one of them knew something, but she didn't wager on it.

Besides, Eadric was hurt and shouldn't be doing anything until he got his wounds treated. She had half a mind to drive him to the hospital, herself. Not that he would go.

"I would be okay by myself." Amorette began to rearrange the books on her shelf.

Her fingers itched to do something. Anything except sit still. Her whole body still shook, though Amorette was pretty sure the adrenaline should have run out by now.

"We're going to stay anyway," Doon insisted.

Hunter snorted. "For once, I agree with the idiot."

"Hey!" Doon glared at Hunter. "I have the authority to kick you out of this room, so watch it."

Amorette giggled. That one giggle turned into a laugh, and that laugh didn't stop. Her legs gave out again. Amorette dropped to the floor, unable to calm her hysterical laughter.

Both boys were by her side in seconds.

Eadric didn't like the idea of locking Amorette's father in the basement, but he didn't know how much of a threat the man posed. He refused to turn a blind eye to the issues around him. Amorette's father knew more than he would like them to think.

Two of Collins' security personnel tailed Eadric to the basement door. Both knew better than to follow him below.

Eadric slammed the door behind himself and jogged down the hard wooden steps. The first room in the finished lowest floor stored seasonal things and old artifacts. Eadric bypassed that room and opened the door to the studio room.

One of Collins' men had duct-taped Amorette's father to a chair. Not that the man seemed eager to get away. His calm demeanor unnerved Eadric. The slope of the man's shoul-ders and the set of his jaw denoted a man at his wit's end. A man ready to be done with it all.

"What is your name?" Eadric asked flatly.

Amorette's father looked up. "Is she safe here? Is she okay?"

"Your name."

"Is my daughter okay?" The man bit out each syllable.

Eadric folded his arms over his chest. "No thanks to you."

The man's shoulders relaxed. In fact, his whole body went slack in the restraints. "Joseph. My name is Joseph."

Such a simple, normal name for a man who, Eadric suspected, had not a single simple thing about his life.

"Well, then, Joseph," Eadric shrugged his coat off his shoulders and tossed it aside, "you're going to answer my questions. For your daughter's sake."

"You wouldn't hurt her." Joseph's eyes went wide, as if he didn't believe his own words.

"No. I wouldn't. Apparently, that's your area of expertise." Eadric unbuttoned one cuff and rolled the sleeve up his arm. "You work for Codex?"

"Codex doesn't have employees."

Eadric paused, his fingers stilling as he thought that over. It went against what he deduced about the organization, but in another way, it enlightened him. "What kind of organization doesn't have employees?"

"The kind that has followers." Joseph looked away, toward one of the mirrored walls. "Blind followers. Ones who don't know what they're in for until it's too late."

"Blind followers... That would make it a movement, rather than an organization, wouldn't it?" Eadric grabbed a chair from the stack in the corner and spun it so he could lean his arms on the back as he sat.

Joseph shook his head again. "The Benefactor. He funds everything for the organization. His most trusted followers recruit other followers. They tell them of the injustices of the world, make them believe they need to find a way to stop the insanity."

"And have they? Found a way to stop the insanity."

Joseph scoffed and remained silent. His eyes darted to the other side of the room.

Interesting, but Eadric didn't have time to psychoanalyze the man right now. Joseph didn't want to answer that question, fine.

Eadric moved on. "Your daughter. Why do you think she's in danger? Why beg me to save her?"

"She has the birthmark."

"The one on her shoulder?"

Joseph nodded. "She's always had it."

"How do you know what that mark means?"

"Codex doesn't sit back and do nothing. They found common denominators." Joseph finally looked back at Eadric. "How do you know about it?"

Eadric sighed and tapped a finger against his arm, thinking. "An information exchange. I'll tell you how I know, and you tell me why she's in danger."

Joseph ran his tongue over his lips as if it was the most difficult decision he made all day. He nodded once.

Eadric nodded back. "I had a friend. He found his true love in 1915. She bore that mark on her shoulder. I made a hypothesis when I first saw it on Amorette. It must denote someone destined to end an immortal's curse. Someone's true love."

Joseph sighed. "She's yours. You wouldn't be acting like this if she weren't."

"I'm keeping her safe because our paths crossed coincidentally." Eadric didn't believe the statement any more than Joseph.

Joseph shook his head. "No. There's no such thing when it comes to you people. You refuse to die until you find your true love. Don't you think destiny uses coincidence to throw you together?"

"Codex wants to end immortals, not the innocent true loves. Is that correct?"

Joseph huffed. "By the very definition, they can't end immortals. Not without using the innocent ones. A few sacrificed for many. You put a target on her back the second you met her."

Eadric blew out a breath. He didn't mean to put her in danger, and he felt there was a lot more to the story than that. "Look. Joseph. I'm being nice to you for your daughter's sake, but don't mistake me for a nice man. I've seen atrocities in my years of this existence. I will use force to stop another atrocity from beginning."

"It's too late for that. There are things in motion you don't even realize." Joseph sneered. "I lost my wife to this. I gave up on years with my daughter to keep her safe. I gave her a surrogate family who hates her, hoping it would cause others to overlook her. There is nothing I won't do to keep her out of their clutches, so don't test my patience, old man."

Eadric stood and kicked his chair to the side. "For a man who wants to protect her, you haven't done a very good job so far. We'll see who can keep her safer."

For Amorette's sake, Eadric retreated. If he stayed, he would hurt the man, and Amorette may never forgive him. Still, someone had to look out for the safety of a woman who never had someone to do it before.

Angry, Eadric stormed out of the back room and toward the exit.

"Mr. Hawkmore!" Doon stopped his descent at the top of the basement stairs. "You're gonna want to come take care of this."

"What's wrong?" Eadric narrowed his eyes.

Doon waved a hand to beckon Eadric to move faster. "We called a nurse, but she's not here yet. I think you're the most solid bet right now."

"Why?"

"Your girl is hysterical and she's freaking me out. Would you get a move on?"

Eadric dashed up the stairs. Leave the boys alone with Amorette for ten minutes, and what happened? They couldn't even calm her down.

"Who's with her right now?"

"Hunter, Collins, Bryant, and that guy you have following Hunter around." Doon fell into step beside Eadric.

Eadric took the stairs two at a time. Why couldn't one of these perfectly competent men find a way to calm down a small woman? She didn't pack that much of a punch.

Bryant and the third man, Miller, stood outside of the room. They stepped aside as Eadric neared. A single push opened the door the rest of the way.

Amorette sat curled in a corner, her arms over her head and her knees pulled to her chest. Her shoulders shook with violent sobs.

Hunter crouched nearby, his hand poised mid-air as if he wanted to comfort her but didn't know how. Collins stood behind Hunter, a bewildered expression on his face.

Eadric rolled his eyes and swooped past both of them. He tucked one arm under Amorette's knees and the other behind her back. She didn't weigh much, so it was a simple feat to carry her the few steps to the bed.

"Doon, the blankets."

Doon sprang into action, racing from the door and pulling the blanket and sheets down so Eadric could lay Amorette under them.

Eadric situated her in the middle of the bed and pulled the blankets over her. Never mind the clothes she still wore or the tears still streaking down her cheeks. She needed to feel safe right now.

Eadric reached out to run a hand over her hair. "It's alright now. You're home, safe. They can't get at you here."

Amorette slowly lowered her arms from her face. "I almost died!"

"But you didn't. I wouldn't let that happen." Eadric sat on top of the blankets beside her. "You're going to be fine. They don't know where you are now. They can't get to you."

Amorette hiccuped another sob. "Are you sure?"

"Sir." Eadric turned in time to see Collins remove his finger from the comm in his ear. "The nurse is here."

"Check her and send her up."

Collins exited.

Eadric turned back to Amorette. "We're going to have a nurse look you over, alright? She might give you something to calm you down."

"I'm not that hysterical." Another hiccupy sob interrupted her words.

Eadric arched a brow. "Oh, aren't you?"

"Of course not. How else am I supposed to get answers unless you're here to answer them?" Amorette lifted her chin defiantly, but Eadric heard the quiver in her voice. She didn't deal well with being shot at. Nor should she.

"Rest now and we'll talk later." Eadric stood from the bed and motioned Doon and Hunter toward the door.

"Eadric?"

Eadric paused to look back over his shoulder. "Yes?"

"Thank you." Amorette attempted a small smile. Dark circles and pale lips made it seem less than cheery.

Eadric inclined his head in a silent acceptance of her gratitude.

"Hey, what about me?" Doon raised a hand as if this were a classroom and he needed the teacher to call on him.

Eadric rolled his eyes and shoved the man toward the door. "You have phone calls to make. Move it." He shot a glare at Hunter next.

Thankfully, Hunter seemed shell-shocked enough to listen.

The security force outside Amorette's room split in half as the three men made their way down the hall. Two remained at Amorette's door.

"I don't feel so well." Hunter pressed a palm to his own forehead. "I'm going to go lie down."

He didn't wait to be excused, nor did he ask permission. Hunter turned and wobbled his way toward his bedroom.

Eadric watched him for a long moment, wondering what went on in that boy's head. He seemed dead set on garnering Amorette's favor, but this level of distress made no sense. Hunter should look for a way to help her, not crumble in on himself.

"Um, excuse me, but I know nothing about these calls which you referred to." Doon slung an arm around Eadric's shoulders.

Eadric flicked Doon's hand away and waited for his arm to follow.

"Just one. You'll enjoy it, I'm sure." Eadric grinned at his friend. "Call the company and have the security team bring Melodia Morris here. There are things I need to discuss with her. You can join."

Doon's jaw went slack. "You... Me and her... How... how did you know?"

"Whoever doesn't know is clearly blind or deaf." Eadric shrugged a shoulder. It didn't take long to deduce Doon's feelings for the woman. Not many women rejected Doon, twice, and caught a second look from him. "Have them bring her in. They know where she lives and a mention of Amorette should be all it takes to bring her willingly."

"Sir, yes, sir." Doon saluted and jogged off.

Eadric stopped at the top of the stairs to look back toward Amorette's room. She should be safe there. With guards outside the door and bullet-proof glass, she should be secure for the night. That didn't stop him from worrying.

"You're sure you'll be okay?" Doon asked Amorette for the

fifth time.

Amorette sighed and folded her arms. "Doon. Seriously?"

"Twelve hours ago you were in hysterics. Besides, *someone* threatened my life if I didn't keep an eye on you today." Doon sighed.

Amorette couldn't help but grin.

She didn't know what shifted between her and Eadric last night, but something did. Something had been brewing ever since the day in the maze. Did it finally break last night? She didn't know the details, she barely knew the emotions she felt, but she was willing to explore them.

Right now, none of that was the problem.

"Why do you need to keep an eye on me?" Amorette arched a brow.

"Amy has a point." Melodia dumped her bag onto the counter and spun to face Doon. "He has security plastered to her shadow, I don't think you're a necessity."

Doon held up a finger, as if to begin an argument.

Amorette swatted it down. "On top of that, even Eadric says this is the most secure building in the city. No one's going to get to me here. I think you can leave me alone to do my job."

"You heard the woman." Melodia brushed her fingers through the air toward the door. "See you later."

"What if I wanted to stay?" Doon pouted.

Both women shot him a look of disdain. "No."

"Oh, come on! Why not? I'm good for business, trust me."

"Make a purchase or come back later." Melodia spun on her heel and marched behind the counter.

"Don't be like that, Mel..." Doon leaned his elbows on the

counter and rested his chin in his hands. "How about lunch? Just you and I? Nice little cafe downstairs. I'll buy and everything."

"Oh, so tempting. I'm gonna have to pass." Melodia logged into the computer and brought up the necessary pages for business.

Doon reached out and snagged her hand in his. "Please? It's lonely eating alone."

"Take Amorette."

"She's not allowed into the lobby without security and a notification to the big boss and... let's just say it's complicated."

"And there isn't an eatery on any other floor?" Melodia arched a brow again.

Doon shook his head. "Not one that I want to take you to lunch at. Please? Please? I'm begging you. Do I need to get on my knees?"

"Don't be ridiculous, Doon."

Amorette raised her hand, unsure whether to interrupt them or not. "Um..."

"No. Don't say anything. I'm so close to getting a second date." Doon lifted wide eyes up to Melodia. "Please, please, please? I promise to be on my best behavior and I'll stay out of the store for the rest of the day."

"The week."

"Two days."

"Three."

"Okay, two and a half but that's as far as I go. And I take exception for any time Eadric makes me come check on her highness over there." He jabbed a thumb in Amorette's direction.

"Again, he has security spies on her. I think they can report pretty well."

Doon sighed and held out a hand. "Okay. Fine. Two and a half days without coming into the store, as long as you'll agree to lunch with me."

Melodia took a deep breath. "Okay. Deal." She shook his hand.

Amorette wasn't entirely sure what happened, but it seemed like their relationship progressed.

Truth be told, she liked them together. Doon was a nice, considerate guy and Melodia needed a guy like that. She deserved a guy like that. Simple, uncomplicated, and willing to treat her like a queen.

Doon tapped a palm against Amorette's shoulder as he headed for the door. "See you at lunchtime."

"Have fun!" Amorette called after him. She had no clue where he went during the day, but she didn't need to know.

Doon merely waved his hand once more and disappeared down the hall.

"What a piece of work." Melodia huffed and shuffled through her bag until she found her current romance novel.

"I'm sorry about security." Amorette ran her hands back through her hair and twisted it up into a ponytail.

Melodia shook her head. "No, he's right about that. After what happened last night, security is a must."

"How do you know about all that?"

Melodia paused. "Um... that's because he brought me over to explain what was going on. Apparently, he didn't want the added guards to freak me out. Or something."

"Wait, you were at the house?" Amorette looped a rubber band around her bunched hair. "When?"

"Last night. You were pretty passed out, so I didn't try to wake you up or anything." Melodia thumbed her book open. "It's all good. Mr. Hawkmore explained the situation and I'm cool with all the extra security. No more running off by yourself, okay?"

"I went to see my dad. It wasn't like I expected invisible crazy people to start shooting." Amorette rolled her eyes.

She didn't run away. She did, however, sneak off for an hour or two. How was she to know that Eadric would freak out and come looking for her? She still didn't understand why her dad said and did the things he did. He and Eadric spoke in a language all their own.

Which meant she needed to learn it.

Which meant she should speak to Eadric.

Despite his promise to "talk later" Amorette hadn't seen him since he tucked her in. Even this morning, Doon drove her instead of Eadric.

From the message Eadric left, she deduced he had some sort of important business to tend to. He apologized, but it still felt wrong. After only a few days, she got used to riding with Eadric to work. When she couldn't, everything felt... off. She didn't have the strength or courage to psychoanalyze herself.

With a sigh, Amorette pulled a box from behind the desk and set to work re-shelving.

[EPISODE 13]
A MATTER OF SINCERITY

Doon burst into Eadric's office and settled in a chair. "Melodia agreed to lunch, so Amorette is all yours during that hour. You're welcome, that's the most groveling I've done in a lifetime."

"You loved every second of it." Eadric swiped a stylus against his tablet to fix a mistake in the graphic.

In every possible scenario, Doon enjoyed this particular mission too much.

Doon shrugged. "So what if I did?"

"I don't meddle in your personal affairs." Eadric saved the graphic and sent it back to the team. One day, someone competent would work for him. He hadn't found that person yet. "Why Melodia?"

"I thought you didn't meddle in my personal affairs." Doon flipped one leg up over the other.

Eadric chuckled. Over the past few months, he came to appreciate Doon's evasiveness, but sometimes Doon overdid it. Then again, Doon's personal life wasn't any of Eadric's business. Perhaps, over the years, Eadric had become something of a busybody.

Eadric threw his hands in the air. "Alright. I won't ask. Did you finish the other preparations?"

Doon stood and extracted an envelope from his inner jacket pocket. "Reserved and waiting. Here are the files you asked for." He dropped the envelope on Eadric's desk. "They were difficult to get and even harder to read."

"You read them?"

"Of course. What kind of valet am I if I don't read the documents you ask me to purloin?" Doon clucked his tongue. "Really, you should have known that when you hired me."

"I didn't hire you, you inherited the position." Eadric tucked the envelope into his own jacket. "If your ancestors hadn't worked my land and discovered my secret, you wouldn't be here."

"Oh, please, you need friends." Doon grinned. "Mr. Hawkmore, can we be friends? I'm sure grandpa would approve."

"I thought we were already friends."

Doon was the closest he could get to friendship. Eadric didn't risk the lives of just anyone. His people consisted of a small group, but he would guard them all with his life.

Doon blinked and made a face somewhere between admiration and confusion. "Oh. And all this time I thought I was your underling or something like that."

"You are." Eadric treasured the absolute disappointment on Doon's face. "At work. After hours, it's a different matter. Those who look after me are qualified into a short list of people I show interest in."

"You're interested in me? Sir, I'm honored and flattered-"

"Don't be." Eadric regretted telling Doon all that. If he knew

Doon would react so over-dramatically, again, he never would have bothered. "Is the car ready?"

"Yes, and Collins has been briefed."

"Good." Eadric stood from his desk and reached for his coat. "And the item?"

Doon patted his pockets, came up empty, and held up a finger. A quick look through his coat, hanging in the corner, revealed the box he'd been looking for.

Doon held it out to Eadric. "Exactly as you ordered it."

Eadric flipped the lid to study the object, then smiled. Yes. It was exactly as he ordered it. Doon didn't need to say more for him to know everything.

Eadric stuffed the box into his own coat pocket. "Thank you, Doon."

"Gratitude? What's that?" Doon grinned wider. "You're welcome, but don't sound too over-eager when you go see her. And put down the coat. It's only ten. You have two hours."

"So do you." Eadric pointed out.

Doon collapsed into a chair. "It's so long. Can you make some gadget that skips time forward?"

"If I could, I would have made it by now."

Eadric sighed. If only that were possible. If only time existed in relativity to one's lifespan. He didn't have those luxuries. Time ticked by slowly and wore him down without ever leaving a visible mark.

Eadric stood again and grabbed his coat. "I'll be back."

"Where are you going? Are you leaving me to suffer alone?" Doon turned as he watched Eadric storm out, each twist of his body allowing him to see the older man's progress.

Eadric chuckled. "I think you'll survive."

"I won't! I'll die of boredom! Mr. Hawkmore, come back!"

That was the last plea Eadric heard before the door shut behind him.

In truth, he didn't know where he would go for the next two hours. But, Eadric knew he couldn't sit behind his desk without anything to distract him. He needed to move.

First, naturally, a stop by The Nook. Once he knew it was secure, Eadric knew he could find something else to do.

Eadric took the elevator down to the fifteenth floor. If he stepped out and then back in, it should be enough time to ensure security presence and view any customer interaction.

Plan in place, Eadric stepped into the hall.

The Nook seemed busy today. Several Hawkmore employees roamed the aisles, despite the obvious security presence at the entrance. Good. At least they knew enough to overlook the men in black.

Eadric was about to step back into the elevator when he spotted it.

Hunter stood at the front counter. Across from him, Amorette leaned on the smooth surface with a smile on her face and her chin on her palms.

Eadric's expression ticked into a sneer. What right did Hunter have to be here, of all places? And what made him worthy of Amorette's attention or affection? Did he do anything to keep her out of harm's way? The answer: a resounding no.

Eadric didn't like Hunter from the beginning, but today he liked him even less. No doubt the boy charmed his way into a visitor's pass to get up here. Eadric made a mental note to crack down on security in the lobby, too.

This instant, he needed to find a way to get rid of Hunter. Not permanently, but long enough to have a heart-to-heart with Amorette. Long enough to woo her for himself.

Sometime in the last twenty-four hours, Eadric somehow accepted that Amorette wasn't meant for someone else. The way she looked at him, the way his heart turned when she was hurt, all attested to the growing bond between them. That's what scared him most.

Eadric reached his fingers up to run them over the scabbed gouges on his cheek. Unlike the dog bite from a few days ago, these wounds hadn't disappeared. The strange part was, they should have. They weren't nearly as deep as the bite. It left only one hypothesis, and the implications terrified Eadric.

His fists clenched and unclenched at his sides as he thought. There didn't appear to be a good solution right now, but he would come up with something.

Eadric stepped back into the elevator and opened his phone. The least he could do was demand someone keep an eye on Hunter. At least find out how he got in.

Eadric phoned the lobby first.

Nicole, the current receptionist, answered on the second ring. "Hawkmore Industries, this is Nicole speaking, how may I assist you today?"

"This is CEO Hawkmore. Did you issue an unauthorized visitor's badge this morning?" Eadric had never been one for pleasantries and, quite frankly, Nicole's voice irritated him. She appealed to visiting elites, the only reason she kept the job.

"Yes?" Nicole hesitated. "Did I do something wrong? He had one of our security personnel trailing him and he said he needed to see someone who works here. Her information was in the computer, so I assumed..."

"No need to apologize. Thank you for the information." Eadric ended the call.

His own fault for having one of the security staff trailing Hunter. Logically, it wouldn't work to kick the boy out, which left one option only.

Eadric texted the guard assigned to Hunter. *The woman doesn't go anywhere with him. Don't let him out of your sight.*

He didn't need to receive an answer to know his order would be carried out.

⚷

Amorette handed the plastic sack of books to the customer and flashed her brightest smile. "Thank you for shopping at The Nook. Please come again."

The customer waved as she left.

Amorette dropped the smile and turned to Hunter. He arrived earlier, but she couldn't get him to leave. Not for lack of trying. He simply wouldn't go.

Amorette was used to Hunter's persistence, but this represented a whole new level of stubborn. Why didn't he leave her alone?

An hour and a half had come and gone, with Hunter still conspicuously situated in the corner. If he was trying to earn her sympathy, it wasn't working so well. The longer he didn't listen, the more tempted Amorette became to have security kick him out. She liked Hunter's company, but she hated his interruption to her work.

"Mi Amor, let's do lunch," Hunter suggested.

A quick glance at the clock revealed the hands at high noon.

Amorette sighed and tossed him a look. "Will it make you leave?"

"I promise I won't come back this afternoon if you agree." Hunter grinned, his classic boyish charm shining through.

Melodia sauntered by and mouthed two words at Amorette. *Malibu Ken.*

Amorette laughed and shook her head at her boss. Melodia's distaste for Hunter didn't surprise her anymore. He was a pretty boy, through and through. Amorette could see how that would turn some people away. But she knew the kind man inside the facade.

"Fine. Let's do lunch." Amorette retrieved her bag from behind the counter.

Hunter grabbed her hand with a wide grin. "Great! Let's go." He dragged her toward the door.

Hunter's security tail stepped into their path and put a hand against Hunter's chest. "I'm sorry, sir. The young lady can't go with you."

Amorette couldn't say she felt any sense of remorse at the thought of not going to lunch with Hunter. He seemed especially clingy today. She didn't want to deal with that if she didn't have to.

"What? Why?" Hunter chuckled and flicked the man's hand away. "Stop joking around."

The man stepped into his path again. "Again, I'm sorry. I'm under strict orders to not allow her to leave the store with you."

"That's ridiculous." Hunter huffed. "We're just going to lunch. You'll be there. Her bozos will be there. It isn't super difficult to go with it."

"I'm under orders."

"Really? Whose orders?" Hunter's voice sounded strained, barely held in check.

"Under my orders."

Amorette recognized the voice immediately. She didn't understand why Eadric didn't want her going anywhere with Hunter, but he saved her from listening to Hunter whine. She could forgive it.

The guards all stepped aside, each with a slight bow. For a split second, Eadric seemed like the king of the world, revered by many and obeyed by all.

With his hands shoved in his coat pockets, Eadric stopped where Hunter's security tail previously stood. "Amorette and I have a standing appointment."

"That's not the story I got two minutes ago." Hunter tightened his grip on Amorette's hand.

Amorette winced and gingerly pried each finger from his grasp. "I forgot. Okay, actually, I didn't know, but I believe him. If he says we have a standing appointment, I should keep that. Right?"

Hunter's laugh sounded more incredulous than amused. "You're dumping me for him right now?"

"I think I made this appointment first."

"You did." Eadric didn't move an inch. He seemed unfazed by Hunter's mood swing.

"We'll do lunch next time. Okay?" Amorette smiled, hoping to appease Hunter's temper.

With a sigh, Hunter shrugged his shoulders and nodded. "Fine. Next time."

"Thank you." Amorette patted a palm against his shoulder. She turned in time to catch Eadric's lip curled in annoyance.

Eadric recovered quickly and offered his arm in Amorette's direction. "Shall we? We shouldn't be late for our reservation."

"Reservation?" With that one word, Amorette's full attention turned to Eadric instead of Hunter.

Eadric effortlessly steered her out of The Nook and toward the elevators. "Yes. I find it makes things easier if you make reservations. I've been doing so for years."

Amorette glanced back to see her guards file in behind them. They kept a larger distance between their bodies and hers this time, as if they trusted Eadric to step in if something happened. Given his quick and resourceful decisions the night before, Amorette couldn't disagree.

"It's more conspicuous if you keep looking back."

Amorette winced before she turned back to Eadric. She lifted her chin defiantly. "Don't tell me what to do."

"I wouldn't dream of it." Eadric released her arm and motioned her into the elevator. He tossed one instruction to the guards before he stepped inside. "Bring her jacket."

Amorette looked down, only now realizing she didn't grab it.

Why was she so scatter-brained today? It took her an extra hour to shelve books and far too long to ring up purchases. *Pull yourself together*.

"Take a breath." Eadric tapped the elevator button that would take them to the underground garage. "I did recommend that you stay home today. If memory serves, you were the one who refused."

"Are you kidding? Staying home with a sprained ankle was tough enough. No way I'm holing up in my room just because some psycho shot at me." Amorette shrugged a shoulder indifferently, even though she felt anything but indifference.

"Besides, I can't prove that he wasn't after you instead."

Eadric nodded his head, clearly thinking. "Let's not discuss the shooter for the time being."

"Fine by me." Amorette blew out a breath.

All the better for her mental state. Even with a sedative in her system, last night's dreams had been torturous at best. If she could forget the panic and Eadric's blood, even for a moment, Amorette would treasure the respite.

Speaking of... she reached a hand up to his cheek. Her thumb ran over the scabs still visible there.

Eadric looked down at her. "What is it?"

"They aren't healed yet."

"Should they be?"

"The dog bite healed faster. These were barely scratches compared to that." Amorette let her palm flatten against Eadric's face. She could feel the tick in his jaw, seconds before he pulled away.

"I told you, the bite was nothing." He looked away from her, as if he still hid part of himself.

Amorette dropped her hand to her side and sighed. "Will you ever tell me the truth?"

"Patience is a virtue."

"It's one I don't have." Amorette grinned. "Come on, it can't be that bad."

"I have things to tell you at lunch. Let's wait until we've eaten."

The elevator thumped to a stop. Eadric wrapped his hand around Amorette's and stepped into the dim garage.

Amorette appreciated the automatic gesture. Her fingers wrapped through his. She didn't like the dark or the shadows, especially after yesterday. Though bright lights sat at appropriate intervals, the garage would never be without shadow. Amorette cringed away from mysterious corners.

"It's secure here. Nothing will happen." Eadric stopped beside his SUV and opened the passenger side door.

Amorette crawled in and reached for her seat-belt. "I know that."

"Of course." Eadric shut her door.

Neither of them believed Amorette's assurances. Even Amorette knew she shouldn't be traipsing around the city so soon after a traumatic experience. However, if she didn't do something, she would go crazy.

Since she didn't want to lose her mind, Amorette pressed forward. One decision at a time.

⚷

Eadric waited for Bryant and Collins to arrive before he even considered unlocking the SUV doors or letting Amorette out. He wasn't foolhardy enough to believe Codex didn't have eyes on one or both of them. However, Eadric also knew Codex wasn't idiotic enough to make a move on either of them in broad daylight. Not when they were together and had security close by.

Besides, there were too many witnesses. Codex played their cards close to their chest.

Bryant and Collins exited their vehicle.

Eadric took that as his cue. "Stay still," he instructed Amorette.

Eadric stepped out of the car first. In a matter of seconds, he assessed the surrounding area. Everything seemed fine, so he circled the car and opened Amorette's door.

"Shall we, then?"

Amorette smiled at him and reached for his offered hand.

Eadric could honestly say he'd grown fond of that smile. The one that spoke of trust and security. She believed in him, and that was something Eadric hadn't felt in a long time.

Collins and Bryant stepped into position behind Amorette. Eadric knew, with their training, that the two men's attention shot anywhere but at the woman they guarded. It was their job to avoid a catastrophe if it could be avoided. They would look for any attacking forces. Which left Eadric to pay special attention to the woman beside him.

He held the door for her and followed her inside the cozy restaurant interior.

It was unusually quiet for a weekday at lunchtime. No chatter filtered from the dining area. No crash of dishes sounded from the kitchen. A lone receptionist stood behind the front desk.

She inclined her head in a respectful greeting. "Welcome to Rosenthal's."

"Thank you," Eadric handed the receptionist a handful of twenty dollar bills. "You've all been quite good sports about everything. We'll return the establishment to you in an hour or so."

"The kitchen and wait staff are at your disposal." The girl stepped aside and motioned Eadric and Amorette into the empty dining area.

Amorette looked around like a child who entered a candy store. Eadric found it amusing to watch her head whip from one side of the room to the other. He doubted she missed much.

Crystal chandeliers hung over their heads. Silk napkins adorned expensive China plates. Fresh flowers created intricate centerpieces on each table.

"Why is it empty?" Amorette asked.

Eadric chose a table away from the windows and pulled out a chair for her. "I made a reservation."

"You rented out the whole place?" Amorette's mouth went slack. "How much does that even cost? Wait, no, don't answer that. I'm sure it's more than my yearly salary. Let's... let's forget I asked."

"It's natural to wonder." Eadric tipped his head toward the chair he still held. "Won't you have a seat?"

"Am I dressed appropriately for this?" Amorette glanced down at her jeans and blouse.

Eadric smiled. He was used to seeing her in things like this. It had become an endearing trait, her casual dress. "You're perfect. Sit down."

Amorette settled in the chair and took out her napkin. "It's a little bit of overkill."

"Think of it this way," Eadric pushed her chair in and circled to his own seat. "An empty room is easier to secure than one with a whole host of unknown variables. With the time limits I had, this was the simplest way to keep everyone safe."

It was a half-truth, but the important bits remained intact. He didn't want to worry during this lunch. If people filled the room, he would fret over spies and assassins and the like. Better to get rid of all the distractions. Besides, he and Amorette had things to discuss.

Amorette flipped her menu open. A shocked gasp caught in her throat.

Eadric winced and reached over to pluck the menu from her fingers. He expected it to give way, but instead, Amorette held tight.

"Amorette..."

"This... I'm hallucinating, right?" Her eyes didn't leave the list.

Eadric sighed and yanked hard. The menu tore from Amorette's fingers long enough for Eadric to tuck it beneath his own.

"Are we on a date right now?" Amorette's head tilted in an expression Eadric knew well. If he didn't stop her soon, she would overthink the entire situation.

He hadn't planned on things going this way, but he could roll with the punches. "That's something I thought perhaps we should converse about."

"Oh my gosh, we're on a date." Amorette averted her gaze.

Eadric took a steadying breath. "Amorette. I realize this is all... very sudden. I can't explain it. Not really. But I can try if you'd like."

"If I get uncomfortable, can I leave?"

"I don't think that's a wise idea, given our situation."

Amorette wrinkled her nose. "Okay, fine, you have until the food is gone. I don't know what to order."

"You like steak." Eadric closed both menus and folded his hands atop them.

Amorette nodded. "Well, yeah, who doesn't?"

"They have a divine prime rib here. You should try that."

This, Eadric felt comfortable with. He could suggest food any day, solve problems as long as they didn't involve his own emotions. It was everything that came next that he couldn't quite grasp.

A single waiter appeared from the kitchen. All business, he offered wine that Eadric refused, took their orders, and disappeared again.

Amorette turned her attention to Eadric. "I suggest you start talking now."

"I'll give you the short version." Eadric leaned on the table again. "Amorette, beyond reason, I find myself attracted to you."

"Seriously? Are you saying what I think you're saying right now?"

"I'd appreciate if you don't interrupt. I only have two more things to say." Eadric reached into his coat pocket. The small box still sat where he put it earlier. He took it out and set it on the table. "From now on, don't give Hunter any hope that he can have you. Give all your hope to me instead."

Amorette nibbled on her lip before she pointed to the box. "Is this for me?"

"Yes, this is a gift if you accept the proposition."

Eadric watched the wheels tick in her head. He hated every second that she thought through this. If only he could make her act impulsively when he wanted. When it would make sense to act impulsively. She barged into his office to complain about a broken phone, yet she wouldn't immediately accept his offer.

"Amorette?"

"Shh, I'm considering what you said." She glanced up. "You like me?"

"Yes."

"*Like* me, like me?"

"That's what I'm saying."

"Then ask like a man." Amorette folded her arms. "You're such a child sometimes. Say the words."

Eadric blinked. Honestly, he should have anticipated

something like this from her. Amorette believed in fairy-tales. She needed the words.

He blew out a breath. "Let's date. Be mine."

Amorette set the tip of one finger on the velvet box. "Ring, earrings, or necklace?"

"Open it and see." Eadric grinned.

He had her on the hook. He saw the way she looked at him, last night and in this moment. He would prove himself every day if she said yes. There was no other way to live.

Amorette's smile was more than enough to appease his worrisome thoughts. She slid the box closer and cracked the lid. Her eyes went as round as the saucers on the table.

Eadric smirked. "You like it?"

"Are those diamonds?" Amorette lifted the box closer to her face.

"They are." Eadric stood and leaned sideways against the table. He plucked the necklace from the box and let the pendant dangle. "Do they satisfy your taste?"

Amorette trailed a finger over the compass pendant. A single diamond adorned each spoke on the wheel. The center contained a large black stone.

Amorette grinned up at him. "It's gorgeous. Thank you."

"Shall I put it on you?" Eadric offered.

Amorette nodded enthusiastically.

Eadric unclasped the necklace and stepped behind Amorette.

Amorette swept her hair up in one hand and tipped her head forward.

It was the most silent they had been around each other in a long while. A silence charged with questions and inexplicable answers. Eadric secured the necklace well and went back to his seat.

Amorette lifted the pendant to study it one last time. "Thank you."

"You still haven't answered my question."

"I didn't exactly hear a question. I think you claimed me." Amorette shrugged. "I'm cool with it. Just know I'm not going to bend to your every whim. I'm human too. We'll work together, and if it doesn't work out, it doesn't work out."

"It will work out." Eadric was more sure of that than anything else. He and Amorette were destined, it was just a matter of convincing her of that. Since she agreed to date him, she must have some inkling. "It will be more dangerous for you now that we're official."

"What do you mean? Official?"

"You didn't know? The people after you already think you're my woman. Now that it's official, they're bound to find out."

"You're saying the security guys are a 'from now on' kind of thing, aren't you?"

Eadric didn't miss the disappointment in her voice. Afraid that she would back out, he reached across the table for her hand. "Until we sort out this Codex situation."

"That reminds me." Amorette held up a finger and reached into her bag. She produced Eadric's journal, bound and just as he remembered it last. "You can have this back now. I finally read it."

"How much?"

"I don't understand how or why, but you don't die." Amorette thrust the journal toward him again. "I don't think it's right to keep someone else's personal journal like this. Not with the memories stored here."

"I don't need it back." Eadric pushed the book back toward her. "You keep it. Until you understand it all. Ask anything you want."

"Why don't you die?" Amorette clutched the book to her chest like a lifeline.

Eadric smiled wryly. "I'm not entirely sure either. I've known several others like me, and I have a hypothesis."

"What kind of hypothesis?"

"I've been waiting for you." Eadric said it with a smile, but deep down he knew it was the truth. He couldn't love just anyone, no matter how hard he tried. Hate was easy. Love defied all logic.

Amorette opened her mouth to speak, then shut it again. "Codex," she finally demanded. "Tell me about Codex."

"From what I've gathered, they believe immortals are monsters, things to be rid of forever. They've run experiments and documented known cases of immortal men and women. Some of my own friends have fallen prey to them. I'm not sure how your father knew who I was, but I believe they must have some sort of dossier on anyone they believe to be immortal."

He didn't mention the most important factor. The one that made no sense but somehow seemed true. The professor. Eadric hadn't quite figured that out yet, so he remained silent on the matter.

"My dad is a part of that group?"

"For years, he has been." Eadric paused, considering his next words carefully. "Your mother, too. May I ask what happened to her?"

"I don't know." Amorette shrugged. "I have no memories of

my mother. She left when I was very little."

Eadric nodded. Of course she wouldn't know anything. Why would her father tell her about things that would endanger her? Any loving father would try to keep his daughter as far from that catastrophe as possible.

The waiter's swift arrival saved Eadric from the most uncomfortable part of this luncheon. Or, at the very least, postponed it.

Amorette and Eadric ate in silence, with only the occasional clink of a fork or scrape of a knife to break it. All the while, Eadric knew he had to tell her. He didn't have Doon investigate it so that he could keep Amorette in the dark. If she chose this path, she needed to know at least this much.

"Amorette," Eadric wiped his lips and set his napkin down beside his empty plate. "This lunch... is also an apology and an explanation."

"Okay, wow. No need to be so cryptic." Amorette set her silverware down and folded her arms. That defiant chin lifted once more, denoting her nerves.

Eadric reached inside his jacket and produced the envelope. She needed to know, for everyone's sake. "I know what happened to your mother. I only need your father to confirm a few minor things, but... I'm excellent at filling in puzzle pieces." He held the envelope out to Amorette. "You should read the files."

Amorette stared at the manila envelope suspended in the air between her face and her new boyfriend.

It still sounded weird, even to think the word. Even stranger, something she sought from her father for years now presented itself at the most inopportune time. She asked her father about her biological mother so often. He only ever shut down.

If there were files, it meant whatever happened to her mother had been meticulously documented. One logical deduction presented itself.

"She died."

"You should read the whole story." Eadric set the envelope on the table. "Take your time. I'll wait."

Courage fled at the thought of discovering the truth. What if she didn't like what she found? What if it broke her all over again?

Amorette toyed with the corner of the envelope. Could she bring herself to do this, when she thought she finally came to terms with her mother's disappearance?

In short: yes.

Amorette snatched the envelope and slid the papers from inside. Not a thick file. In fact, far too thin. As if someone let it slide by, without ever questioning the findings.

Page by meager page, Amorette skimmed her mother's story. A story that told of chaos. Words stood out like spotlights along the way.

Dead on arrival.

Defensive wounds.

Distraught husband.

Infant daughter.

"She was murdered?" Amorette's voice caught in her throat.

No wonder her father never said anything. Who would so easily overcome their wife's homicide?

Eadric folded his hands as if he had more to say. "Do you want to know what happened the night she died?"

"There aren't any witness statements." Amorette dropped the file and swiped at a tear as it escaped her eye.

Eadric nodded. "That's right. No one said anything about seeing it, but there were two witnesses to this murder. Three, if you count the culprit."

"Who are they? Can we talk to them?"

Eadric took her hand in his. Amorette had to admit the gesture made her feel better. Safer.

His gaze met hers, all serious. "You. Your father. You were both there."

"Then why didn't dad say something? He should have said something. He wouldn't just let her die."

"Amorette." Eadric tightened his grasp on her. "Your mother died trying to save you. If I'm right, your father hatched a deal with Codex after that. Your life for his silence."

"Why? I was a baby, why was I in danger?" She couldn't grasp it. Codex didn't make sense and her parents' involvement even less so.

Eadric tugged her forward until he could reach a finger to tap the back of her shoulder. "This. This birthmark. I'm sure your parents didn't know the extent of Codex's corruption when they signed on, but there's no going back once you're in. They must have told someone about their marked daughter. Your mother is noble for taking a stand against them. Your father, as well."

"You don't know that. You're speculating." Amorette pulled back from him.

Her mother and father wouldn't endanger her like that. No way.

Eadric sighed. "Shall we ask him, then?"

It was in that moment that Amorette realized what she truly believed. Years of strange dreams now made sense. One recurring phrase that she thought her overactive imagination made up on its own.

Not this. Not her.

Did her parents set her up to be murdered? Was her whole life a lie? How could anyone trade one life for another? None of it made logical sense, but somehow the knowledge forced her whole world to fall into place.

Her father's absence. Her mother's disappearance. The strange conversations she overheard as a child. For years, she lived in the serpent's den, and she didn't even know it. How deep did it go?

"Amorette."

Eadric's voice barely registered. Amorette didn't know what to believe anymore. Her loving home? Gone. Her imaginations of finding her mother strong and healthy? Impossible.

"I need to talk to him."

"Right now?"

Amorette nodded. It was the only way anything could make sense. If she asked her father directly. If she heard the story from his lips. "Can we go talk to him now?"

Eadric slipped from his chair. He slid the envelope into his pocket and took out his phone. "Collins? Start my car. We have places to go."

[EPISODE 14]
A GAME OF CHESS

Amorette never liked the idea of her father locked in a basement, but somehow she understood the precaution now. He was still her dad, but that didn't mean he was entirely innocent. The people he followed tried to shoot her. Judging from his reaction before the incident, he had an idea that they would.

Now, here she stood, ready to demand answers to questions he had ignored for far too long. Eadric's steady presence in the shadows behind her lent to Amorette's determination.

Joseph looked up from the cot in the corner. Sometime between his arrival and this meeting, Amorette figured Eadric provided him with the basics. She didn't know why, but she was grateful.

Amorette folded her arms and lifted her chin. "Why didn't you tell me?"

"I don't know what you're talking about." Joseph turned back to the magazine in his hands. Every action spoke nonchalance, as if he didn't care about the turmoil in his daughter's head.

Amorette stormed across the room and ripped the magazine

from his grasp. "Answer me! Why didn't you tell me about mom? What really happened?"

"How do you know about that?" Joseph shot a look past her, the accusation in his gaze aimed toward Eadric.

Amorette didn't care. "They killed her. And you let it happen."

"Don't blame me for saving your life." Joseph snorted a humorless laugh. "Your mother didn't understand how dangerous these people are. I loved her with all my being, but I wasn't about to let her die in vain."

"What did you do, dad? How much of your soul did you sell?"

"Codex isn't the devil." Joseph sat up and draped his arms over his knees. "But they're the next best thing."

"Tell her."

Amorette looked over her shoulder at Eadric. Did he know more than he said? Did he know the whole story, without a doubt? Had he already asked?

"There's nothing to tell her. It will only put her in more danger."

"I'm dating Eadric, dad." Amorette winced at her own words.

She didn't mean them to sound so sharp or calculated. She figured he might tell her more if she had already thrown herself into the lion's den.

Joseph laughed as if Amorette had meant it as a joke.

Amorette felt Eadric's presence close in on her, until she could feel him standing over her, behind her. His fingers brushed the center of her back. Whether he meant it as encouragement or reassurance, she couldn't tell.

"You said it yourself," Eadric intoned. "She and I are destined, so why fight it?"

"She's a child."

"I'm a woman! I know my own mind. And twenty-three is hardly a child."

"Says the *woman* staying with her step-mother and enduring abuse she didn't have to take." Joseph shrugged a shoulder. "You could have moved out a long time ago."

Amorette paused. He had a point. She never had to take the beatings her step-mother gave, verbally or physically. But... "You wouldn't have been able to find me."

"All the better."

"No, it isn't." Amorette shook her head. "You don't get it, do you? You're the only happy memory I have."

Joseph worked his jaw back and forth. "I shouldn't be. Because of me, you almost died twice now."

"That's not true."

"It is true!" Joseph shot to his feet.

Eadric pulled Amorette behind his back. "Joseph, calm down. She deserves to know. Don't be angry with her because of her ignorance. That's your fault, not hers."

Amorette peeked out to watch the following stare-off. Her father didn't seem happy with Eadric's interference, but all of them knew Joseph wouldn't win in a one-on-one fight.

Finally, Joseph nodded. He sank back onto the cot. His head fell into his hands. "You were two the first time. Your mother and I argued all that time about whether to tell Codex about your mark. We'd seen the things they did to immortals and their mates. The experiments."

"Why didn't you leave? You could just run away." Amorette stepped out from Eadric's hold. As much as she enjoyed his protective streak, she had to face this one on her own.

"You don't know Codex. Once we reached a rank high enough to learn of the experiments, we were required to take part. To report anyone who bore the birthmark." Joseph scrubbed his fingers through his hair. "Your mother refused to hand you over. So I reported, hoping they would understand because you were the daughter of their followers. I was wrong."

"You were going to hand me over to them for... experiments?"

Amorette couldn't quite believe what she heard. Her father loved her. She always believed that. Why would he do such a thing?

"No. I wouldn't. Codex requires blind obedience, but I wouldn't turn a blind eye this time. It's different when it's your child's life." Joseph glanced up. "So they came to retrieve you. Your mother stood in their way. They threatened her. There... was a fight. I should have intervened, but I didn't. In the end, I made a deal. You could live, untouched, as long as I didn't testify to the death."

"You told emergency services that you didn't see anything." Amorette huffed a disbelieving breath. "How could you?"

"So you could live! Your mother died protecting you, I wasn't about to let Codex take you."

"So why call them now?"

"Because you're with him." Joseph jutted his chin in Eadric's direction. "As far as we know, he's the original immortal. The oldest and the most dangerous. Someone who isn't on anyone's side but his own. Someone who kills the innocent without remorse."

"I'm not sure you should be one to judge on that." Eadric chuckled. "And I have never, in my life, harmed an innocent person."

"Think again." Joseph laid back down and reached out to snatch the magazine back. "I'm done offering information. I'd appreciate it if you both left."

Amorette blinked at the sudden tears. After so many years, her father felt more like a stranger. Had she ever been safe, for a single day in her life? What kind of person was she, that she assumed the people around her would protect her? How innocent and naive did she have to be to believe all the half-truths?

Her attention traveled to Eadric, who stood as poised and unfazed as ever. Did he really kill people? On occasion, he seemed dangerous. But homicidal? It didn't quite fit what she knew about him.

"Let's go for now." Eadric held out an arm, a silent way to usher her toward the stairs.

Amorette let him lead her while her brain processed. Though the mother she hoped would one day return was dead, there was a certain level of comfort knowing that woman loved her enough to protect her. If only she understood why Codex so desperately wanted her, she might be able to live.

Amorette stepped out of the stairwell into the bright afternoon sunlight that streamed into the house.

Eadric's hand reached forward. He laced his fingers through hers. "I'm sorry, Amorette."

"Why?" She shrugged her shoulders. "You didn't do anything wrong. Did you?"

Amorette didn't want to have doubts about herself or Eadric, but suddenly they flooded her. What if her father was right and Eadric had been manipulating her this whole time? What if she wasn't strong enough to get through this?

"I'm sorry you had to find out about your mother this way." Eadric took a step closer. "I thought you should know so you could understand what we're dealing with."

"Did this all start because of the journal?"

"It did. I told you, you should have given it to me."

"It's too late now. I tried and you refused." Amorette wrapped her free hand around their intertwined fingers. "You hated me at the beginning. What changed?"

"I did."

"How?"

"I realized I became so accustomed to shutting everyone out, that I didn't know how to understand others. No one questioned my orders and everyone did as they were told, without any emotional attachments." He chuckled softly. "Then an energetic young lady entered my life. She didn't want my money, she refused to do as I told her, and she had so many emotions I worried for her mental health. She made me understand that people aren't always what you see on the surface."

"Why me?"

Eadric tucked a finger beneath her chin and tilted her head back until her eyes met his. "No one else has dared to draw me out before. That's what started it. Now... I simply can't imagine coming home to a house devoid of your presence."

"That's a pretty good explanation. As far as explanations go." Amorette couldn't deny the rapidity of her heartbeat or the clamminess of her palms.

Eadric had a way with words, and it made her like him that much more. Forget the doubt and all that about him manipulating her. She understood what he meant. As if some strange connection wound itself through each of them.

Amorette couldn't think of anything else to say. As far as days went, this one had been full of ups and downs. She still had work to do this afternoon, but part of her didn't want to break this moment between herself and Eadric.

With a sigh, Eadric dropped his fingers from her chin. "We should return you to The Nook."

"Yeah. We should." Amorette scuffed a toe on the ground. "Can I do one thing first?"

"Of course. What is it?"

"It's... embarrassing." Amorette lifted one hand and crooked a finger at him. "Come closer."

Eadric bent closer, his head turned so she might whisper in his ear.

Amorette took a breath. Blew it out. Slowly untangled her fingers from his. She raised on tiptoe to press a quick peck to Eadric's cheek, then fled toward the car.

She didn't look back to see his reaction, but if she had, she might have cherished the memory of Eadric's genuine, wide smile.

⊶

For a while, things returned to normal. Days flew by in a flurry of activity. Collins and Bryant never left Amorette's side during the day. Customers came and went through The Nook with a gusto never before seen in the establishment. Eadric holed up in his office to perform mundane tasks delegated to the CEO of a major corporation.

Somehow, Amorette and Eadric managed to hide their blossoming romance from Hunter. A wonder, since nightly dinner became a tradition in the manse.

Eadric developed a habit of sending too many affectionate smiles in Amorette's direction. Amorette's reaction depended on Hunter's and Doon's level of attention. Some evenings, she would glare. Sometimes, when Eadric timed their silent conversation right, Amorette would blush and smile back shyly.

Joseph remained a guest in the basement, guarded but allowed free reign of his own level of the house. It wasn't for lack of trying to kick him out. Eadric couldn't resist the man's pleas for refuge. Apparently, the mansion remained the only shelter in the swirling hurricane of chaos. Joseph refused to leave his new hermitage.

No one heard anything more from Codex. Eadric received no more threatening phone calls, which unnerved him the most. Silence meant planning. Planning meant it was only a matter of time until the shoe dropped.

Still, everyone pressed on. A sort of daily routine developed between the four of them. One that threatened to crack should anyone take one misstep.

Eadric found stress relief in his practice. Deep in the bowels of Hawkmore Tower, he shut himself inside the studio and took up his staff. With nothing but dark memories, Eadric rehearsed battle with the skill of a seasoned dancer.

In his talented hands, the staff became an extension of his arm. A weapon meant not to destroy but to lend aid to those less fortunate.

For hours, Eadric practiced each movement. Stretched each muscle. He didn't mind the sweat dripping into his eyes or the body heat warming the room. Here, he could strip off any pretense and be himself. Completely, totally, and without fail.

His phone chimed in the corner. Eadric paused to open the

text message.

Running late tonight. Thirty extra minutes? Melodia needs organizational overhaul.

Eadric chuckled to himself. Amorette's frustration with her boss came more from affection than annoyance. They both knew it. He typed a quick reply and dropped the phone in his pocket. He could use the extra time.

For so long, Eadric fought his imagination and memory with his training. Sometimes, he wished he could end all his suffering. That urge seemed less nowadays. Now that he had something to look forward to.

Still, Amorette didn't know some of the things he had done. She would be surprised if he told her. The difference between traitors and patriots was merely on which side one stood.

Those things were the things he purged these days. Mistakes he made. Incidences where he regretted his choices. Most of all, he came here to purge the fear of hurting Amorette. No one had been around him without getting hurt before. It was the blessing and curse of his existence.

Eadric lost himself once more to the pull of his muscles and the *whoosh* and *clack* of the staff.

Ancient battles played in his mind, memories of people he outlived and things he wished never to see again.

Regrets.

Losses.

Failures.

Eadric's phone buzzed in his pocket. The longer tones indicated an incoming call.

Amorette must need more time than she originally suggested. She only ever called when she needed to beg forgiveness or make a request.

"What is it this time?" Eadric answered good-naturedly.

"I was thinking we should play a game."

Eadric's blood ran cold. He knew better than to let his guard down. He should have expected this. The voice on the other end. The man who disguised himself behind the curtain of Codex. "What kind of game?"

"Chess seems appropriate. White knight. Black king." A chuckle. "You pick who you think you are out of the two."

"Alright. Tell me the time and place. We'll sit down and play." Eadric struggled to keep his voice calm, his tone even. He couldn't let on about his rage or annoyance.

Another chuckle assaulted Eadric's ears. "You foolish man. I've already made my first move."

The room went black. Sudden silence echoed around Eadric. His fingers tightened on the staff. A dull green light slowly illuminated the room.

A power outage. Something Hawkmore Tower had prepared for but never experienced.

Eadric made his way to the door and unlatched it. "What's this, then? Sabotage? It won't hurt the business much."

"I'll take this as your first move and make my next. You may want to catch up if you have any hope of winning."

He acted nonchalant, but Eadric's mind accelerated. If Codex caused the power outage, what good did it do them? It wouldn't do anything to bring down Eadric's business empire. Which meant they wanted something else.

He ran through the list of emergency protocols for this instance. Computers automatically backed up every five minutes, so they wouldn't lose much work. The building itself remained unchanged. Employees would evacuate through emergency stairwells since the elevators wouldn't work.

Eadric paused.

The elevators didn't work, which meant neither did the security gates or the automated locks. In fact, everything could be manually unlocked in this state. Anyone could go anywhere.

"It isn't fair if you don't tell me what your second move is." Eadric kicked the door open and dashed for the emergency stairs.

There was now only one reason Codex would attack his building. They were after someone.

The voice sighed. "So you finally came to your senses. Did you know that your little flower looks especially radiant today? I hear she has a smile to combat sunshine."

Eadric read through to the threat. They'd had eyes on Amorette, or at least wanted him to think they did. He slammed the stairway door open and blinked against the flashing red emergency lights.

Amorette should still be secure on the fifteenth floor, but that was fifteen flights of stairs between them. If he was on the phone, he couldn't contact Collins. He had no way to know what the plan was or if she was still safe.

"I swear, if you touch one hair on that woman's head, I'll kill you myself." Eadric took a breath and took a running start, two steps at a time.

"Oh, as if you could."

"I'll find a way. Look forward to it."

"I see you've reached the stairs. I'll give you a minute's head start before I make my next move."

Eadric rolled his eyes. "I think I'm at the disadvantage here.

You won't tell me what your moves are."

"I've been nothing but open and honest since the moment you picked up the telephone."

"Oh, really?" Eadric checked each floor number as he passed it. A minute wouldn't be enough. His fingers shifted around the staff he still held. If he ever met this man face to face, he wouldn't hesitate. "Then why won't you tell me what your next move is?"

"We're on your turf right now. I think you have the advantage despite all that."

Eadric didn't think arguing would get him anywhere, so he didn't try it. Why bother to waste time when it wouldn't solve anything? "I'm at floor five."

Eadric rounded another corner. Five wasn't close enough. He could call it a strategic move, one after which he hoped his opponent showed his hand.

"Well, then. Let me reveal my next move. I've taken one of your pawns."

That could mean anything. In this wretched game, he could consider any number of people pawns.

Eadric didn't answer. He focused instead on speeding up. Each second that ticked by meant one more second that something could happen.

"I think it's only fair I tell you that I already have one of yours." That should at least throw the man off the scent for a while.

A clatter from the stairs above him disrupted Eadric's private strategy meeting. He raised his head and held tighter to his staff. No way would he stop to wait for whoever or whatever it was to come to him. Eadric wasn't that kind of man.

He hugged the wall and kept his pace up the stairs.

The footsteps coming down echoed through the stairway along with Eadric's. Eadric counted steps, calculating approximately how far apart they were.

When they approached the same corner, Eadric swung the staff.

He pulled it up just shy of hitting the man's head.

Doon held up his hands and skirted away from the solid wooden staff. "I'm sorry! I should have announced my presence. What's going on? Why the power outage? Why aren't you in the lobby?"

"Come with me." Eadric flipped the staff over his shoulder and took off running again.

"Okay..." Doon sounded incredulous, but he didn't argue. Eadric liked to think that had something to do with the no-nonsense attitude he portrayed. It may have had more to do with the fact Eadric almost clobbered Doon with a bow-staff.

The voice on the other end of the phone clucked his tongue. "I see you've made another move. You're running out of time, you know. I didn't want to do this, but I have no choice but to take a knight."

Eadric set his jaw. Each second that ticked by upped the stakes. First a pawn. Now a knight. If he didn't hurry, it would be his queen.

Eadric's sneakers and Doon's designer shoes clanged against the metal stairs. Floors sped by.

Seven.

Eleven.

Fourteen.

Eadric threw open the door to the fifteenth floor and stepped into the haunting green lights.

"Have you arrived yet? I can't stand the anticipation any more."

He didn't feel the need to let the man on the phone know his progress. The less he said, the more likely he would win.

Doon tugged on Eadric's sleeve. "Over there." He jutted his chin in the general direction of The Nook's open doors.

Collins and Bryant lay in a crumpled heap by the glass entrance. Shadows etched their features with the ghoulish contrast of peace and pain.

Eadric gripped his staff and pointed the end toward the floor, prepared for anything and anyone. He bent before Collins first.

A needle protruded from the man's neck. Eadric used two fingers against the other side of Collins' neck to check for life. A rapid, sporadic pulse met his touch.

Doon did much the same for Bryant and sent a nod in Eadric's direction.

Eadric expected as much. Codex had no real reason to kill the guards. Their only transgression was standing in the way of Codex's path to an immortal and his woman.

"You're surprisingly quiet."

Eadric winced. He had almost forgotten about the man on the phone. Eadric's lips opened to answer, but Doon's cry cut him off.

"Melodia!"

Eadric spun to his feet as Doon raced inside. Signs of a struggle littered the front of the store. An overturned shelf. Books and bags scattered across the floor. What drew Eadric's attention, however, was the blonde woman sprawled in the middle of it all. He jogged closer.

Doon knelt beside Melodia's limp body and took her face in his hands. Blood trickled down one temple and matted the hair by her ear.

Eadric spun in a circle, the panic rising as he realized the one thing missing from The Nook.

"Where is she?"

"Now you ask the pertinent questions."

"Tell me!" Eadric shouted at the phone.

"Touchy, touchy." A sigh, then a pause. "I suppose this is where the game gets fun. It would be a shame if you run out of moves and your queen falls to her death."

"The roof." Eadric shot a look at Doon.

Doon waved him on. "Go get Amorette. I've got Melodia. Go. Now."

Eadric shot for the stairs. If only the elevators worked. He would need to rethink that. The lights hadn't gone out too long ago, which meant he wasn't too far behind the culprits.

A sudden, throbbing pain ripped through Eadric's abdomen. He doubled over.

The phone clattered to the stairs.

For a moment, the staff was the only thing that held him up.

Eadric grimaced and reached for the phone again.

"Something the matter, Oh Great One?" The voice taunted.

"Absolutely not." Eadric spat. He took a breath and went running again. "She hasn't done anything to you."

"Her existence is vexing."

Eadric didn't like the tone with which the man said it. As if he could do without Amorette and all she embodied. Eadric couldn't climb the steps fast enough. Why did the Tower have to be so tall?

"Your fight is with me."

"She's a part of you, though. Isn't she?"

He couldn't argue with that. Each new tidbit of information made Eadric that much more irate.

Since he couldn't keep the truth from this foe, he might as well give in. "If she's hurt when I find her..."

"You'll kill me? Yes, we've been over this. It's dull to rehash the whole thing, don't you think?"

Eadric ignored the man and climbed the last few sets of stairs to the roof. He emerged into the cold night air. Thankfully, the darkness inside lent to his ability to assess the situation immediately.

Nearly a dozen men stood in formation facing the stairs. In the middle, doubled onto her knees with her hands bound, sat Amorette. A split decorated the corner of her pretty lips, but other than that she seemed none the worse for wear.

Eadric clenched his fingers around his staff. "I think we've reached the endgame, don't you? Sorry to rush off, but I have business to attend to."

He didn't wait for an answer. Eadric ended the call and tossed his phone to the ground.

Codex wouldn't have sent just anyone to do this job. These men had been specifically chosen, and he knew it. They weren't high enough in the political inner workings of Codex to compromise anything. Instead, they must be the ones trained to fight. The thugs. An apropos title for the work they were doing this evening. They wouldn't let him leave with Amorette if they could help it.

Eadric widened his stance and motioned the closest thug

closer. "I'm sick of chit-chat. Let's get this show on the road."

The men rushed forward like a pride of lions descending on their prey. Except these lions didn't know when they were outmatched.

Fists and feet flew in Eadric's direction. Eadric met each blow with his staff or a fist of his own. Having studied defensive tactics in The Orient paid off now. Thankfully, none of them seemed to have weapons aside from a few knives and a bat. Those he could deal with.

The distinctive fluttering of a helicopter interrupted the fight. Eadric glanced over his shoulder to see red lights nearing the rooftop he stood upon.

As much as he wanted to lay eyes on Amorette, Eadric forced himself to focus on the task at hand.

He understood now why they cut the power. They made him run stairs in an attempt to weaken his stamina. What no one counted on was the dogged determination of a man fighting for his woman's life.

The time crunch didn't faze him. Eadric had dealt with more difficult situations in numerous wars. Obviously, no one told these men they would be fighting an experienced warrior.

From the corner of his eye, Eadric saw one of the men wrap a hand around Amorette's arm and roughly pull her to her feet. A gun appeared in that man's hand.

Eadric's staff cracked against one thug's neck and sent him to the ground. There were still too many. He wouldn't be able to get to her in time.

A distinct *pop* ricocheted in the air.

The man holding Amorette cried out and released her to grab his own arm.

Eadric spotted two of the security team members at the top of the stairs. "Get Amorette to the manse. Now!" He spun to allow his staff to make contact with another thug's knee.

The security staff bolted into motion.

It was only after Amorette was below again that Eadric truly let loose. In a matter of minutes, he had every last one of the assailants writhing in pain.

Sirens from below reminded him that Doon would have already called the paramedics. Good. These men were going to need them.

The helicopter swerved and disappeared into the night sky.

Eadric's phone trilled from where he dropped it. He glanced at the screen from where he stood, then stooped to answer. "Checkmate."

"For now." The man laughed. "Until next time. Look forward to it." The line clicked.

Eadric pocketed the phone and bent over to breathe. The dull pain in his abdomen hadn't stopped, but it had lessened. Whatever happened, he would heal. He always did. For now, he needed to clean this up and get home to Amorette, if only to ensure she was alright.

[EPISODE 15]
MORE QUESTIONS THAN ANSWERS

If she could sit still, she would. Amorette wished she had control of herself, but all thoughts of control fled hours ago.

The power outage had been surprising, but even more so were the men who stormed into The Nook seconds later. Amorette and Melodia never had time to think about evacuating.

For a few minutes, they stood off against the girls. Then someone made a call to their leader. After that, everything seemed blurry. Someone attacked Melodia, not knowing the woman took self-defense classes on a weekly basis. There was a struggle. Someone hit Melodia, who went down.

Amorette remembered fighting back when they dragged her toward the stairs. She remembered doing her best to get away and getting punched in the stomach as a result.

The roof... The roof, she remembered too well. The men forced her to her knees and tied her up. Then they all waited.

Eadric's appearance didn't surprise Amorette. She expected him to come after her, but she had never seen him so enraged. Not even when he retrieved her from her father's house. She rooted for him the whole time, even when someone put a gun against her head.

Amorette glanced her fingertips against the spot on her temple. One wrong move and that man could have shot her. She never appreciated Eadric's security team more than at that moment.

She couldn't stay in her room anymore. She needed to know what was going on. Amorette flung the door open.

The guards from the Tower spared her a glance. One raised an eyebrow.

Amorette didn't care what their orders were. She brushed past them and jogged down the stairs.

Their footsteps followed.

Amorette found a sort of peace in knowing someone watched over her in Eadric's absence. The other half of her quickly grew annoyed with their overbearing presence.

Amorette hit the main floor at the same time the front door clicked open. One of the guards stepped in front of her like a human shield.

Hunter took a step back. The door shut behind him. "Okay, wow. Didn't expect that. Who are these guys? Where are Collins and Bryant? Aren't they your shadows?"

Amorette dodged around the guard. She pressed a palm against the man's arm to reassure him that this was normal. "You didn't hear? No one told you?"

"Ma'am, I really think it will be safer if you return to your room." The guard eyed Hunter suspiciously.

Amorette rolled her eyes. "He's kosher, he lives here."

The guard took a step back, but neither of the two moved very far.

"What happened? Are you okay?" Hunter's eyes shot between Amorette and her current entourage.

"Okay" didn't begin to describe how Amorette felt. Of course, she knew better than to lie to Hunter, but no one said she couldn't omit some of the truth. "There was an incident at Hawkmore Tower. It's probably on the news right now. I don't want to relive it."

"That bad?" Hunter scratched the back of his neck, a bad habit of his when he overthought something. "You're sure you aren't hurt?"

Amorette nodded, even though that was only a partial truth. "I'm fine. Thanks for asking. Why weren't you home at this hour?"

"I had some things to do." Hunter stepped forward and gathered her into his arms for a hug. "I'm glad you're okay. You sure you don't want to tell me what happened? If it's on the news, it's a big deal."

"I'm okay," Amorette repeated like a mantra. She should have known Hunter wouldn't believe her, but it would be worse if he heard about the incident on the news. She had to at least warn him. Now that she did her duty, Amorette wasn't so sure she did the right thing in tipping him off.

A little wiggling wormed her way out of Hunter's hold.

Amorette tucked her hair behind her ears. "I'm really okay, Hunter. You didn't happen to see Eadric or Doon on the way in, did you?"

"Not a trace of them. Just the car from the Tower." Hunter motioned to the guards. "I assume it's theirs."

"Yeah. I guess they went to the hospital." Amorette traced a thumb against her bottom lip.

"Hospital?!" Hunter's eyes went wide.

It would make sense for them to go. Doon probably wanted to be sure Melodia survived. Eadric would want to know everything, and the simplest way to figure that out was to follow everyone to the hospital. The police would want him to fill out a report, as well.

"Earth to Amorette!" Hunter snapped his fingers in front of her eyes. "Hello! Explain. What hospital? Is someone hurt? Do we need to go, too?"

"I'm under lock and key." Amorette shot a look to the security duo.

She didn't resent it, but frustration set in easily when she didn't know what was happening with everyone else.

"Okay, fine, we won't go anywhere, but who went to the hospital?"

"Melodia."

No use denying it. The news would report that, too. Anything that happened in Hawkmore Tower was a matter of public interest. Amorette understood the curiosity.

"What happened to Melodia?"

"She got hurt." Amorette blew out a breath. Vague answers wouldn't get her anywhere with Hunter. She opened her mouth to explain.

The door flew open.

The guards sprang to position between Amorette and the door.

Eadric brushed them both aside and gathered Amorette close to his chest. He didn't utter a word, but Amorette already knew he assessed the situation and made note of everyone in the room.

"Eadric, I'm sorry. I—"

Eadric cupped his fingers against her jaw and bent his head to kiss her. As always, his actions spoke louder than his words.

Amorette leaned into the embrace, accepting the fact that Eadric had been worried. Both of them ran high on adrenaline at a time like this.

She never imagined her first kiss like this, but somehow Amorette couldn't think of a more fitting scenario. True feelings often shone through when lives were placed at stake.

Eadric pulled back from the kiss, leaving Amorette to realize that Hunter stood a foot away. She spared him a brief glance before she turned back to Eadric.

"How's Melodia?"

"They say she'll be fine. Doon is bringing her here. Just in case." Eadric stroked a thumb over Amorette's cheek. "You must be tired. Let's get you to bed."

"Um, hello?" Hunter waved a hand. "Literally right here."

"We'll talk later." Eadric tucked Amorette's arm through his and headed back upstairs.

This time, Amorette didn't mind holing up in her room quite as much. Especially since everyone and everything seemed to have worked out as best as it could in this situation.

Amorette heard Melodia before she even made it below the second floor. Only Melodia would complain about the quality of the food. No one else denied its absolute excellence. Then again, Melodia didn't care much about what other people thought. She liked to raise trouble.

"How is there not apple juice in this house? Really?"

Amorette laughed as she skipped into the dining room. "I see you're making a mess of things already, my dear boss."

"Shut it, Amy. I didn't sleep much last night and I have a killer headache. Which reminds me..." Melodia narrowed her eyes. "Doon! Where are my painkillers?"

"You already took them." Doon shuffled into the room from the kitchen.

"I don't feel like I took them." Melodia pouted.

Doon rolled his eyes and set a tray of fruit in front of her. "Give them time to kick in, you wuss."

Melodia arched a brow, but she didn't argue anymore. Instead, she focused on spearing a piece of orange and shoving it in her mouth.

"What time did you get in last night?"

Amorette spun to see Eadric entering the room. He focused solely on the tie in his hands, as if it would tie itself if he stared hard enough.

"Melodia... Mel, stop it." Doon hissed from the table.

Amorette peeked back in time to see him struggle to pull the butter knife from the woman's hand.

"Let me at him. Give me thirty seconds in the ring with him." Melodia tugged at her arm, but Doon held it tight.

Amorette laughed. "It's okay, Mel. He was the one who got me out of there. He's still a good guy." She bent closer. "And I ditched Malibu Ken for him, so you should be happy. It was your advice."

"I'm glad you two are together. I'm ticked that I got hit over the head. Since I can't nail the culprits, he's the next best thing." Melodia kicked her chair back and stood.

Doon shot to his feet and wrapped both arms around her to

hold her back. "Mel... Mel, calm down. Take a few deep breaths. There's cake in the kitchen. You like cake, right? Do you want a piece?"

Melodia stopped struggling in his hold. "What kind of cake?"

"I believe it's chocolate."

"Cream cheese frosting?"

"As far as I know."

"Are there nuts?"

"No."

Melodia pushed Doon off and shoved her curls out of her face. "Fine. Go get me a piece of cake."

"This isn't a trick, is it?" Doon pointed a finger at her, clearly suspicious of her easy acquiescence.

Melodia shot him a glare. "Cake, now. Or else."

"Fair enough." Doon scurried back to the kitchen.

Amorette skipped to Melodia's side and wrapped her arms around the woman's waist. "I'm glad you're okay, Mel. I don't know what The Nook would do without its fearless leader."

"Oh, please, you'd take care of it just fine." Melodia rolled her eyes, but her lips ticked up at the corners. Deep inside, Melodia wasn't as bossy as she portrayed herself. Her heart melted with the right incentive.

"We have a lot of cleaning up to do today, are you sure you're up for it?" Amorette laid her head against Melodia's shoulder and smiled sweetly. "I can do it on my own."

Eadric cleared his throat. "The Nook is closed for today. A few of my direct employees will straighten it up." He took his seat at the head of the table.

Only Amorette noticed his too-stiff demeanor. Something

worried him, but she wasn't sure what that could be. Everyone was safe and sound. He made sure of it last night.

"Why wouldn't we go in to work?"

"Melodia is still injured and under strict medical surveillance. Head injuries aren't anything to play with."

Amorette frowned and dropped into the seat beside him. "Okay, but that doesn't mean I couldn't go to work. I'm okay."

Eadric's tongue snaked out to wet his lips. When he looked up, Amorette half expected his expression to be closed off again. Instead, his eyes softened and his frown turned up into a brief smile. "I would appreciate it if you would stay here today. I'll leave the guards."

"Why?"

It didn't make sense. Out of all the places she could stay, right by his side seemed safest. Amorette would rather be with him than anywhere else in the world.

Eadric cupped her cheek in his hand. "For your safety. There are still many reporters at the Tower. Many strangers going in and out. We don't want a repeat of last evening. Please, Amorette? Please stay home today. Rest. Relax."

Part of Amorette bristled at being told what to do. Still, he didn't command. He asked. As far as improvement went, that's about all she could ask of Eadric.

To appease his concern, Amorette nodded. "Fine. I'll stay home today. But only today. Tomorrow, I'm going to work."

"Tomorrow is Saturday."

"So?"

"Normal people tend to take Saturdays off from work."

Amorette shrugged her shoulders and flicked Eadric's hand away from her cheek. "You have no right to control my schedule."

"Control your schedule? Is that what I'm trying to do?" Eadric leaned closer, one arm on the table. Their faces inches from each other.

Okay, so maybe saying he had no right was an overstatement. They were in a relationship, after all. And he made a good point about her being in trouble. Frequently, as of late.

"Maybe... we could discuss it?"

"That's better. Exactly what I was aiming for in the first place." Eadric smiled and leaned back in his seat. He plucked an orange slice from Melodia's tray.

"Hey, get your own food!" Melodia slapped at Eadric's hand. "I'm being a good girl, honestly. This mushiness is killing all of us, but are we saying anything? No. We're just letting you two lovebirds cheese it up."

"Melodia, cake." Doon dropped a plate in front of her.

As quickly as her rant started, Melodia shut up. Within seconds, the only sound coming from Melodia's seat was the clink of her fork against her plate.

"Trouble at nine o'clock." Doon jutted his chin that direction as he dropped into his chair.

Eadric turned to look. Amorette followed suit.

Hunter stood with his arms folded, eyes shooting flames in Eadric's direction. He didn't spare Amorette a glance, but she knew he spoke to her when he opened his mouth. "Can we talk for a minute?"

"Sure." Amorette stood from the table.

Eadric's fingers wrapped around her wrist.

Amorette turned to look at him. A reassuring smile eased the strain on his face, but she saw the concern still in his eyes. With a gentle tug, Amorette pulled away to trail Hunter out into the living room.

Hunter stopped once they reached the stairs. "So... you and Eadric."

"Yeah." Amorette nodded. "For a while now."

"The whole thing at the Tower last night... they tried using you to get to him?"

"That's what I heard." Amorette didn't like the stiff way Hunter stood or the way his eyes looked everywhere but at her. "Look, Hunter. I'm... Well, I'm not sorry I'm dating Eadric. But I am sorry if I hurt you."

"Me? Hurt?" Hunter snorted a laugh. "Why would I be hurt? No. It's okay. I'm okay. I just... you know I don't like that guy. It's tough seeing my best friend with someone I didn't approve." He batted a palm at Amorette's shoulder in a futile attempt at play.

Amorette raised her eyes heavenward. She didn't know how to smooth this over. She knew it would be hard on him, but she didn't realize he liked her that much. Sure, Amorette crushed on Hunter for a while, but in the end it was Eadric who stole her heart. Even someone as stubborn as Amorette couldn't refuse true love for a fleeting infatuation. Besides, Hunter would spring back. He always did.

"Well, now that I've confirmed that..." Hunter pasted on a smile. "I have places to be. You have a good day at work."

"I'm not going. We decided it's too dangerous."

"Then, have a good day with Doon and the guards. Make sure Melodia doesn't injure anyone, including herself."

"Will do." Amorette laughed. "Thanks for understanding, Hunter. It means a lot that we're still friends, you know that right?"

"Of course I do." Hunter clasped Amorette's hand for a brief moment before he pulled back. "I'll be back later. Don't do anything I wouldn't do." The door slammed as Hunter pulled it closed.

"I didn't hear any shouting."

Amorette smiled over her shoulder at Eadric. "We didn't shout. He just needed to confirm it. I think he's been suspicious for a while."

"He accepted it?" Eadric's forehead furrowed. "Strange. He doesn't seem the type."

"Maybe you've been underestimating Hunter's sportsmanship." Amorette smiled and wrapped her arms around Eadric's torso. "You're going to be late for work."

Eadric tucked her hair out of her face. "I can be fashionably late to my own party if I wish."

"That's not your style." Amorette kissed his cheek and weaseled out of his arms. "You should get going. The sooner you leave, the sooner you can get back."

"Will you miss me that much?" Eadric laughed.

Amorette nodded. "Yes. So get going."

She almost hated to admit that she would spend most of the day waiting for him to get back. She was sure she could figure out something to distract her. Maybe she could go play with the dogs for a while.

No matter what, Amorette was determined to make the most of her day off.

⚸—⚷

Eadric didn't like the idea of leaving Amorette alone, but she had a point. He had to go to work. People needed reassurance.

Confused employees needed the truth. He had a whole mess of PR to care for. Such were the problems of someone of his caliber.

As usual, Eadric parked beneath the building and took the elevator up to his office. First things first. He needed to assess the amount of damage control needed.

The company would sustain a significant dent from last night's sabotage, but that didn't worry him too much. He had years' worth of savings tucked away. Instead, Eadric worried more about those employed by his company. They all had families and debts. If the company sustained damage, so did they.

Collins waited outside Eadric's office. It didn't surprise Eadric that Collins discharged himself from the hospital. Despite the use of a strong anesthetic, Collins seemed none the worse for wear.

"It's a relief to see you." Eadric offered a handshake.

Collins accepted with a nod. "I came early. I'm no secretary, but a good one would advise you to make a statement. The reporters are swarming like bees. Should I have Nicole call a conference?"

"That's too calculated for what happened." Eadric slid his tablet from his desk and logged in. "Where are they swarming?"

"The lobby, mostly. Everywhere else is too heavily protected."

"And what is the local news reporting right now?"

"Mostly what they know about the blackout. Some are throwing in suspected victims. Critical conditions. They took the ambulances' presence and ran with that footage."

Eadric nodded. So, first, he needed to give them the real story. "Good. We'll head down to the lobby first. Post discreet security presence at the perimeter."

"Yes, sir." Collins stepped out with his finger pressed to the comm in his ear.

Eadric didn't specifically like working with the press, but he understood the importance of a good public image. He understood the importance of those who depended on him, more than anyone knew.

It took five minutes to assess his working schedule for the day. Eadric rearranged the things he didn't find essential in favor of stabilizing the situations within his tower.

Collins fell in line behind him as Eadric headed for the elevator. He didn't often descend from his office, but today demanded his attention. For others' peace. For the secrets he held dear.

The elevator opened to a sea of flashing light-boxes.

Eadric lifted his chin and marched toward the gates that cordoned off the Hawkmore employees from the general public. Unintelligible questions intermingled in a mesh of confusion.

Collins motioned for a few of the reporters to take a step back. They begrudgingly obliged.

Eadric nodded in thanks and held up a hand. On cue, the lobby went quiet. Perfect.

Eadric examined each face near him before he folded his hands and began. "The blackout last night is still under investigation, but I have been granted special permission to insinuate that it may not have been an accident. Hawkmore Industries requests that you politely turn to the investigating detectives for further information."

"Can you confirm the number of casualties?" An overeager blonde shouted.

Eadric pasted on a polite smile. "No casualties have been reported to me. I personally visited the hospital to visit the injured, but no fatal injuries were incurred. Thank you for your concern."

That should about do it. Eadric nodded and turned back for the elevator. That should appease them for a while.

Collins fell in behind him again.

Eadric barely spared him a glance. They had work to do. "Call in the maintenance crew and the security team. I have questions."

Despite the best-laid plans, hours seemed longer than usual. Amorette tried her best to preoccupy herself. She looked into Codex on the internet. Baked an entire batch of cookies. Walked through the maze with Cronus and Kratos.

The sun rose overhead and lowered to the horizon, all in sync with Melodia's constant grumpiness.

By dinnertime, Doon cut Melodia off from television and ice cream and forced her up to her room. It calmed the atmosphere considerably but left Amorette without much else to do.

In the end, she jogged up to her room for paper and colored pencils. She couldn't draw so well, but it would pass the time. With Doon holed up near Melodia's room, the living room should be clear and quiet until Eadric came home.

Amorette skipped down the stairs. Her feet came to a stumbling halt as they met the floor at the bottom. The basement door stood ajar by a fraction of an inch. The barest sliver of light glowed through the recess.

A quick glance around the room didn't present any sign of the guards usually on assignment. Of course, maybe they took a break or went downstairs to check on her father.

Amorette tapped her fingers against the box of colored pencils. Should she go check? It seemed like the smartest thing to do. What if something went wrong with her dad? She should take responsibility for him since she dragged him into this mess in the first place.

She set the paper and pencils on the bottom step and reached for the basement door handle. The door swung open.

Amorette glanced behind her once more before she stepped into the dim stairway. Honestly, someone needed to fix the lighting situation at the top of the stairs. Someone could fall and hurt themselves.

Her bare feet tapped against the steps, creating minimum noise. Still, in the silent basement, it echoed. Strange, the noiselessness of the basement today. Especially if the guards came down here. They were chatty when other people weren't around. She should know, since she spied on them more than once.

"Dad?" Amorette worked her way through the first room and toward her dad's room. "Are you awake? Sleeping? Ignoring me?"

A crash resounded from the other side of the door.

Amorette startled back a step and a half. "D..." she cleared her throat. "Dad?"

A second clatter sounded less lethal than the first.

Amorette made a split-second decision. She couldn't leave. Not when something definitely seemed wrong. Despite his flaws, he was her father.

Amorette pulled the door open and hastened into the next room. She froze at the sight before her eyes.

Both security guards lay sprawled on the floor. If not for the rise and fall of their chests, Amorette might think them dead.

Her father cowered in the corner against a shattered studio mirror. Blood lined the distorted reflection of a weak and drowsy victim.

"Dad?"

"Amorette." Joseph held up a hand to stop her. "Go... get..." He heaved a breath as his eyes fluttered closed.

"Dad!" Amorette raced to Joseph's side. Her fingers went to his pulse. It felt fast, but she didn't know how it should feel in the first place. Still, he still breathed.

Amorette wasn't sure what happened here, but she knew better than to try to handle it herself.

She scurried off the cot and toward the stairs. Doon could handle something like this. In the past, she saw him at work. Doon was resourceful.

"Doon!"

Whether it was the panic in her voice or the volume of her cry that brought Doon running, Amorette would never know. It didn't matter, anyway. As long as he came.

"What's wrong?" Doon leaned over the second-floor banister to ask the question.

Amorette pointed at the basement. "The guys... my dad..."

Doon turned his head toward the third floor. "Hey! Idiots! Get down here now! We have a situation."

Amorette knew who Doon yelled at. Her guards. Probably her fault for ditching them outside her room. As far as she knew, this house was the safest place she could be. Whatever happened in the basement didn't need to have an effect on the rest of the day.

The guards came running from the top floor. Doon didn't

wait for them to arrive. He dashed for the basement ahead of them. "Bring the first aid kit, Amorette. Whatever happened, we should at least try to do something."

Amorette had never been happier to oblige. They could use some ice packs, too. Since she didn't see any obvious wounds on the guards, that meant they must have hit their heads. Judging by Melodia's headache this morning, it would make sense to ice their injuries.

Urgency roiled inside of Amorette as she headed for the kitchen. Someone needed to wake up and tell her what went on down there. She couldn't stand the suspense. Something about the whole situation nagged at her, but Amorette didn't have time to place it.

She pulled an empty ice pack from a cabinet and turned for the refrigerator.

A silent silhouette in the doorway dragged a sharp yelp from her throat.

"Hunter!" Amorette pressed a hand over her heart. "You're back?"

"Your head hurts?" Hunter nodded toward the ice pack in her hands.

Amorette shook her head and yanked the freezer open. "Something happened downstairs. The guards are knocked out and my dad is sick. I thought it might help."

"Sometimes, what we think will help actually hurts people more."

Amorette tossed a confused smile over her shoulder. "Wow, okay. You're angsty today. What's with the deep thinking?"

Hunter blew out a breath. "I really didn't want things to end up this way. I genuinely developed feelings for you, you know?"

"I thought we discussed this earlier." Amorette paused. "Wait, earlier, you said..."

Something small and sharp pricked the side of her neck. Amorette's hand flew up, only to meet a needle and Hunter's fingers. She turned to look at him. Hunter blurred in her vision.

"H-Hunter?"

She didn't understand. Hunter was her friend. What was going on? The world rocked on its axis.

Amorette heard only one thing before everything went black. One simple sentence.

"I'm sorry, Mi Amor."

[EPISODE 16]
FINAL EPISODE

Traffic jams. Of all the times to be stuck in traffic, it had to be tonight.

Eadric tapped the brake for the fortieth time in half as many minutes. He should be home by now, but no. Cars crept along beside him as if yielded by molten tar. If he could, Eadric might tar whoever started this craziness.

The concept remained simple. Drive the car at the posted speed limit. How did this happen? How did traffic come to a complete stand-still?

Eadric slammed a hand against his horn, more out of frustration than actual anger.

The cars trailed along the highway in all directions. If he could get out of the downtown area, getting home wouldn't be as bad. He needed an exit.

Eadric checked the time and sighed. He should call and explain he got caught in rush-hour traffic for the first time in his life. Eadric tapped Amorette's number and settled a blue-tooth device over his ear.

The phone rang. And rang. And rang.

Strange, that she wouldn't answer his call. Amorette always answered. Maybe she left her phone up in her room again.

He tried Doon's number instead with much the same result.

In a last-ditch attempt not to panic, Eadric phoned the only person on the planet he hated more than Codex. Hunter's phone didn't even ring, but instead directed Eadric straight to voicemail.

Eadric tossed the blue-tooth onto the other seat and laid on the horn again. Two might be a coincidence. Three? He didn't believe in coincidence that much.

The nearest exit pointed him toward his home, so Eadric took it. If he took the back roads, he could speed without much repercussion.

A few quick taps on the screen of his cell phone pulled up Collins' emergency number. Eadric pressed dial and coasted around another corner.

"Yes, sir."

"Something's wrong at the house. Bring as many of the personal security detail as you can."

"Yes, sir."

The conversation took all of three seconds, but both men knew the stakes. How could they not, after the night they endured?

Eadric worked his jaw from side to side. Even the terrible scraping noise his grinding teeth made didn't help ease the anxiety.

He dialed Amorette's number again. Still, nothing.

Only two miles left.

Eadric pressed the gas pedal to the floor and disregarded any twinge of conscience about disobeying the law. Lives were at stake this time. The traffic law could bow to the urgency of the situation.

The gates hung open, which should have been Eadric's first clue to the gravity of the situation.

Eadric climbed from the running SUV and opened the guardhouse door. The guard on duty lay sprawled in the chair, a needle still extended from his neck. Thankfully, Eadric found a pulse on the first try.

A glance to the security panel showed all the cameras had been turned off. Of course. Codex wouldn't make anything easy.

A rush of nausea nearly brought Eadric to his knees. He raced back to his vehicle and sped up the drive. At the front door, he yanked the keys from the ignition and dashed inside. The house was suspiciously devoid of all sound.

Everything seemed in order, which worried him more than any signs of a struggle might.

Eadric did a quick assessment of what he could see. A scuff mark on the polished floor by the basement door caught his attention first.

The basement. He could start there.

Eadric slipped and slid down the stairs. His heart beat so hard he feared it might explode. In his wildest dreams, he didn't expect to find two needle-pricked guards at the bottom of the stairs.

Eadric rolled one man over to check his pulse. Realization dawned upon seeing the man's face. These weren't the guards from the stairs. These were Amorette's guards. The two he left specifically to keep a close eye on her.

Eadric scrambled to the next room and flung the door wide.

"Doon!" He sank to one knee beside the unconscious man. "Doon, wake up! Tell me what happened." A strong shake of Doon's shoulder did little to rouse him.

A quick glance around the room revealed two more unconscious guards, but no Joseph.

How could the man have disappeared? Could it have been Joseph that instigated all this? A man on the inside... was that their plan all along? How did he not anticipate such a thing from Codex?

There were plenty of men on their way to take care of these casualties. Eadric sprang to his feet and skittered up the stairs like a rabid dog. There were others that resided here. Other people he felt a responsibility for. Eadric silently prayed they were all well. That, perhaps, this was all a dream.

He took the stairs three at a time up to the second floor.

A quick glance into the room adjoining Doon's offered a small breath of relief. Melodia slept peacefully, sprawled under a single blanket. At least one inhabitant remained untouched by whatever cruelty invaded the manse.

With Melodia's safety ensured, Eadric sprinted up to the third floor. *Please, please be here.*

Eadric came to a halt outside Amorette's open bedroom door. Despite all his knowledge, he had hoped to be wrong this time. His fingers twitched at his sides, ready to do battle with whoever dared to invade his personal asylum. Hunter had better be missing too, or so help him, he would throw punches at the negligent youth.

Eadric raced down the hall, only to find Hunter's room empty, as well.

Three missing, and no conclusive story to show for it. With the evidence presented, a few scenarios seemed plausible, but Eadric still couldn't quite figure it out. Until the others woke, he wouldn't know what happened. The security cameras wouldn't show anything since they had been turned off.

This job reeked of inside information, but he didn't have time to ponder that. Under the assumption that Codex took Amorette, Eadric needed a plan and a way to find her.

He opened an app on his phone first. He'd been too chicken to plant a tracking device in the phone he gifted her. Thank God he came to the decision that he needed another way to find her if something like this happened.

Unfortunately, once the application triangulated a position, it didn't give him a definite area. Which meant either someone discovered the GPS tracking device or too much cement surrounded her. Even the best satellite couldn't deal with cement too thick.

Though the app narrowed it down to a part of town containing storage units and warehouses, it couldn't pinpoint her exact location.

Eadric growled and slammed a hand against the wall. Fine. He would start elsewhere. He couldn't traipse around an area so large without some insight. He needed to research. He needed someone who might know something about the vanished persons.

But, who?

A voice floated through his mind. A voice that sounded familiar, as if he heard it recently. Then, for the first time, Eadric remembered the face behind it.

Shoving his phone in his pocket, Eadric bolted back

downstairs.

His SUV waited where he left it. It took seconds to ignite the engine, a minute to make his way back to the road.

By the time Eadric sped his way across town, the sun had set. He didn't care. Amorette's old neighborhood was the only place he could find answers.

Eadric parked the car at the top of a hill and shoved the keys into his pocket. He wouldn't take chances tonight. Codex may not be lingering around this neighborhood anymore, but he couldn't say that for certain. Especially when Joseph was one of the people vanished from the house.

His boots pounded against the sidewalk with the purposeful rhythm of a man on a mission. The street lights still flickered around here, but it didn't bother him. Eadric could hold his own in a fight. Yet, tonight, he didn't come here to start a brawl.

Instead, he stopped before a pile of scarves and blankets.

Eadric squatted down and rested one arm over his knee. "It's been a long time, hasn't it... Nanette?"

A face full of drawn lines turned up. Nannie grinned.

Waves of nausea rolled over Amorette like a rip-tide. Her eyelids felt heavy, as if cement weighed them down. Still, she managed to open them halfway. The scene before her morphed through a haze of hair.

"You promised not to hurt her."

That voice. She knew that voice, almost as well as she knew her own. *Come on, Amorette, pull it together. Focus.*

"You said you could keep her from falling in with that malefactor. You failed." A second voice seemed familiar, as well.

"You're the one who had me keeping an eye on her. You think I didn't develop feelings during all that time?"

"If you had, I expect you would have fought harder." A cluck of a tongue. "Pity. In the end, she's brought to this demise by your own hand. You shouldn't have gotten so involved."

"Demise? Professor, you promised not to hurt her!"

"Do you think there's any other option at this juncture?"

One of the men turned. For a brief moment, everything clicked into focus. A soft gasp parted Amorette's lips. Hunter.

Of course. She remembered now. The kitchen, his odd behavior. He must work for them. Them... Them... Why couldn't she remember who they were?

Amorette let her head loll. She wanted to go back to sleep. At least then she didn't have to deal with harsh reality.

"You have to save her!" Hunter cried.

The second man sighed. Amorette glanced up in time to see him rest a hand on the back of Hunter's head. "Don't worry over it. I've cared for you until now. I won't let a silly girl get in the way of that. This is the way of things. All we've worked for. Don't you trust your own father?"

Silence met the question.

Amorette closed her eyes and gave in to the darkness begging to take her under. Eadric would come, or she would die oblivious. Either was preferable to the truth before her.

⚷

Nanette uncurled a scarf from around her neck and tugged the wig off her head.

"There. That's better." She positioned her fingers in front of the vents in Eadric's front seat. "I'm surprised it took you so long to recognize me. But, then, you were preoccupied last time."

"How long have you been keeping an eye on her?" Eadric tapped a hand impatiently on the steering wheel.

Nanette shrugged a shoulder. "Since she was small. When one doesn't have a family, it's advantageous to treat someone like they matter. After that incident as a child, I made sure to stay close."

"Codex didn't recognize you?"

"You didn't even recognize me." Nanette tilted her head, sharp eyes piercing Eadric's indifferent demeanor.

Eadric sighed and nodded his head. "You always were a good spy."

"There must be a reason you sought me out."

"You know more about her than anyone else. I need to know who betrayed her and where they took her." Eadric didn't beat around the bush. Nanette wasn't the kind to take kindly to that kind of political diplomacy.

"They got their grimy hands on her, then?" Nanette blew out a breath. "Fine. Ask what you need to ask. I'll try to answer what I know."

"Nanette, I need your honesty." Eadric frowned. It had been decades since he last saw her, but she hadn't changed much. A loner, easy to talk to but harder to get information from. "If you don't help me, she'll die."

"You think I don't know that?" Nanette whipped her head to face him. "That child is more my daughter than her own father's. I don't plan on letting her meet the same fate as..." Her lips snapped shut. "No matter, she won't die if we have anything to do with it. So tell me where to start."

"How did Codex get into my house? Was it her father?"

Nanette laughed. "You really know nothing, do you? Joseph is on the very fringes of the organization. He couldn't have orchestrated something like that."

"Then who..."

"Listen carefully, Eadric. Codex has had their eye on her from the time she was born. They've orchestrated ways to keep her under their thumb. They've sabotaged every avenue of escape from that household. Until recently. Now, why do you think they allowed her to move out so suddenly? Could it be that they wanted her in your house?"

"Stop talking in riddles." He didn't have time for this kind of nonsense.

"You weren't the first place she stayed after running away, you know. Amorette found refuge elsewhere for a while."

"Yes, with that school chum of hers."

"That *school chum* has attended the same class as Amorette since they were ten years old." Nanette folded her arms across her chest. "You don't find it odd? Since he lives on the other side of the city?"

"He moved there after he graduated high school. You're not making any sense." Eadric gripped the steering wheel harder.

"You're not looking past the obvious. Hunter has never lived in this area. They only know each other because an anonymous benefactor paid for all her tuition bills. Coincidentally, even though they didn't move in the same circles, Hunter attended all her classes and showed an interest in her."

Eadric's suspicion peaked, a wailing siren in his logical mind. "He was a child when they met. He couldn't be..."

"Oh, he could." Nanette bit out. "I watched him because I

thought he might grow apart from them, but blood ties are hard to break."

"Blood ties?" Eadric's head spun.

Of all people, could the culprit really be Hunter? The one man who challenged Eadric's fascination with the lovely Amorette. The only one who protected her regardless.

Nanette nodded. "Now you understand."

"Exactly who is that boy?" Eadric gritted his teeth. If Hunter so much as laid a finger on Amorette, he wouldn't spare him.

"That boy..." Nanette arched a brow, "is The Benefactor's offspring."

Eadric sneered at the term. He felt the same way. "He has a son?"

"You'll have to ask him the details, but yes. If I had known the child wasn't trustworthy, I would have taken care of the matter long ago. I'm as cross as you are about this matter." Nanette sat straighter, as if a sudden thought occurred to her. "Take me with you. I'd love a shot at that weasel."

"You can't kill him." Eadric shook his head.

Nanette scoffed. "You never studied up on lore and legend, did you? Whatever will I do with you?"

"Hopefully nothing scandalous." Eadric rolled his eyes. How did she not change over the course of her long life? Always talking in circles and riddles. "Tell me."

"There's always a way to die, silly goose." Nanette patted a hand against Eadric's shoulder. "Even for those of our kind."

"Nanette."

She smiled patronizingly. "Alright. I'll tell you on the way. She may not have time."

"Are you going to tell me where they're holding her?"

"I don't know. Not really. But I followed Imran to an old factory once. Recently. You could try there. Be prepared for a fight." Nanette batted her eyelashes. "Let me come? It's been too long since I fought. I'm afraid my skills might get rusty."

Eadric put the car into drive, not because he wanted her to come along, but because she wouldn't stop arguing if he said no. Right now, he needed all the help he could get.

"We have a stop to make first."

"Of course. Who are we picking up? It isn't Lim, is it? You know I can't stand him."

"It isn't Lim."

"Oh, thank heaven."

Eadric gritted his teeth again. Nanette reminded him of times he would rather forget. Not because of regret, but because those times brought them to this day. If he acted differently back then, they wouldn't have so many problems now.

He knew now what started all of this. No one meant for it to happen, but one person placed blame. Eadric feared the retribution that Imran planned.

On the way back to Eadric's mansion, Nanette peeled layer after layer from her slim body. Scarves littered the back of the SUV, along with two coats and a pair of gloves. Everything that added bulk and changed her appearance eventually sat in a mountain behind her. Nanette swept her hands back through her raven hair and pulled it into a ponytail.

Without the makeup and the clothes, Nanette looked entirely different. She had always been striking, but this woman held an aura of danger Eadric didn't remember from last time. He was glad she was on his side.

"Stay here." Eadric shot her a fierce look as he slid out of the car. A quick jog inside revealed everyone huddled in the living area.

"Oh, you're back?" Melodia jogged over and looped her arm through his. "The EMTs have been here and gone. The guard puppies are taking it well, but Doon is complaining. We can't find Hunter or Amorette, and apparently the guy you locked in the basement is gone, too."

"I know." Eadric extracted his arm from Melodia's. A quick nod in Doon's direction had the man up and running behind Eadric.

A quick trip upstairs took Eadric straight to his bedroom. Doon entered the room at the same time Eadric snatched the broadsword from its wall mount.

"What's going on?" Doon eyed the weapon suspiciously.

Eadric reached for the stand of bow-staffs nearby. "You know how to use a staff, don't you?" He plucked one of the choicer ones from its confines and tossed it to Doon.

Doon caught it in one hand. "Codex has her, don't they?"

"Are you going to fight with me or stay here?"

"Of course I'm fighting. Not even a question." Doon anchored the staff against his shoulder. "You're leaving the security guys with Melodia, right?"

"She's not in danger. Codex has what they want."

Still, Eadric wondered why they needed innocent little Amorette in the first place. It never made sense to him, why they attempted to kill her as a child.

Doon nodded and motioned to the door. "After you, then."

Eadric didn't waste time or words. The car still waited, one door open and a dark-haired immortal in the front seat.

Doon paused before he slid into the back seat. "Okay, I give. Who's this?"

"Nanette, meet Doon. His family has served me well for a long time." Eadric slammed his door and sped down the lane.

"A pleasure to meet you." Nanette smiled.

Doon huffed. "You mean there are more people like you and I'm just now getting an introduction? This seems unfair."

"I think it's unfair that Eadric is bringing a child to a mature fight, but you don't see me complaining."

Eadric slammed a hand against the steering wheel. "Stop it, both of you. I refuse to listen to your bickering."

"Ooh, the tiger arises." Nanette laughed. "You always did burn hot."

"I'll thank you to shut your mouth before I take matters into my own hands." Eadric shot Nanette a look that brooked no argument. He couldn't take any sass or attitude right now. They had places to be and he couldn't get there fast enough.

⸻

The second time, Amorette woke to a sharp pain against her scalp. A breath caught in her throat.

"Wakey, wakey, little one."

The voice still sounded familiar. Amorette pried her eyes open, only to find another face inches from hers.

Imran Blakely smiled and gave her hair another tug. "There she is. Did you think I'd let you sleep to your heart's content? I know how the drug works. It wore off ages ago."

"Hunter..." Amorette didn't bother to finish the sentence. She knew he betrayed them. She wished she could understand why.

"Don't try calling for help. You're pitiful enough as it is." Imran sighed. "I had a modicum of respect for you, you know. Always a survivor. Always the first to admit her wrongs. It's a pity, really. I didn't want to end you this way."

"Why..." Amorette swallowed. If her mouth weren't so dry, she would ask all kinds of questions. "Why do I have to die?"

"You're his." Imran released her hair.

Amorette took a deep breath, mentally preparing for whatever came next. If she could keep him talking, she could buy some time. Unfortunately, Amorette didn't have that luxury.

"Let's see how quickly we can summon him, hm?" Imran motioned to someone behind Amorette. "Hold her still. If she moves, use force."

Amorette tried to struggle, but her limbs felt heavy. Ropes tied her too tightly to the chair. She couldn't stop the hands that pulled her head back and held it still.

Imran tapped his fingers on the rim of a bucket. "Now. You tell me what I want to know, or you get hurt."

Amorette snorted her disdain. "I'm not telling you anything."

"I respect that, but it's the wrong decision." Imran swept the bucket of water from the table. "Hold her mouth open."

There was no way to fight the onslaught of water that burned her lungs.

The minimal instructions from Nanette steered them right into the middle of a field of factories and warehouses. Eadric parked the SUV and glanced around outside. They were on Codex's turf now. No doubt guards or cameras were stationed somewhere nearby.

"We should go on foot from here on out," Nanette suggested.

Eadric opened his mouth to answer, but nothing came out. Instead, a burn started in his lungs and stole his breath. Eadric sputtered and coughed, bracing against the steering wheel in an attempt to free himself from the pain.

"Mr. Hawkmore!"

"Eadric!"

Nanette and Doon reached for him at the same time. Doon slapped a hand against his back, while Nanette checked vitals.

As suddenly as it started, the burning stopped. Eadric waved a hand, breathless. "I'm... fine." He tried to take deep breaths. Whatever that was, it didn't bode well.

Nanette slipped out of her seat-belt. "Keep an eye on him, Doon. This isn't normal."

"Oh, you're telling me?" Doon rolled his eyes. "You should keep an eye on him too."

"I'm fine." Eadric opened his door. "We don't have time for this, let's go."

Nanette and Doon spared each other one glance before they jumped out of the car.

Eadric clenched a fist around the hilt of his sword. He didn't like the implications of the pain in his chest. No matter the hypothesis, it seemed hopeless.

Three sets of boots clopped on the concrete below them.

Nanette rolled her shoulders and stretched her arms.

Doon kept the staff securely against his shoulder.

Silence echoed through the buildings. A stiff wind swept through the alleys and swirled around the three intruders.

Eadric listened for any sounds of life. The distant thrum of machinery rumbled from one of the factories. A generator, perhaps? He pointed two fingers in that direction.

With each camera they passed, Eadric drew to one conclusion. Imran wanted him here. If Imran didn't want him, Codex would already have countermeasures in place. The quiet spoke volumes more than their usual outcry.

Eadric tried the factory door first, somehow unsurprised to find it unlocked. As if an invitation had been extended.

The main floor might have once held all kinds of machines, but today it sat mostly empty. A few tables scattered here and there, but that wasn't the focal point of Eadric's attention.

A chair near the tables held the only thing that mattered. Amorette's hair and clothes were drenched with water, her breathing labored but rhythmic. Eadric bounded two steps toward her.

"I wouldn't do that if I were you." Imran stepped from the shadowy corner behind her. In one hand, he twirled a sharp dagger. In the other, he carried a sword very similar to Eadric's.

Eadric paused and held a hand behind himself, signaling Nanette and Doon to hold still.

"What have you done to her?"

—⚷—

Amorette couldn't believe he came. The longer she spent strapped to this chair, the more she convinced herself she wouldn't live to see another day. Yet, Eadric stood before her, a sword in one hand. This had to be the end. He would keep her safe.

Imran appeared in her peripheral vision, making his way in front of her. "It's not so much what I've done to her, but what I'm doing to you."

"I thought we were past these childish grudges." Eadric's gaze remained locked on Amorette.

Amorette offered a soft, weak smile. He needed that much reassurance. At the rate he frowned, his face would get stuck like that.

Imran chuckled. "Childish? No. This is far from childish. I'm only doing to you what you did to me."

"I told you then, I didn't know it was her."

Amorette blinked. This conversation turned stranger the more she heard. She forced her head higher, hoping to catch an explanation in the way they looked at each other.

"Of course it was her. You know where I met her. You knew where her loyalties lied." Imran sneered. "You killed mercilessly."

"I did my duty as a soldier serving my nation." Eadric took a step forward.

Imran took a step back and flipped his dagger in his fingers. "Stop. Or she dies."

Eadric halted mid-step.

Amorette looked past him to see Doon creep along the wall, a long stick in his hands. Whatever his plan, he couldn't see the dozen or more Codex members on the balcony above. She glanced between Eadric and Doon, unsure which to deal with first.

"Don't, Imran. Kill me instead. I'm the one you want. Now that I've found her, it's possible." Eadric's fingers tightened on his sword until his knuckles turned white. "Leave her alone."

"Like you left Brigit alone?" Imran shook his head. "Pathetic creature. You don't know, do you? Her pain is your pain. Anything that happens to her, you feel a hundred-fold."

"You want me to suffer, so make me suffer. I'll die in her place."

"Eadric..." Amorette couldn't let him do that, no matter what happened. She couldn't explain it, but she needed him. He couldn't leave her like that.

Eadric shook his head, an infinitesimal movement that Amorette hardly even saw. "Just end me now, Imran. It's the punishment you think I deserve."

"No. It isn't." Imran's fingers flexed around his dagger. "You deserve a much worse punishment. Don't you know that an infinite life of pain is worse than death?"

Amorette flicked a glance to Doon, who stepped out from under the balcony. One of the Codex members crawled to the balcony railing, ready to spring.

Amorette pooled her strength and projected her voice. "Doon! Above you!"

Everything began in a flash.

Doon looked up and side-stepped the man who launched himself downward.

Eadric sprinted forward toward Amorette.

Imran spun and crouched, one arm extended.

A searing heat blossomed in Amorette's gut and stole her breath. Her head jerked forward, sending her wet hair into her face.

Eadric doubled over with a cry.

"I'm truly sorry, little one," Imran shrugged a shoulder.

Amorette met Imran's steely gaze, then let her eyes trail down.

Imran's hand clutched the intricate handle of a sharp blade.

Blood seeped out and stained his fingers. Another tug on the blade pulled it back out.

Amorette gasped a breath as her body jerked. Warm liquid seeped through her shirt and dampened her skin.

A shout cleared the cotton from Amorette's ears. Eadric sprang into action, his sword poised to slice Imran in half.

Imran was quicker.

Swords clashed and sparks flew in time to Amorette's attempt to breathe. Blood dripped from Imran's dagger as he swung it at Eadric's stomach.

The clack of the staff hitting bone and flesh resounded from the other side of the room. Amorette managed to focus long enough to note a tall, dark-haired woman fighting alongside Doon.

A scream wormed its way out from Amorette's throat as Imran's sword whizzed just above her head.

Eadric swung his sword again and used the momentum to switch places with Imran. A single foot planted to the center of the chair tipped it over.

Amorette's head and back hit the floor. For a moment, she couldn't breathe. Her vision blurred and warped. The warmth that had started seeping onto her abdomen had wormed its way over the majority of her shirt.

Amorette rolled her head to see the progress of the fight, but it was useless. She couldn't focus enough to see anything. Despite her mental fight, Amorette gave in to the blackness.

⚿

Eadric forced his muscles to work, despite the ache in his abdomen and the blur of his vision. If it was the last thing he did, he would make Imran pay for this. He needed one chance. One straight shot. If Nanette were right, Imran's weakness sat closer than anyone realized.

"It's in our nature," Nanette had said. *"We can't help it that our hearts begin to thaw when we meet our true love. Imran's heart is soft. Everything else may heal, but not his heart."*

Eadric slammed his sword against Imran's again and held, long enough to squeeze his eyes shut.

Focus. He had to focus and end this quickly. Amorette didn't have much time. Imran knew what he was doing when he stabbed her. His aim wouldn't have missed.

"Giving up so soon?" Imran clucked his tongue and shoved Eadric off of him.

Eadric opened his eyes to glare. "Not hardly." He motioned for Imran to proceed.

The heart. He needed a straight shot to Imran's heart. Eadric didn't know how he would manage it, but he would. It had to be him who took care of Imran, The Benefactor. Imran's own personal grudge had manipulated too many lives over the years. No longer.

Eadric waited for Imran to charge and swept for the professor's legs. The broadsword made contact with a knee at the same time Imran's sword made contact with Eadric's shoulder.

It was a glance, at best. Eadric could pay that price for the woman he loved.

Imran fell to one knee, but it didn't deter him from lunging again. Eadric dodged sideways and swiped at Imran's wrist. The dagger fell to the floor and skittered a few inches away.

Imran growled and angled his sword toward Eadric's arm. Their weapons clashed again, this time hard enough to entangle them. Feet and arms shuffled together as each tried to pull away. In the end, both tossed their sword.

Eadric threw the first punch, landing it squarely against Imran's jaw.

Imran barely flinched. Their fists launched at each other, bloodying and bruising faces and arms and chests.

Imran sprang at Eadric and managed to clamor atop him. Punch after punch landed by Eadric's eye, on his jaw, against his cheek.

Eadric took each hit with the steely determination of a skilled fighter. His arm extended, his fingers searching for something to even the score. They met with the handle of a bloodied dagger.

Eadric slowly tucked it against his palm. He had one shot to get this perfect. His aim needed to hit the target the first time.

As best he could with fists flying against his head, Eadric judged the measurements of Imran's body and mentally drew an X over the target.

A breath centered him.

Focus distracted Imran from the obvious.

Eadric pulled his arm back and plunged the dagger into Imran's chest.

Imran froze, his eyes wide in surprise. A question hung silently between the two men. Neither bothered to answer. Crimson blood leaked from the corner of Imran's lips.

Imran huffed a raspy chuckle. "It doesn't matter. She's as good as dead."

Eadric shoved the man off of him. He didn't care that the dagger still lay embedded in Imran's chest. He didn't notice the sirens in the distance. All that mattered was the unconscious woman bleeding out onto the floor. Eadric crawled his way to her side.

The ropes binding her had been tied too tightly. He could see the red where the skin rubbed raw. Eadric clawed at the knots until they fell apart. Until Amorette fell limp against the floor.

"Amorette..." Eadric gathered her into his arms, oblivious to his own injuries. "My love... come back to me." He smoothed a bloody hand against her cheek.

She couldn't leave him like this. He couldn't lose her, not after all he went through to get her. She looked so pale.

A set of knees hit the ground beside him. "Mi Amor..." Hunter stuffed a towel against her abdomen and pressed his hands down.

Eadric shoved Hunter's hands away. "You brought her to this. This is your fault."

"He promised he wouldn't hurt her. I didn't think he would..." Hunter sat back on his heels. His fingers scraped through his hair. "He promised."

"If you're going to blame everyone else for your incompetence, leave now." Eadric pressed his own hand against the quickly reddening towels. "If not, do something useful."

"I called an ambulance. They're on their way." Hunter swallowed. "She's going to be okay, right? She can't die like this."

"If you don't want to be wrapped up in this, get out now." Eadric sighed. For Amorette, he would give Hunter one chance. He didn't believe Hunter was truly evil, but he had been manipulated by a lying father. "Go now. Leave, run far away, and never show your face in front of me or Amorette again."

"Will she be okay?"

"I'll make sure of it. Go."

Hunter scrambled to his feet and backed away, slowly at first and then faster. Until he raced out the doors and disappeared.

Eadric turned his attention back to the woman in his arms. "Please, my love, don't leave me..."

A steady beep chimed in the cool air. The fog cleared slowly, parting to make way for coherency.

Amorette's eyes fluttered open, then closed again. The bright lights blinded her, and her body screamed its protest. A groan slipped from her lips.

"Amorette?"

The feminine voice seemed familiar, but in her groggy state, Amorette couldn't place it. If she wanted to know its owner, Amorette knew she would have to open her eyes. She pried first one, then the other open.

The room seemed nicer than she expected, almost homey. Flowers littered a desk near the windows. Amorette scanned other insignificant furnishings on her way to the source of the voice.

A black-haired beauty reached for a glass of ice chips and procured one to place it to Amorette's lips.

Grateful, Amorette accepted it and let it coat her dry and cracked throat. "Who... are you?"

The woman smiled, a stunning sight. A familiar beauty. Bit by bit, Amorette's hazy mind pieced it together.

"Nannie?" It couldn't be right. Nannie was older and wider and, quite frankly, Amorette always assumed the woman was homeless.

"Nanette." Nannie shrugged a shoulder. "You would have figured me out in time. I'm a master of disguise, but you're a clever girl."

"How... who..."

"It's better not to ask questions right now. I'm glad you're awake." Nannie smoothed Amorette's hair back from her face in a motherly touch.

Amorette nodded slowly. "Why are you the one here?"

"I've watched over you since you were small. I saw no need to stop now."

"But you're... so young." A sudden idea dawned on Amorette. She opened her mouth to ask.

Nannie put a finger to her lips. "Let's keep that little secret between the two of us." She rose to her feet. "Now that you're awake, I'll leave you to the others. Heal well, my child."

"The others?" Amorette followed Nannie's progress to the door.

The woman waved and disappeared into the hall. Seconds later, Melodia waltzed through the door.

A shriek left her lips. "You're awake!" She poked her head out the door. "Doon, get in here! She's awake!"

"Can you be a little quieter?" Amorette tried to lift a hand to press it to her head, but it stuck fast. A quick perusal identified an IV as the culprit.

Doon darted in behind Melodia. "Oh, good. I was beginning to worry. You're okay, right? They said they got everything all stitched up, but it's gotta sting. Don't move. Don't do anything. Just relax."

Amorette studied Doon's busted lip. With the odds he'd been fighting against, she was surprised at the minimal injuries.

"Sweetie, let's not overwhelm her, okay?" Melodia wrapped an arm around Doon's.

"Sweetie?" Amorette locked her eyes on their intertwined arms. She clearly missed something.

"Hey, this guy fought to save your life. I'd be an idiot not to date him." Melodia smiled up at him.

Amorette grinned despite everything. At least something good came out of the whole ordeal. "Where's Eadric?"

"He had to go cover—I mean *clear* some stuff up." Doon motioned Melodia to the chair beside Amorette's bed. "He said for us to take care of you until he gets back. There were some PR and news conferences. He may be a few days."

"Days?" Amorette sighed. She wanted to see him now. He was injured, too, she was sure. "Why isn't he in the hospital?"

"He's not entirely mortal yet." Doon chuckled. "He's well enough to run the story. Then he'll slow down. You focus on getting better. That's what Eadric would want."

Amorette nodded, but she didn't like the idea. Part of her needed him by her side. Even though she understood his public presence, she didn't want him to run off when she needed him most. What a depressing way to wake up.

True to their word, Doon and Melodia stayed by Amorette's side as she began to heal.

Due to the serious nature of the injury, the hospital refused to discharge her until they were sure it could be taken care of at home. Amorette remained stuck in the hospital for a solid week before anyone mentioned the word "home".

Eadric didn't come to escort her back to the mansion, but he sent flowers and chocolate. They were a poor stand-in for what Amorette really wanted.

Even at home, Amorette wasn't allowed to go far, for fear of opening her stitches. For the first day, she stayed in her room, but after that, she moved to the couch. The TV was more accessible from there, as was the food.

Sleep seemed to attack her more often, but Amorette didn't mind. If she slept, she wouldn't think of the things missing.

She watched the news religiously, waiting for any sign of Eadric. Doon said he would be back soon, that he had to travel out of town to wrap up the story.

For the most part, Doon and Melodia left her to sleep. Both knew the anxiety she felt. Neither wanted to deal with it.

Amorette's seventh day home consisted of constant news, until she curled up and closed her eyes. She meant to sleep for just a few minutes.

A gentle touch of fingers to her hair woke Amorette.

The living room seemed dark, like the sun had set. She sighed and pushed up to one elbow, only for her elbow to meet the side of a jean-clad thigh.

Amorette raised her eyes to meet the quiet, calm storm that existed only in Eadric's gaze.

"Eadric?"

Great. Had she finally lost it? Was she hallucinating?

"I'm sorry it took me so long." Eadric stroked a hand over her hair. "How are you feeling? Better?"

Amorette looked past him to the television screen, where the film of the factory and ambulances played continuously. So the story broke the way they wanted it to.

She smiled. "I'm better now that you're here."

"Doon said you've been sleeping a lot. Is that normal?"

"I think it will get better now." Amorette couldn't help but smile wider.

He looked so concerned, which gave her the answer she'd been looking for. She wasn't hallucinating.

Eadric scooped Amorette into his lap and wrapped his arms around her. "I intend to make up for the time I spent away from you."

"I like cuddles." Amorette rested her head against his shoulder.

Eadric laughed. "I know you do. Where are the others?"

"I don't know."

"It doesn't matter so much." Eadric tipped up Amorette's chin. "I missed you."

"I missed you more."

"I'm never leaving you again." Eadric placed a series of sweet, soft kisses to Amorette's lips. "Not ever."

Amorette wrapped her arms around his neck. "I believe you."

This kiss was seal and promise, a solemn vow to always remain by each others' side. Both knew, without a single word, that nothing would separate them again. Because this was meant to be. Because destiny didn't change.

ACKNOWLEDGEMENTS

First and foremost, I would like to thank God, without Whom I would not have managed to finish this project. He truly brought me through so many obstacles, physically and mentally, to come to this point.

My family – as always, thank you for putting up with all the emotional craziness that comes with writing and publishing a book. You are all superstars and the most valuable people on my writing journey.

Hannah – I covered you in the family acknowledgement, but I also want to give a huge shout-out in your own little section. For helping me with photography and thus helping me push forward with the release of this book, thank you.

The King's Pen – You always provide valuable feedback, even when we're not close together. Thank you for supporting me even from afar. You are all beautiful souls and amazing encouragers.

The Caffeinated Goblins – You know who you are. Without your full support behind me, I probably wouldn't have taken this step to publishing. You all rock, no matter where you're from, and I'm so thankful that you are my writing family!

My social media tribe – I can't do what I do without fans, followers, and friends. Thank you to everyone who shows me support online. I hope we have many more fantastic adventures together!

My readers, new and old – I'm so excited that we get to go on this journey together! Thank you for jumping on this crazy boat ride of writing with me. I appreciate all of you. Without you, I could never do what I do.

AUTHOR'S NOTE

Thanks for reading Eadric and Amorette's story!

There are no words to describe the journey I went through from start to finish of this book. Characters rearranged their own stories, revealed things I never imagined, and told me their woes like never before.

I hope you enjoyed this story, and that you will use it as a measure for stories in the future. I promise to provide a good read every time.

Much love to all my readers,

Megan